ELVES

VOL. 3

INSIGHT
COMICS

San Rafael, California

ELVES

PART 1:
"THE DYNASTY OF THE DARK ELVES"

WRITTEN BY MARC HADRIEN

ILLUSTRATIONS AND COLORS BY MA YI

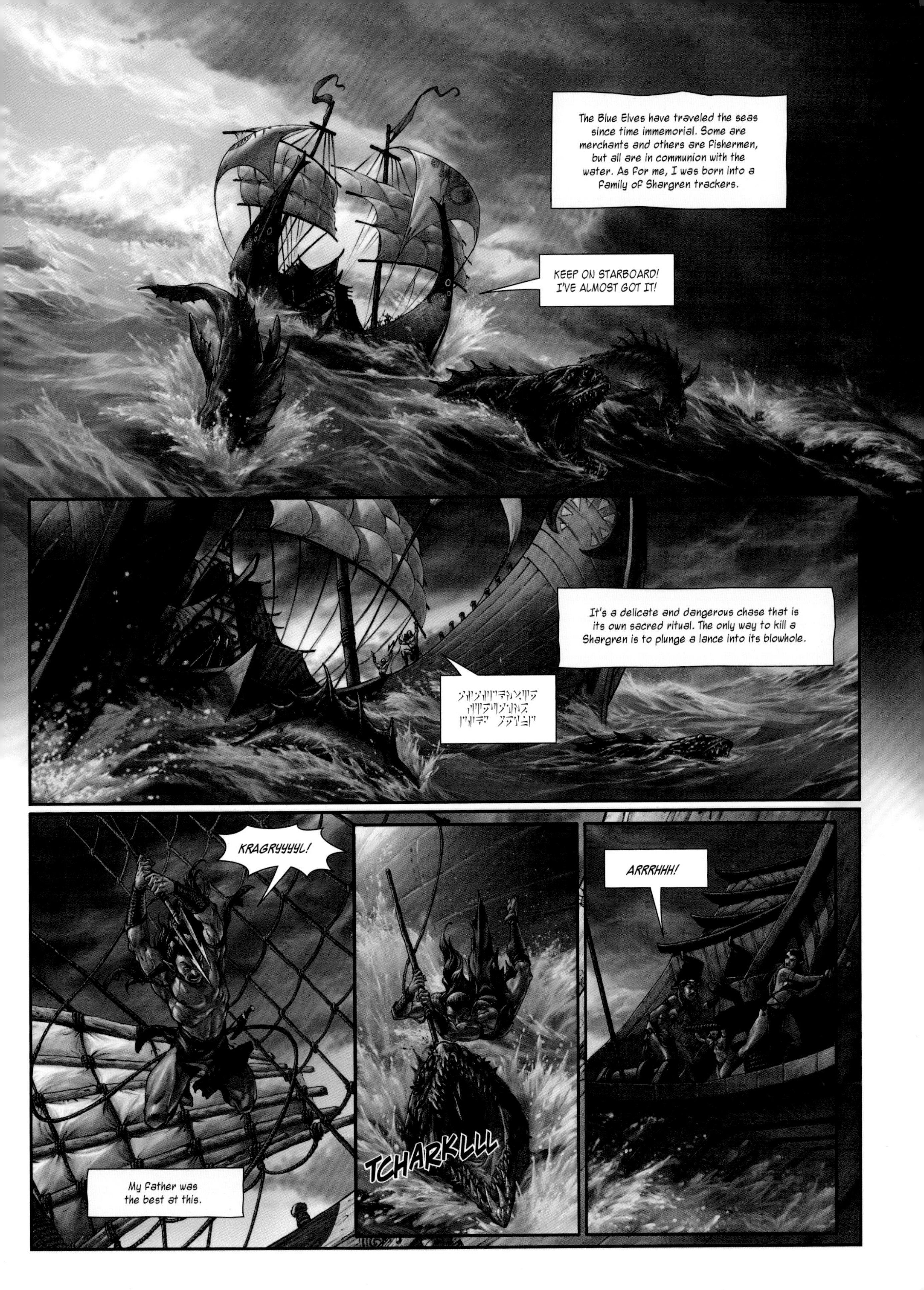
The Blue Elves have traveled the seas since time immemorial. Some are merchants and others are fishermen, but all are in communion with the water. As for me, I was born into a family of Shargren trackers.
KEEP ON STARBOARD! I'VE ALMOST GOT IT!
It's a delicate and dangerous chase that is its own sacred ritual. The only way to kill a Shargren is to plunge a lance into its blowhole.
KRAGRYYYYL!
My father was the best at this.
TCHARKLLL
ARRRHHH!

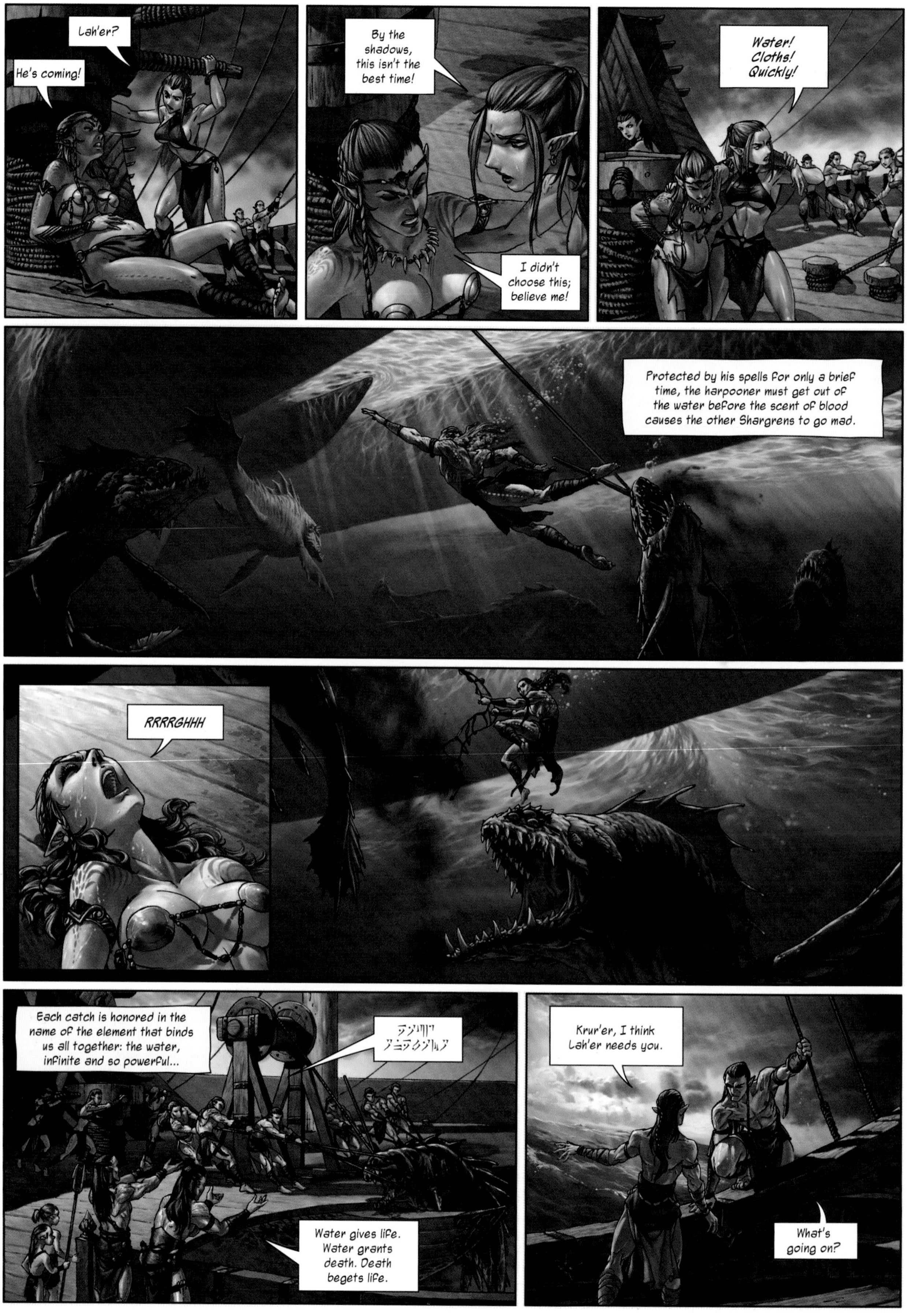
He's coming!
Lah'er?
By the shadows, this isn't the best time!
I didn't choose this; believe me!
Water! Cloths! Quickly!
Protected by his spells for only a brief time, the harpooner must get out of the water before the scent of blood causes the other Shargrens to go mad.
RRRRGHHH
Each catch is honored in the name of the element that binds us all together: the water, infinite and so powerful...
Water gives life. Water grants death. Death begets life.
Krur'er, I think Lah'er needs you.
What's going on?

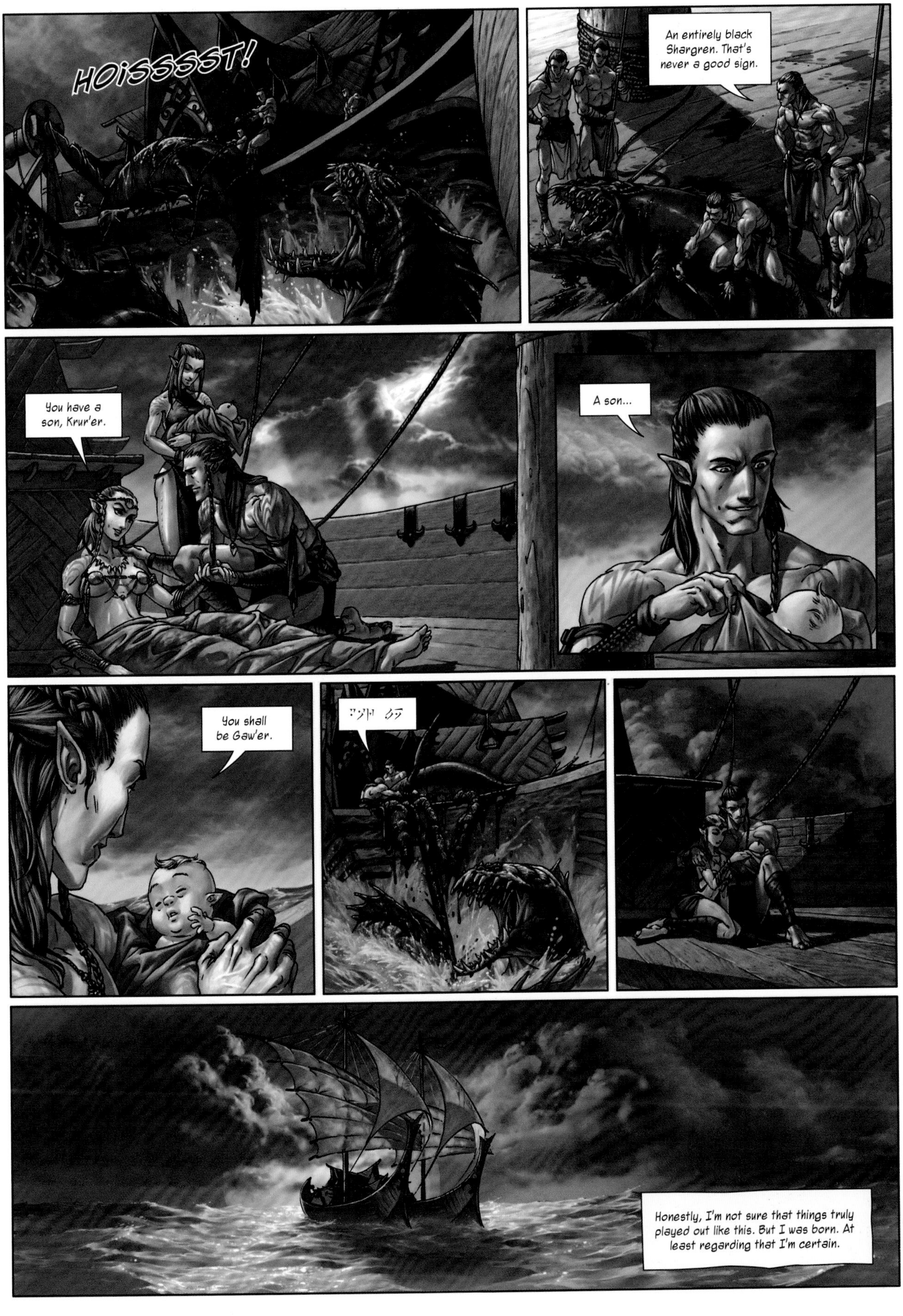
HOiSSSST!
An entirely black Shargren. That's never a good sign.
You have a son, Krur'er.
A son...
You shall be Gaw'er.
Honestly, I'm not sure that things truly played out like this. But I was born. At least regarding that I'm certain.

Like all Blue Elves, I was raised on the water. At four years old, I knew how to climb a mast. At six, I had become a decent butcher of Shargren carcasses, and at eight, my father began to teach me how to wield a harpoon.

The important thing is to hold it perfectly upright to make it carry your weight when you jump.

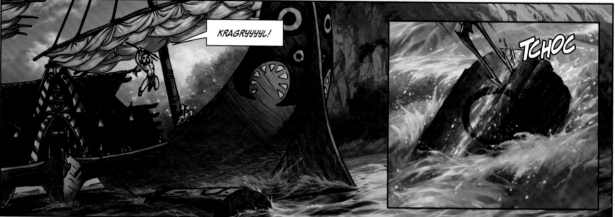

KRAGRYYYYL!

TCHOC

You missed the blowhole, Gaw'er. The Shargren is only injured. It'd whip around and devour you.

So I'll stab it until it does die!

TCHACK TCHACK TCHACK

TCHACK TCHACK

DIE! DIE!

GAW'ER! STOP THAT IMMEDIATELY!

What's going on?

Gaw'er is worrying me. Sometimes he has these fits of uncontrollable rage...

Children are all like that, Krur'er!

Plus he's excited because we'll be arriving at Port Vogue soon.

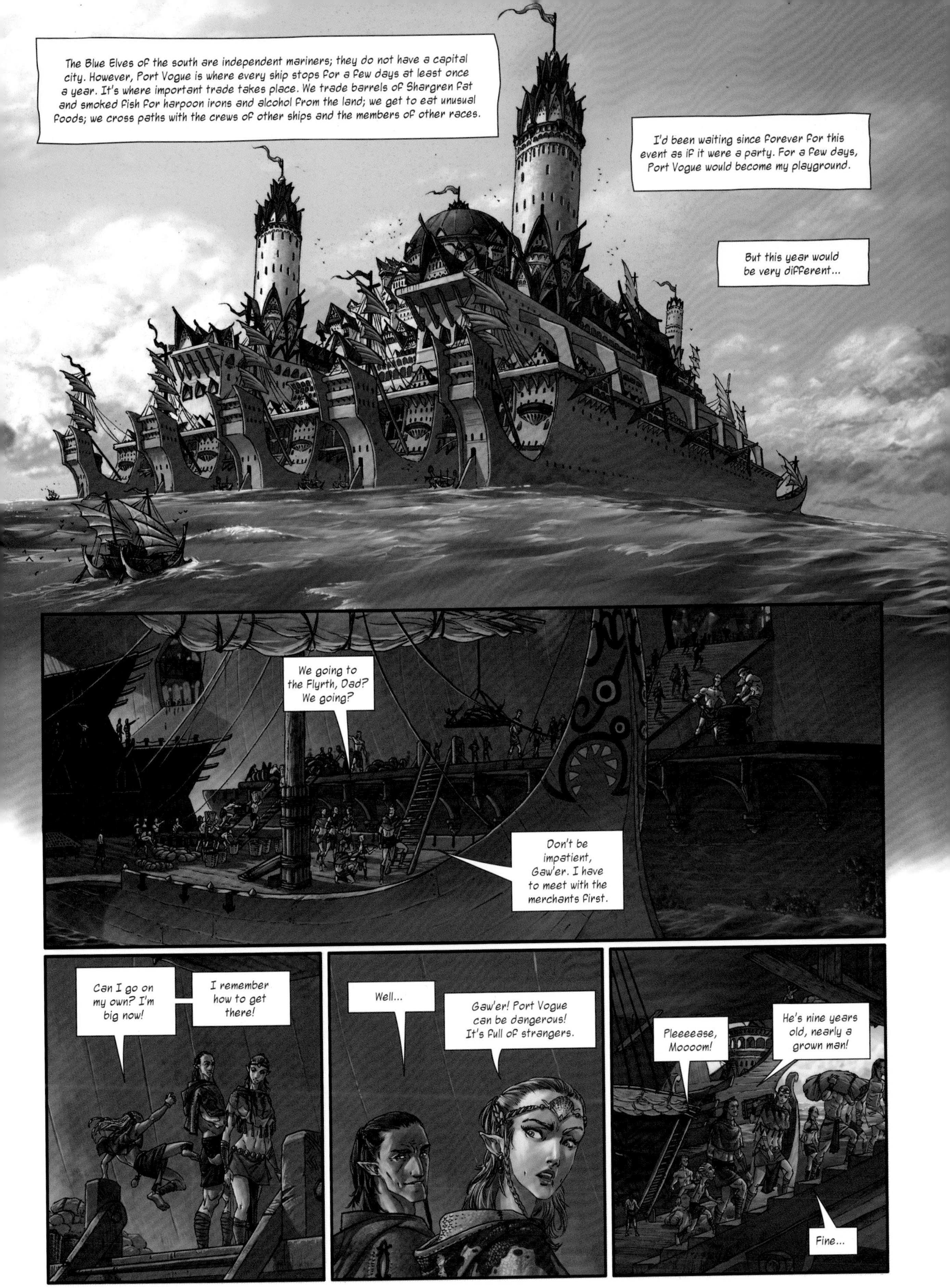
The Blue Elves of the south are independent mariners; they do not have a capital city. However, Port Vogue is where every ship stops for a few days at least once a year. It's where important trade takes place. We trade barrels of Shargren fat and smoked fish for harpoon irons and alcohol from the land; we get to eat unusual foods; we cross paths with the crews of other ships and the members of other races.
I'd been waiting since forever for this event as if it were a party. For a few days, Port Vogue would become my playground.
But this year would be very different...
We going to the Flyrth, Dad? We going?
Don't be impatient, Gaw'er. I have to meet with the merchants first.
Can I go on my own? I'm big now!
I remember how to get there!
Well...
Gaw'er! Port Vogue can be dangerous! It's full of strangers.
Pleeeease, Moooom!
He's nine years old, nearly a grown man!
Fine...

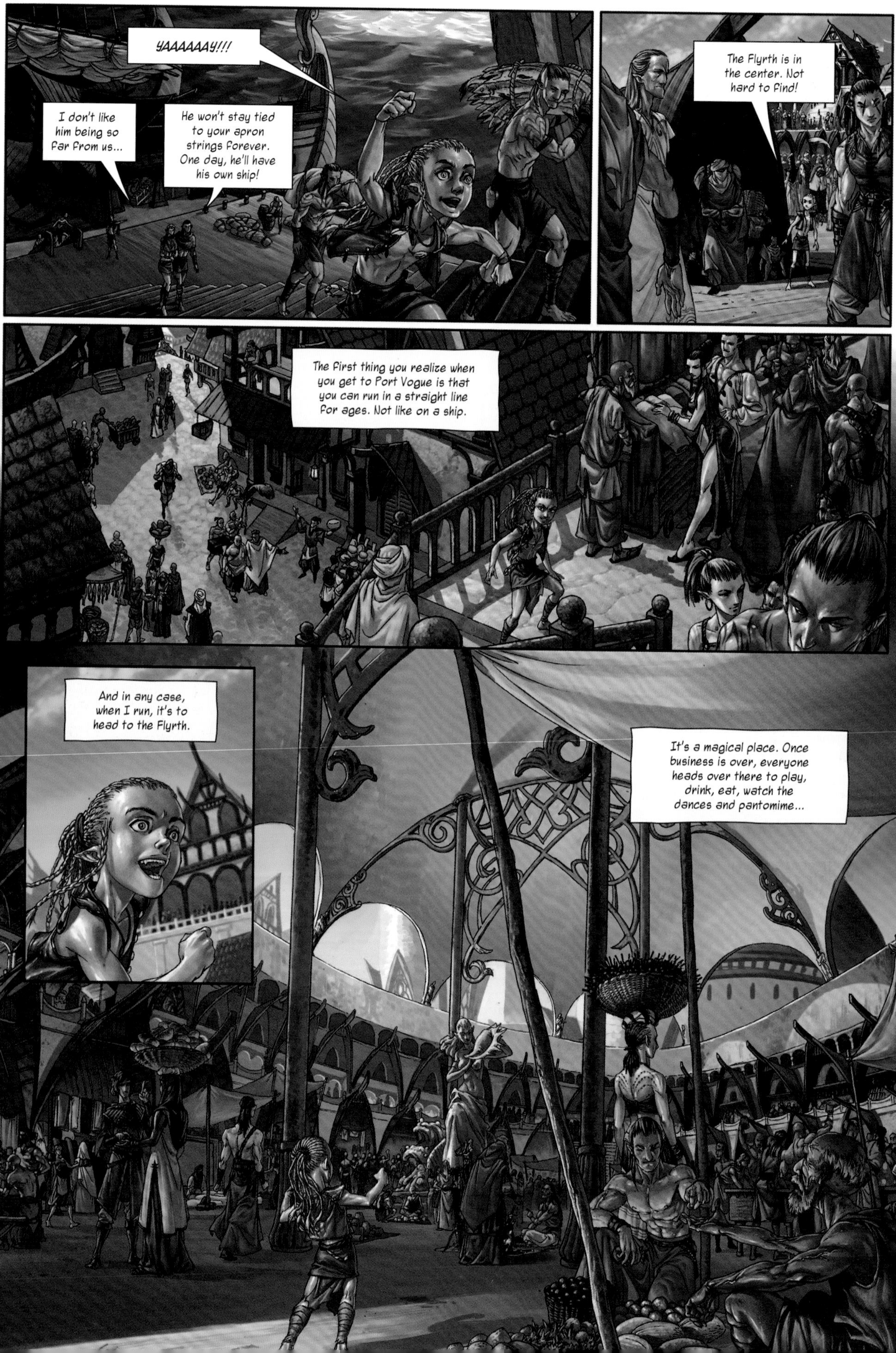
YAAAAAAY!!!
I don't like him being so far from us...
He won't stay tied to your apron strings forever. One day, he'll have his own ship!
The Flyrth is in the center. Not hard to find!
The first thing you realize when you get to Port Vogue is that you can run in a straight line for ages. Not like on a ship.
And in any case, when I run, it's to head to the Flyrth.
It's a magical place. Once business is over, everyone heads over there to play, drink, eat, watch the dances and pantomime...

And there's eel racing and fighter crab matches. I love watching fighter crabs.

GO ON!

EAT HIM!

THE RED ONE!

TEAR HIS PINCERS OFF!

SIX PIECES ON THE BLUE!

TCHARK

SKRSHHH

GO ON! TURN--

SKRSHHHH

FRRTSHHBLLL

YAAAAAY!

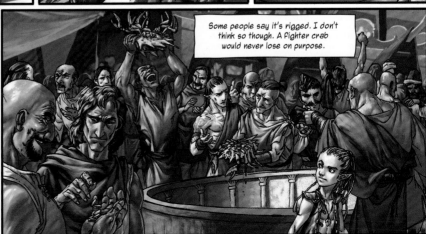

Some people say it's rigged. I don't think so though. A fighter crab would never lose on purpose.

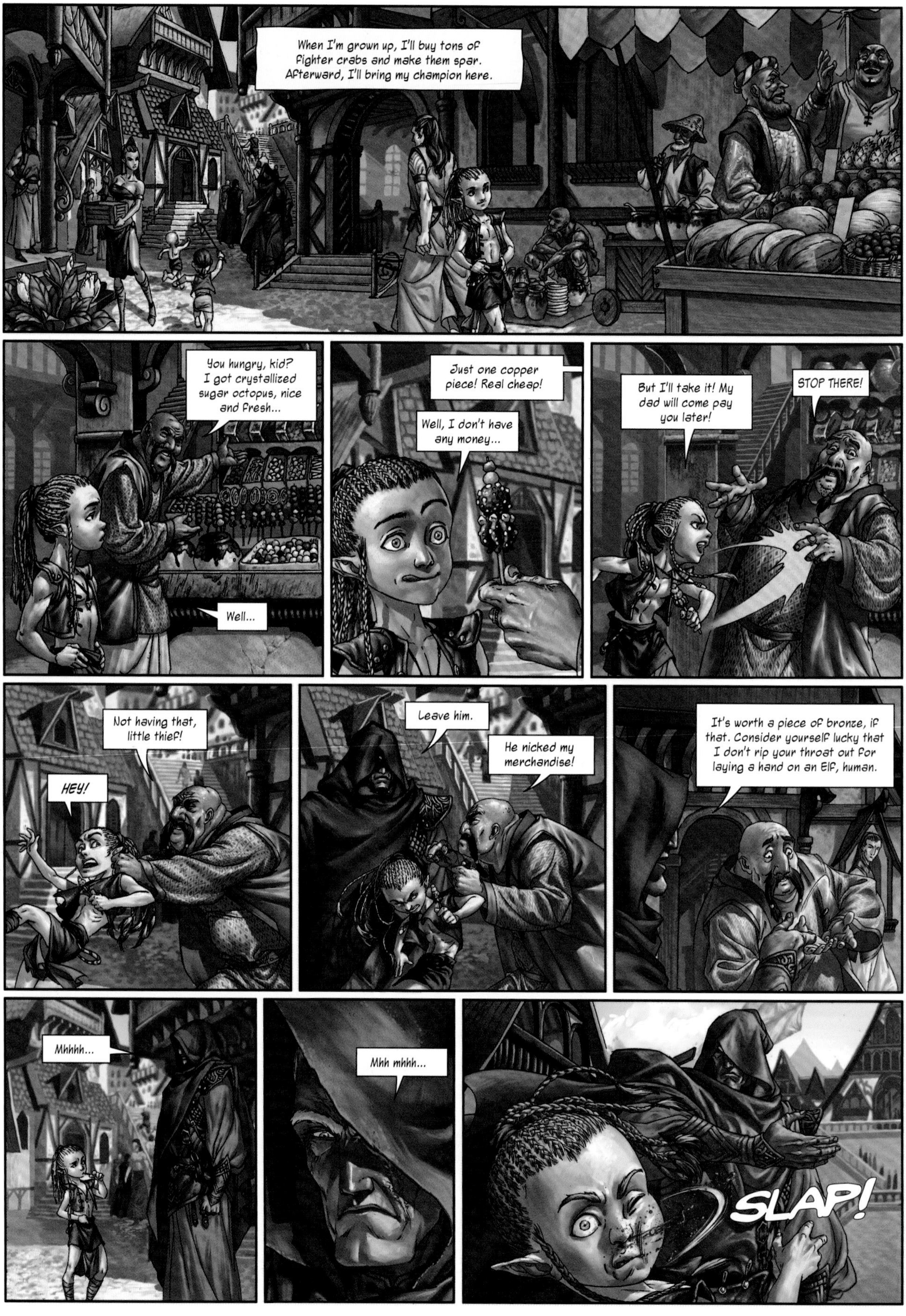
When I'm grown up, I'll buy tons of fighter crabs and make them spar. Afterward, I'll bring my champion here.
You hungry, kid? I got crystallized sugar octopus, nice and fresh...
Well...
Just one copper piece! Real cheap!
Well, I don't have any money...
But I'll take it! My dad will come pay you later!
STOP THERE!
Not having that, little thief!
HEY!
Leave him.
He nicked my merchandise!
It's worth a piece of bronze, if that. Consider yourself lucky that I don't rip your throat out for laying a hand on an Elf, human.
Mhhhh...
Mhh mhhh...
SLAP!

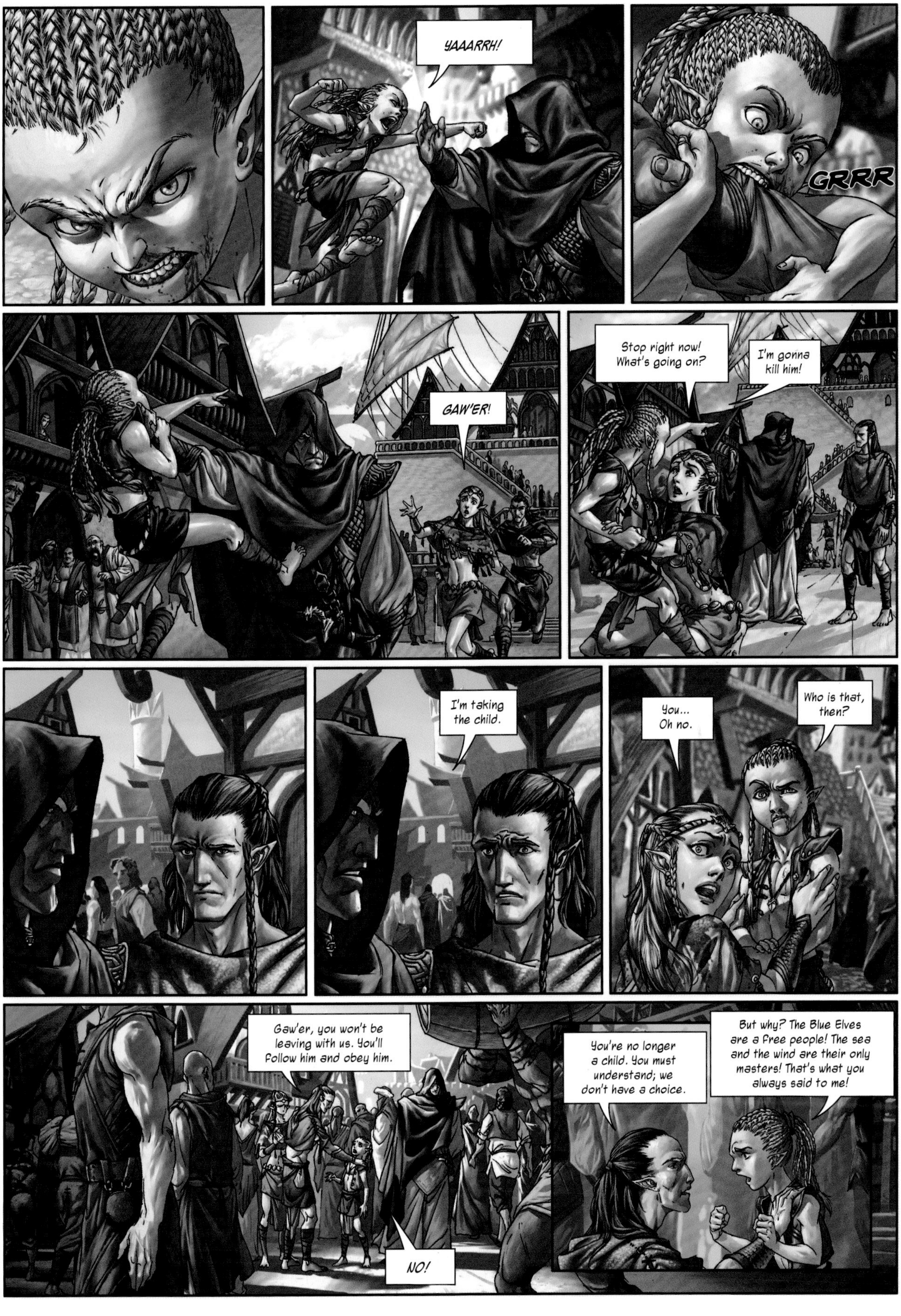
YAAARRH!
GRRR
GAW'ER!
Stop right now! What's going on?
I'm gonna kill him!
I'm taking the child.
You... Oh no.
Who is that, then?
Gaw'er, you won't be leaving with us. You'll follow him and obey him.
NO!
You're no longer a child. You must understand; we don't have a choice.
But why? The Blue Elves are a free people! The sea and the wind are their only masters! That's what you always said to me!

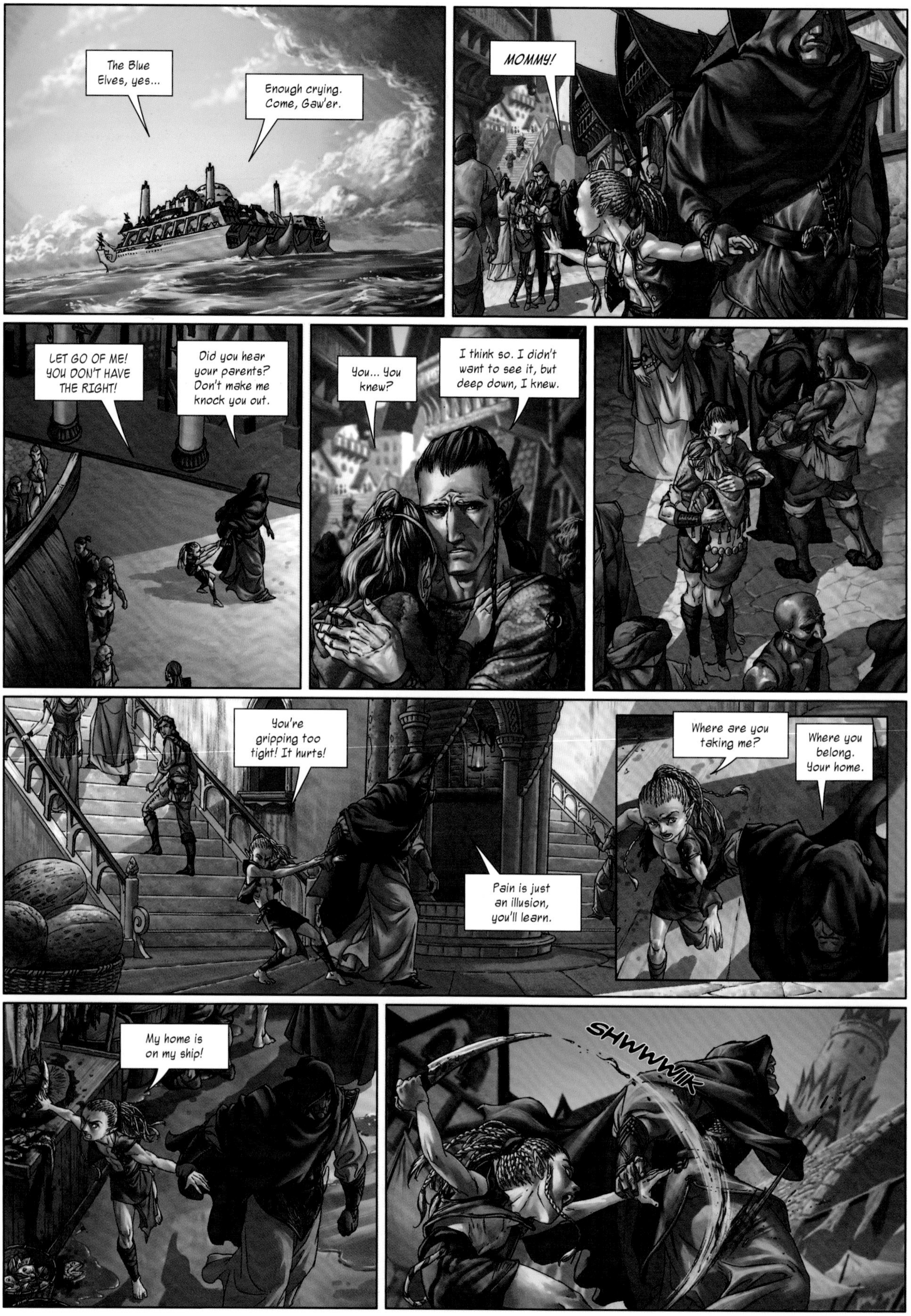
The Blue Elves, yes...
Enough crying. Come, Gaw'er.
MOMMY!
LET GO OF ME! YOU DON'T HAVE THE RIGHT!
Did you hear your parents? Don't make me knock you out.
You... You knew?
I think so. I didn't want to see it, but deep down, I knew.
You're gripping too tight! It hurts!
Pain is just an illusion, you'll learn.
Where are you taking me?
Where you belong. Your home.
My home is on my ship!
SHWWWIIK

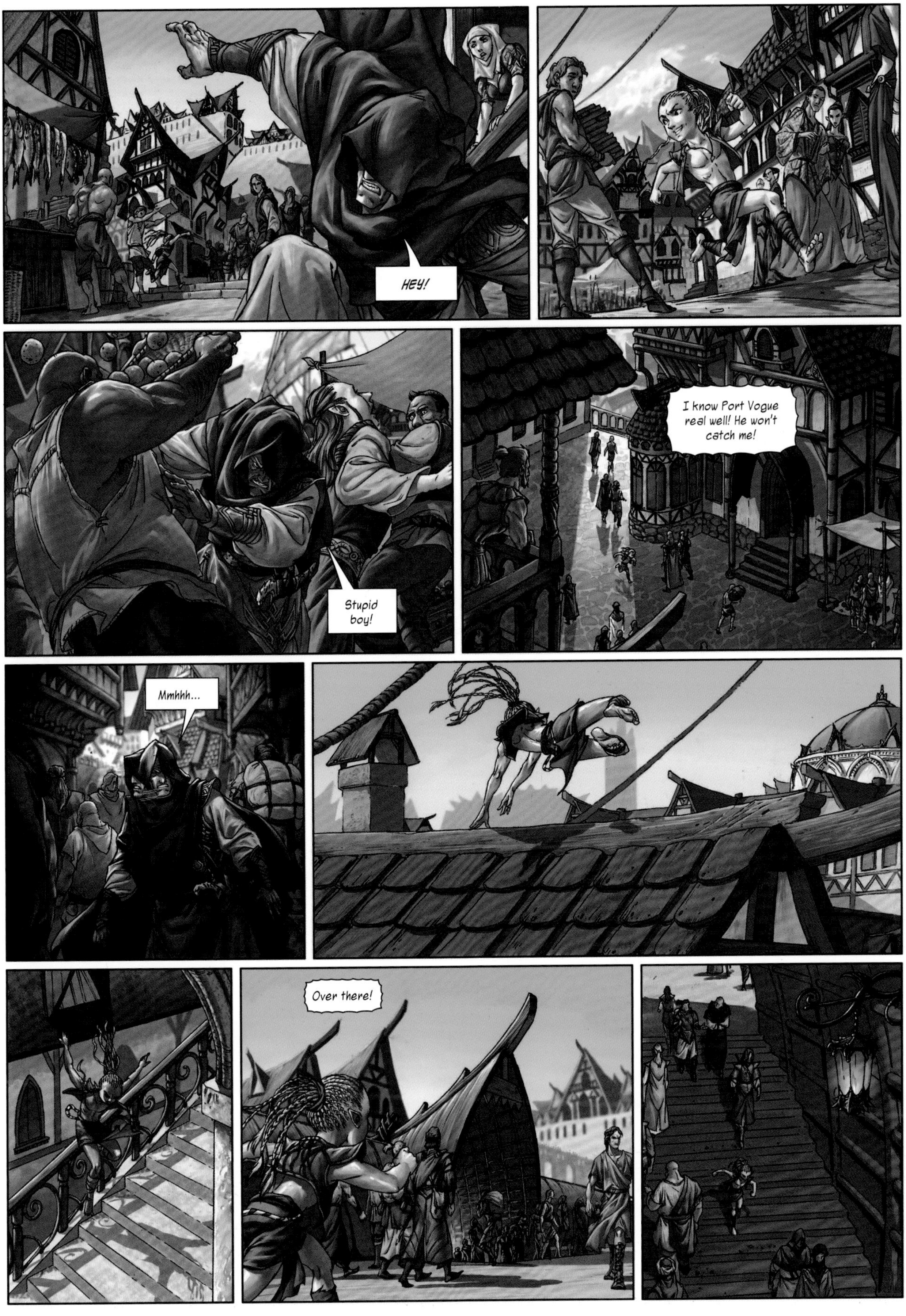
HEY!
Stupid boy!
I know Port Vogue real well! He won't catch me!
Mmhhh...
Over there!

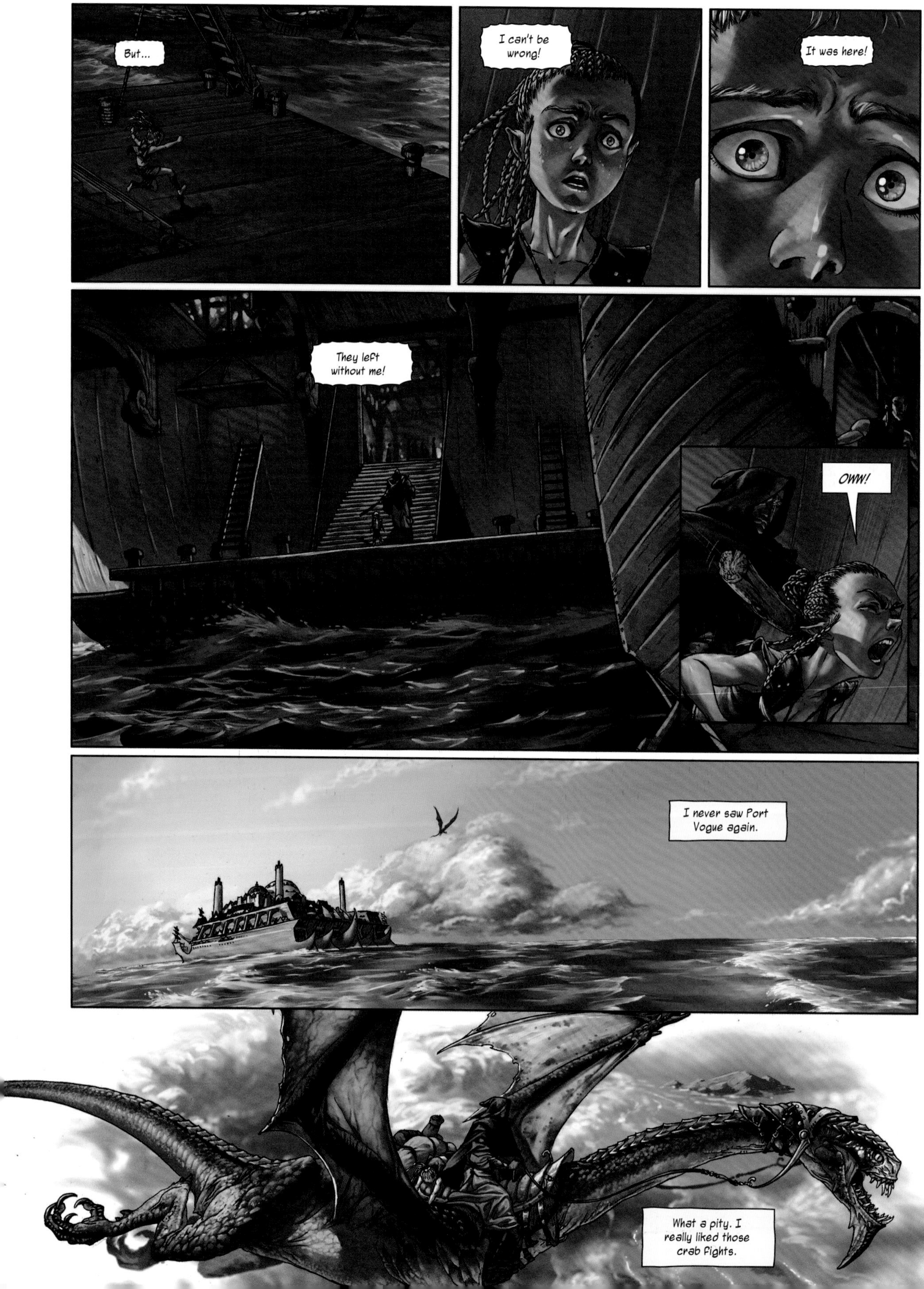
But...
I can't be wrong!
It was here!
They left without me!
OWW!
I never saw Port Vogue again.
What a pity. I really liked those crab fights.

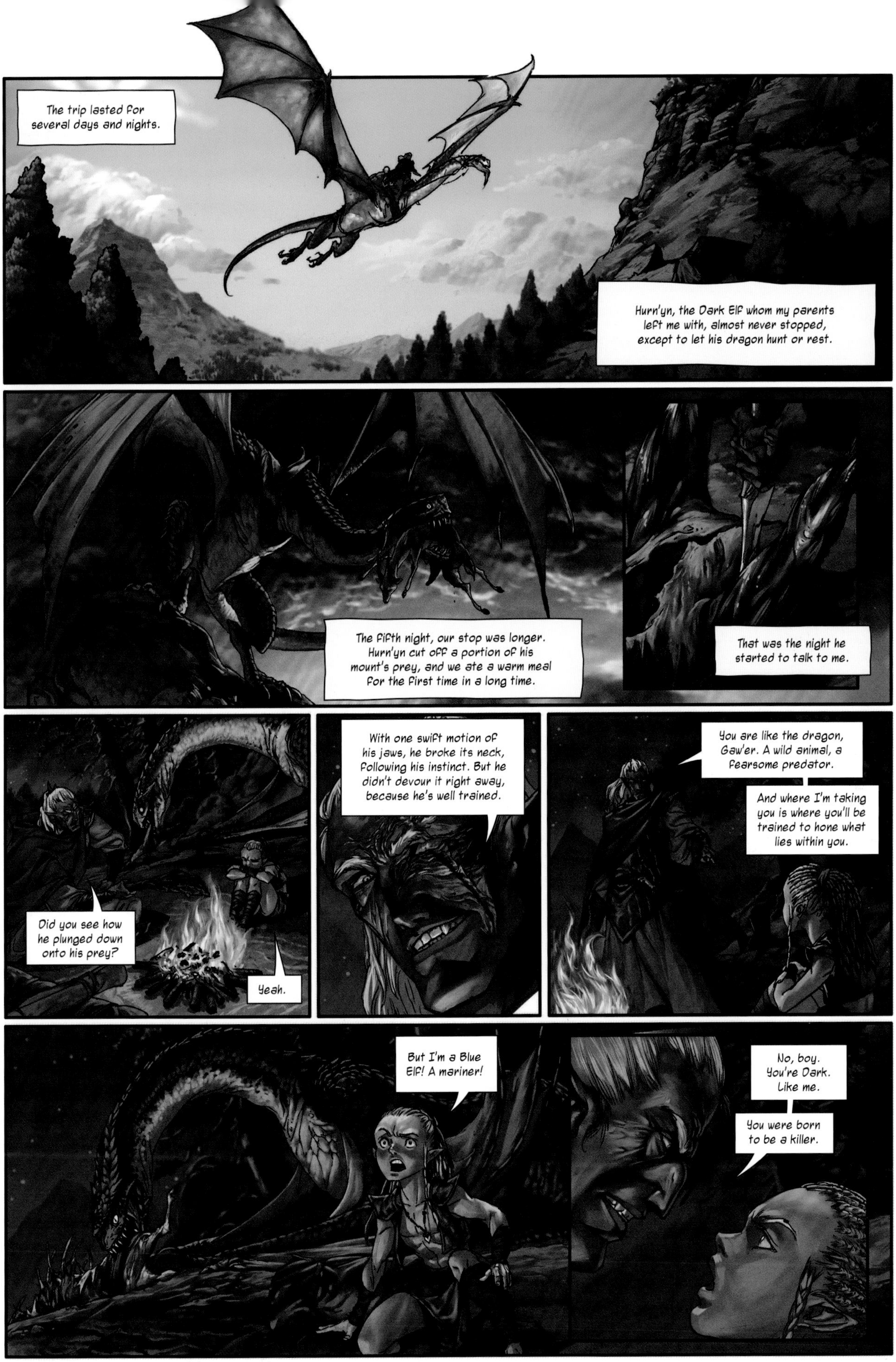
The trip lasted for several days and nights.
Hurn'yn, the Dark Elf whom my parents left me with, almost never stopped, except to let his dragon hunt or rest.
The fifth night, our stop was longer. Hurn'yn cut off a portion of his mount's prey, and we ate a warm meal for the first time in a long time.
That was the night he started to talk to me.
Did you see how he plunged down onto his prey?
Yeah.
With one swift motion of his jaws, he broke its neck, following his instinct. But he didn't devour it right away, because he's well trained.
You are like the dragon, Gaw'er. A wild animal, a fearsome predator.
And where I'm taking you is where you'll be trained to hone what lies within you.
But I'm a Blue Elf! A mariner!
No, boy. You're Dark. Like me.
You were born to be a killer.

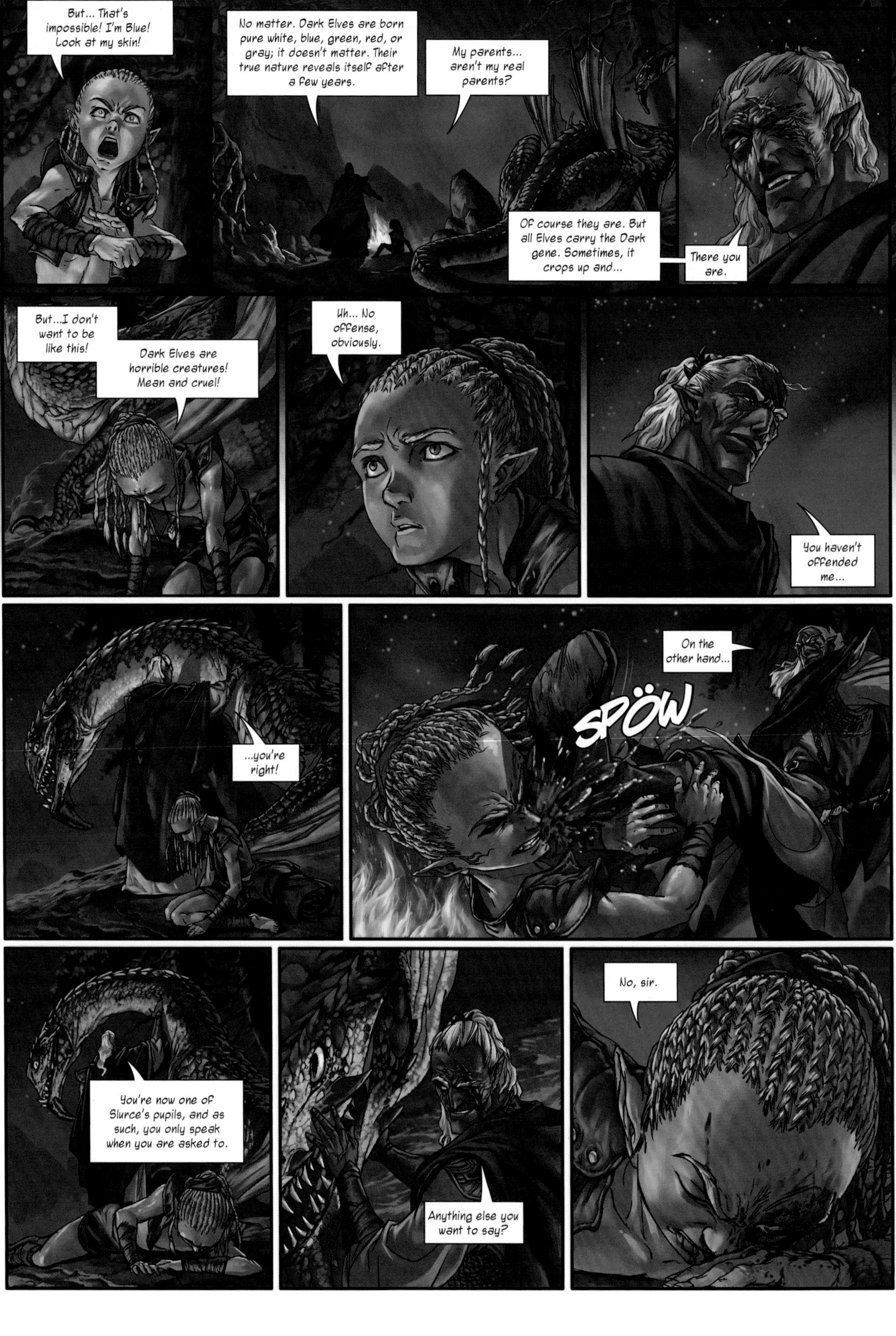
But... That's impossible! I'm Blue! Look at my skin!
No matter. Dark Elves are born pure white, blue, green, red, or gray; it doesn't matter. Their true nature reveals itself after a few years.
My parents... aren't my real parents?
Of course they are. But all Elves carry the Dark gene. Sometimes, it crops up and...
There you are.
But...I don't want to be like this!
Dark Elves are horrible creatures! Mean and cruel!
Uh... No offense, obviously.
You haven't offended me...
...you're right!
On the other hand...
SPÖW
You're now one of Slurce's pupils, and as such, you only speak when you are asked to.
Anything else you want to say?
No, sir.

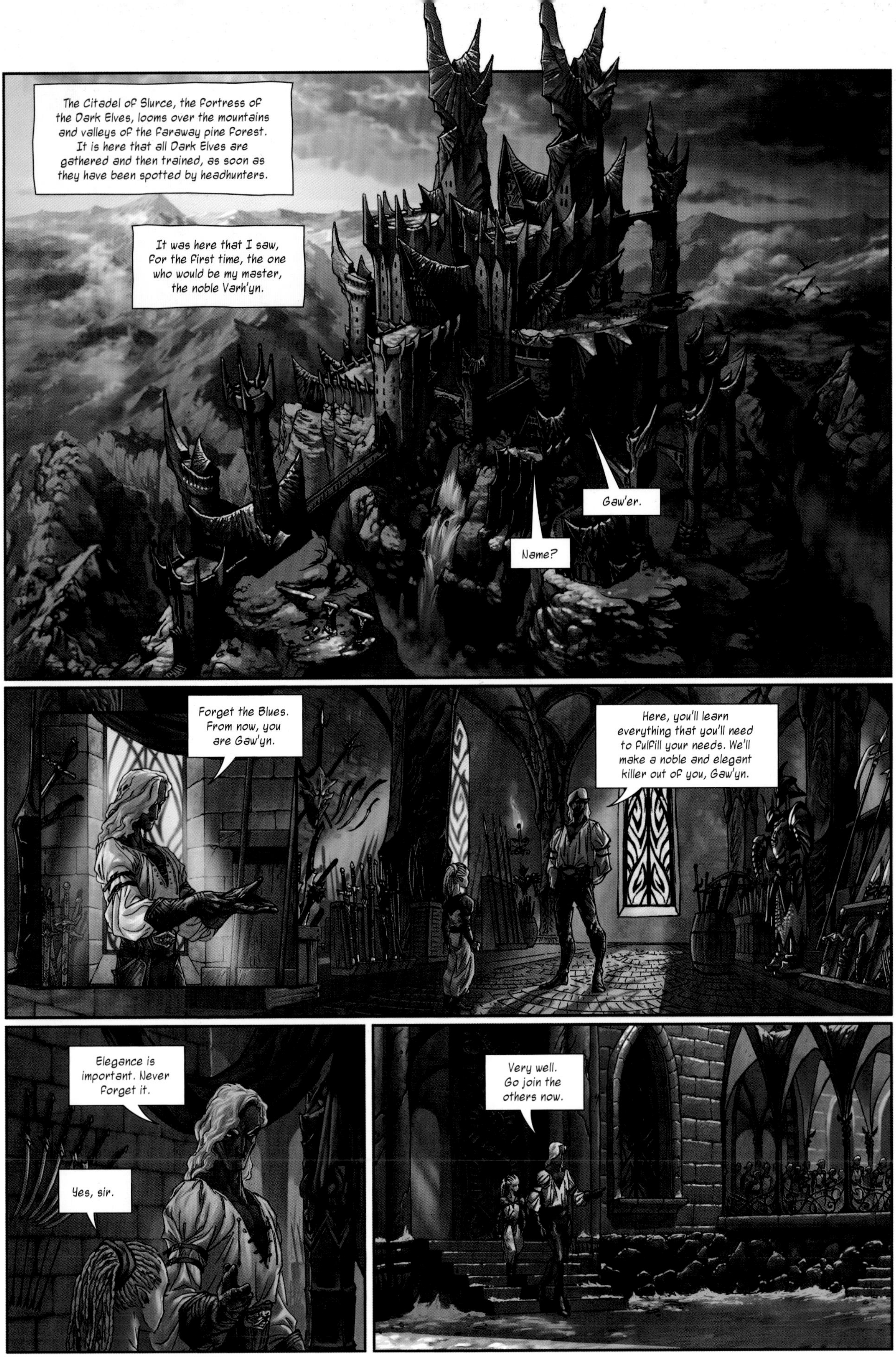

The Citadel of Slurce, the fortress of the Dark Elves, looms over the mountains and valleys of the faraway pine forest. It is here that all Dark Elves are gathered and then trained, as soon as they have been spotted by headhunters.
It was here that I saw, for the first time, the one who would be my master, the noble Varh'yn.
Name?
Gaw'er.
Forget the Blues. From now, you are Gaw'yn.
Here, you'll learn everything that you'll need to fulfill your needs. We'll make a noble and elegant killer out of you, Gaw'yn.
Elegance is important. Never forget it.
Yes, sir.
Very well. Go join the others now.

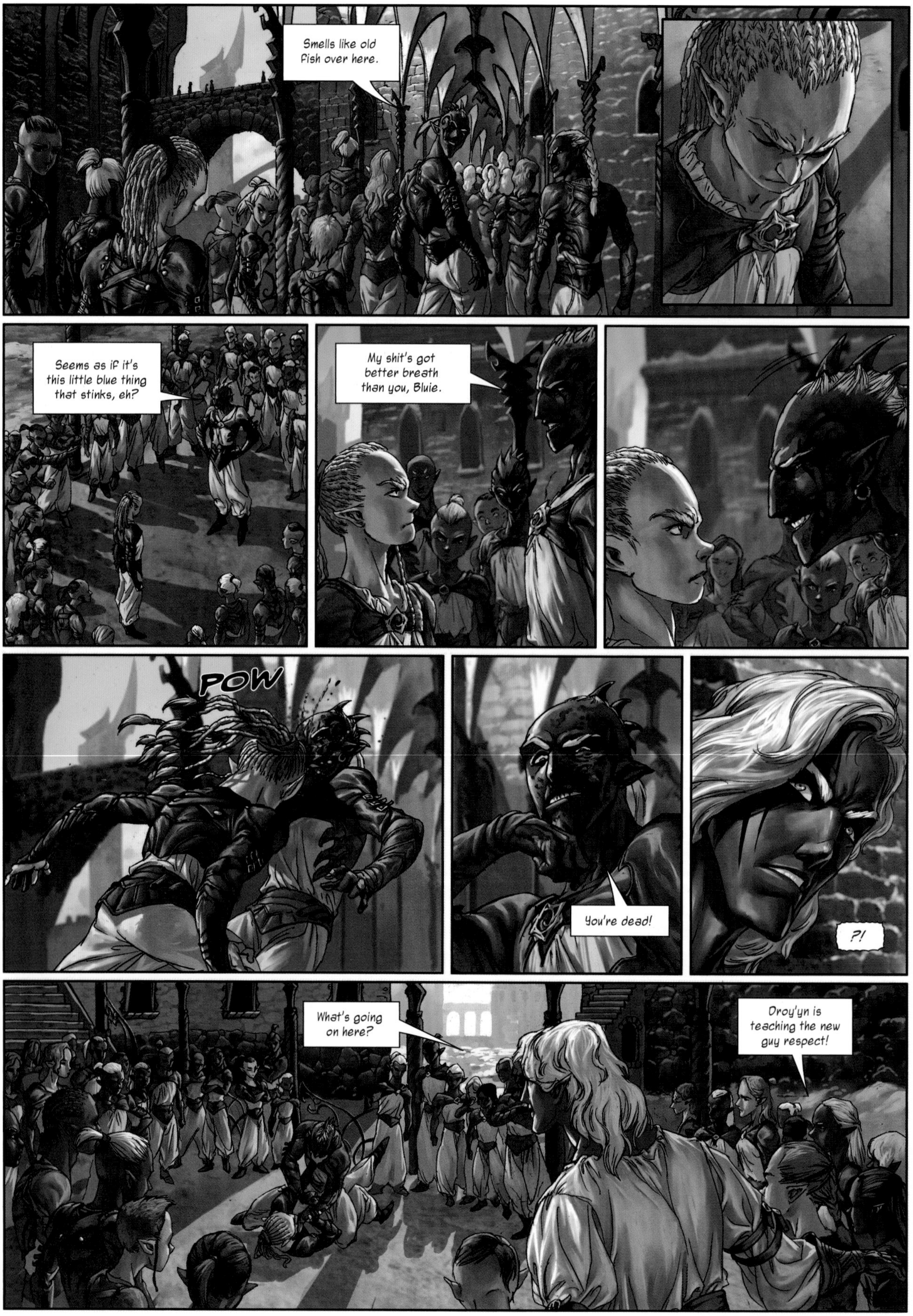
Smells like old fish over here.
Seems as if it's this little blue thing that stinks, eh?
My shit's got better breath than you, Bluie.
POW
You're dead!
?!
What's going on here?
Droy'yn is teaching the new guy respect!

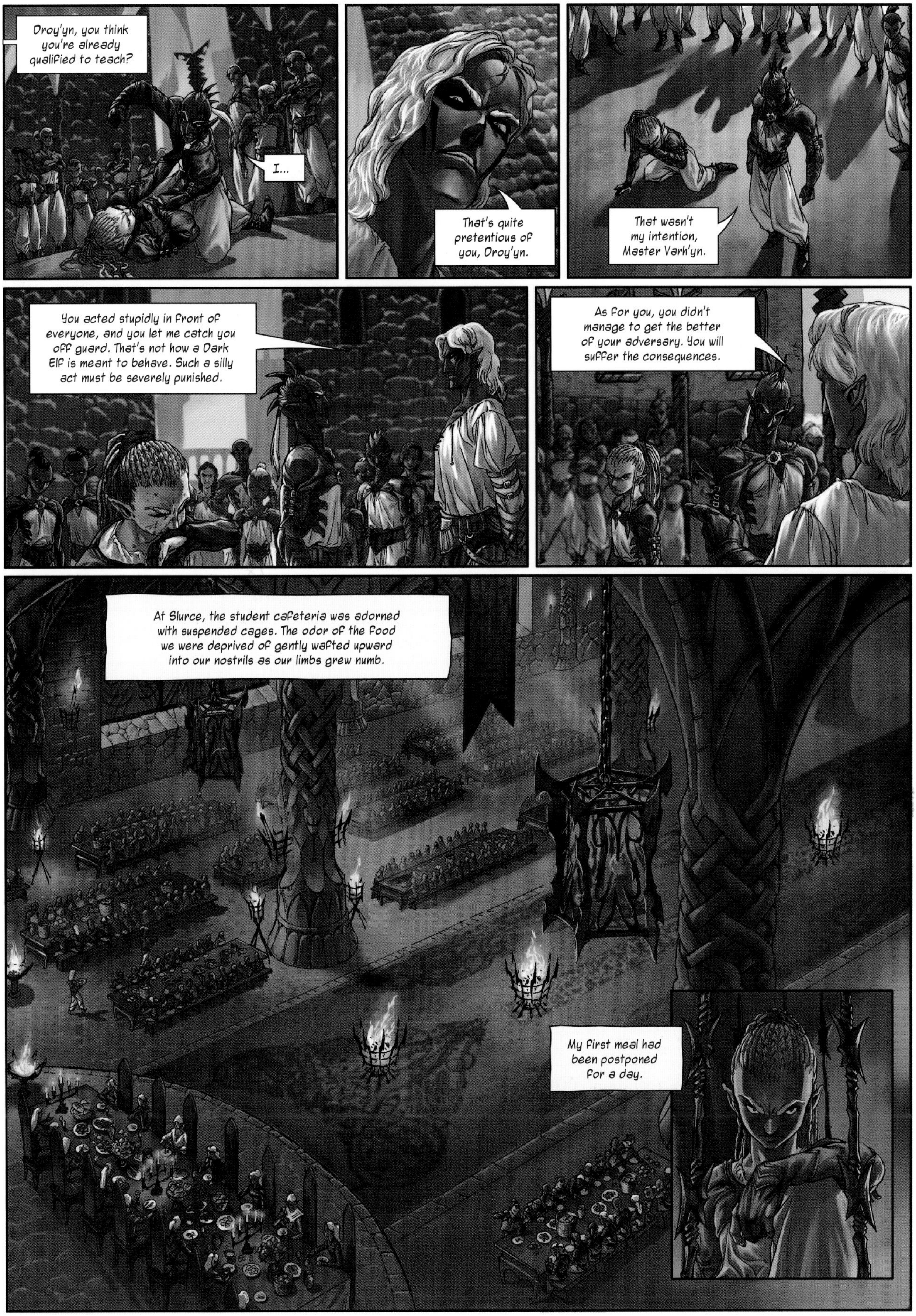
Oroy'yn, you think you're already qualified to teach?
I...
That's quite pretentious of you, Oroy'yn.
That wasn't my intention, Master Varh'yn.
You acted stupidly in front of everyone, and you let me catch you off guard. That's not how a Dark Elf is meant to behave. Such a silly act must be severely punished.
As for you, you didn't manage to get the better of your adversary. You will suffer the consequences.
At Slurce, the student cafeteria was adorned with suspended cages. The odor of the food we were deprived of gently wafted upward into our nostrils as our limbs grew numb.
My first meal had been postponed for a day.

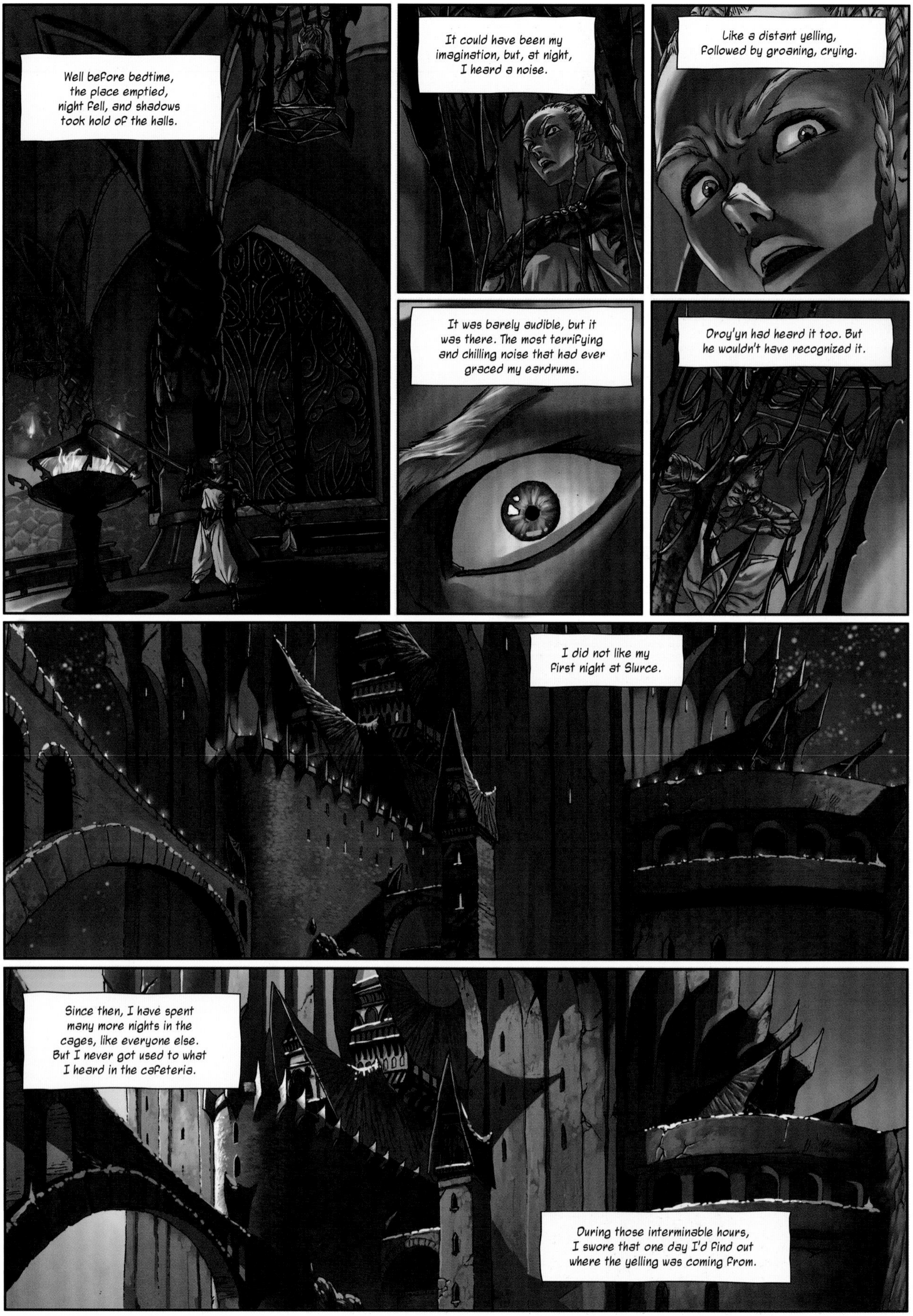
Well before bedtime, the place emptied, night fell, and shadows took hold of the halls.
It could have been my imagination, but, at night, I heard a noise.
Like a distant yelling, followed by groaning, crying.
It was barely audible, but it was there. The most terrifying and chilling noise that had ever graced my eardrums.
Droy'yn had heard it too. But he wouldn't have recognized it.
I did not like my first night at Slurce.
Since then, I have spent many more nights in the cages, like everyone else. But I never got used to what I heard in the cafeteria.
During those interminable hours, I swore that one day I'd find out where the yelling was coming from.

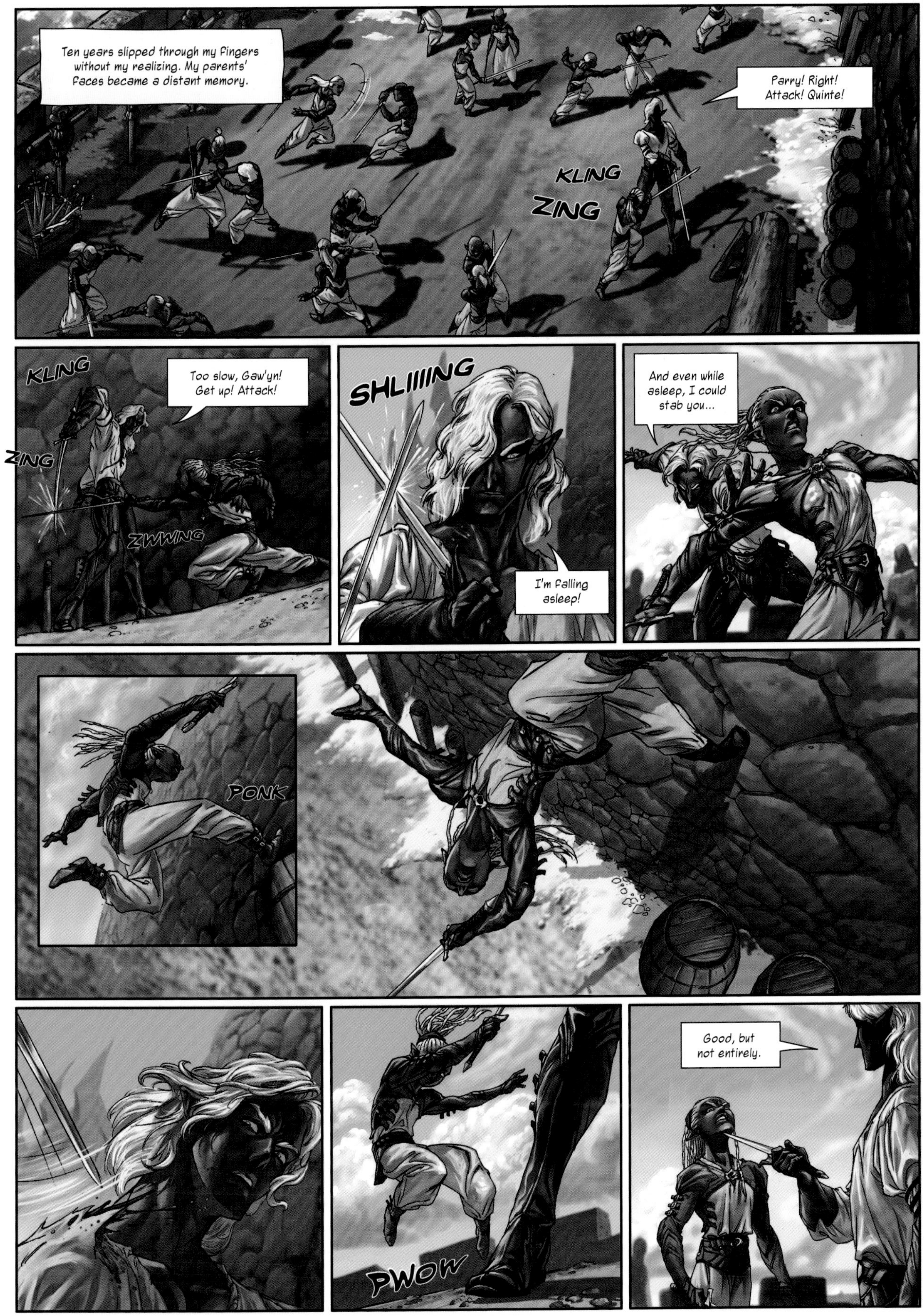
Ten years slipped through my fingers without my realizing. My parents' faces became a distant memory.
Parry! Right! Attack! Quinte!
KLING
ZING
KLING
Too slow, Gaw'yn! Get up! Attack!
ZING
ZWWING
SHLIIIING
I'm falling asleep!
And even while asleep, I could stab you...
PONK
PWOW
Good, but not entirely.

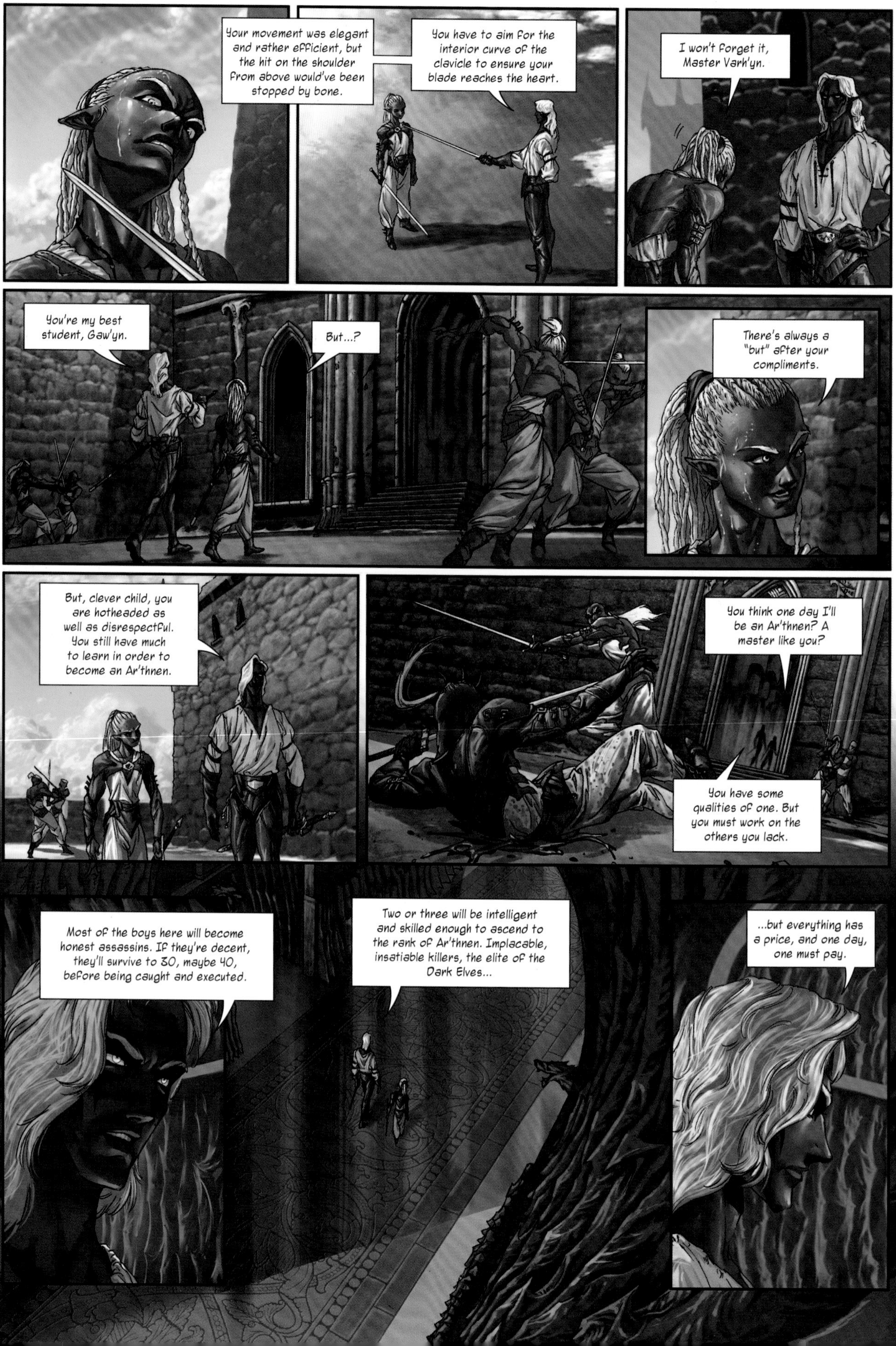
Your movement was elegant and rather efficient, but the hit on the shoulder from above would've been stopped by bone.
You have to aim for the interior curve of the clavicle to ensure your blade reaches the heart.
I won't forget it, Master Varh'yn.
You're my best student, Gaw'yn.
But...?
There's always a "but" after your compliments.
But, clever child, you are hotheaded as well as disrespectful. You still have much to learn in order to become an Ar'thnen.
You think one day I'll be an Ar'thnen? A master like you?
You have some qualities of one. But you must work on the others you lack.
Most of the boys here will become honest assassins. If they're decent, they'll survive to 30, maybe 40, before being caught and executed.
Two or three will be intelligent and skilled enough to ascend to the rank of Ar'thnen. Implacable, insatiable killers, the elite of the Dark Elves...
...but everything has a price, and one day, one must pay.

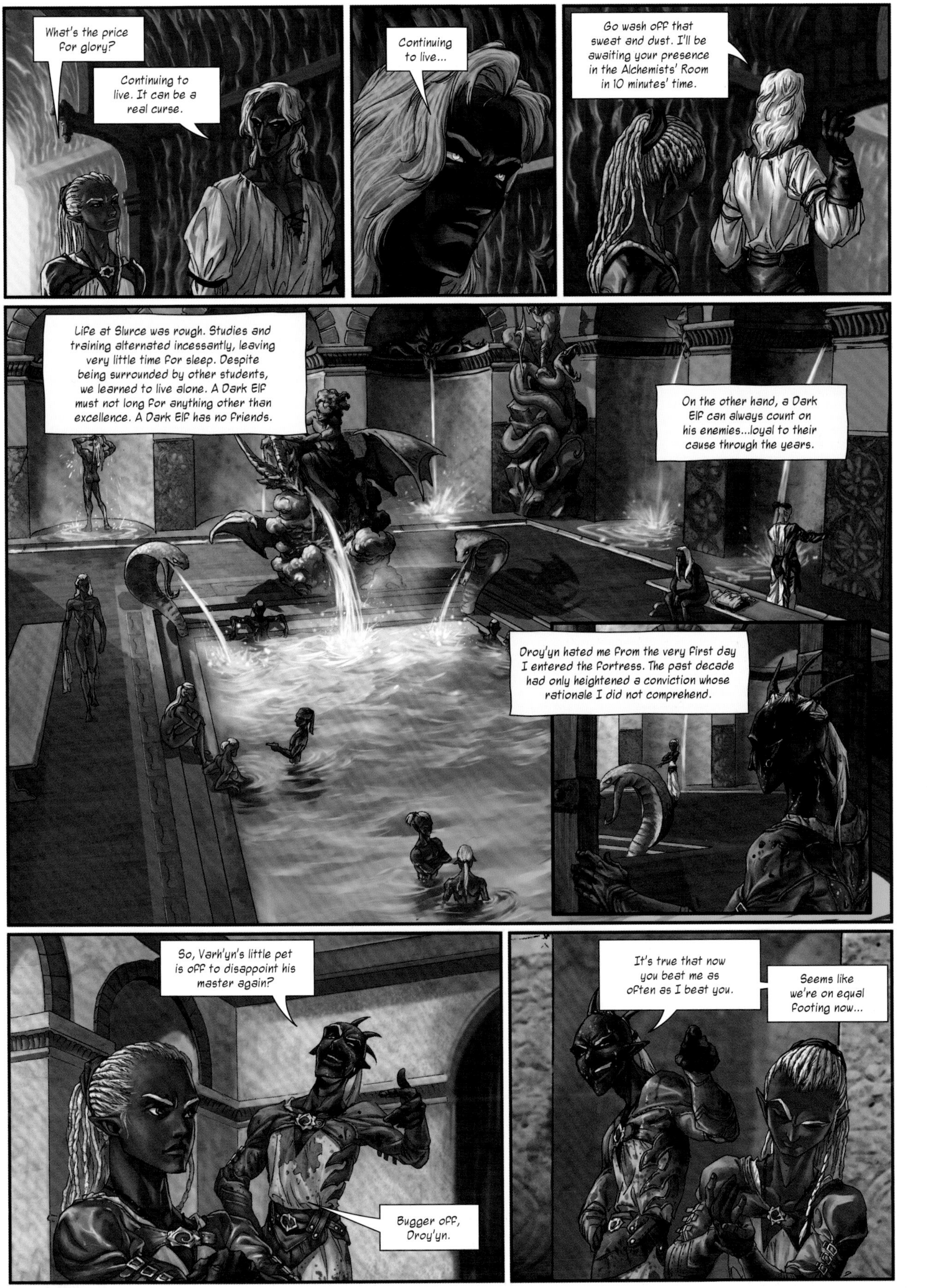
What's the price for glory?
Continuing to live. It can be a real curse.
Continuing to live...
Go wash off that sweat and dust. I'll be awaiting your presence in the Alchemists' Room in 10 minutes' time.
Life at Slurce was rough. Studies and training alternated incessantly, leaving very little time for sleep. Despite being surrounded by other students, we learned to live alone. A Dark Elf must not long for anything other than excellence. A Dark Elf has no friends.
On the other hand, a Dark Elf can always count on his enemies...loyal to their cause through the years.
Droy'yn hated me from the very first day I entered the Fortress. The past decade had only heightened a conviction whose rationale I did not comprehend.
So, Varh'yn's little pet is off to disappoint his master again?
Bugger off, Droy'yn.
It's true that now you beat me as often as I beat you.
Seems like we're on equal footing now...

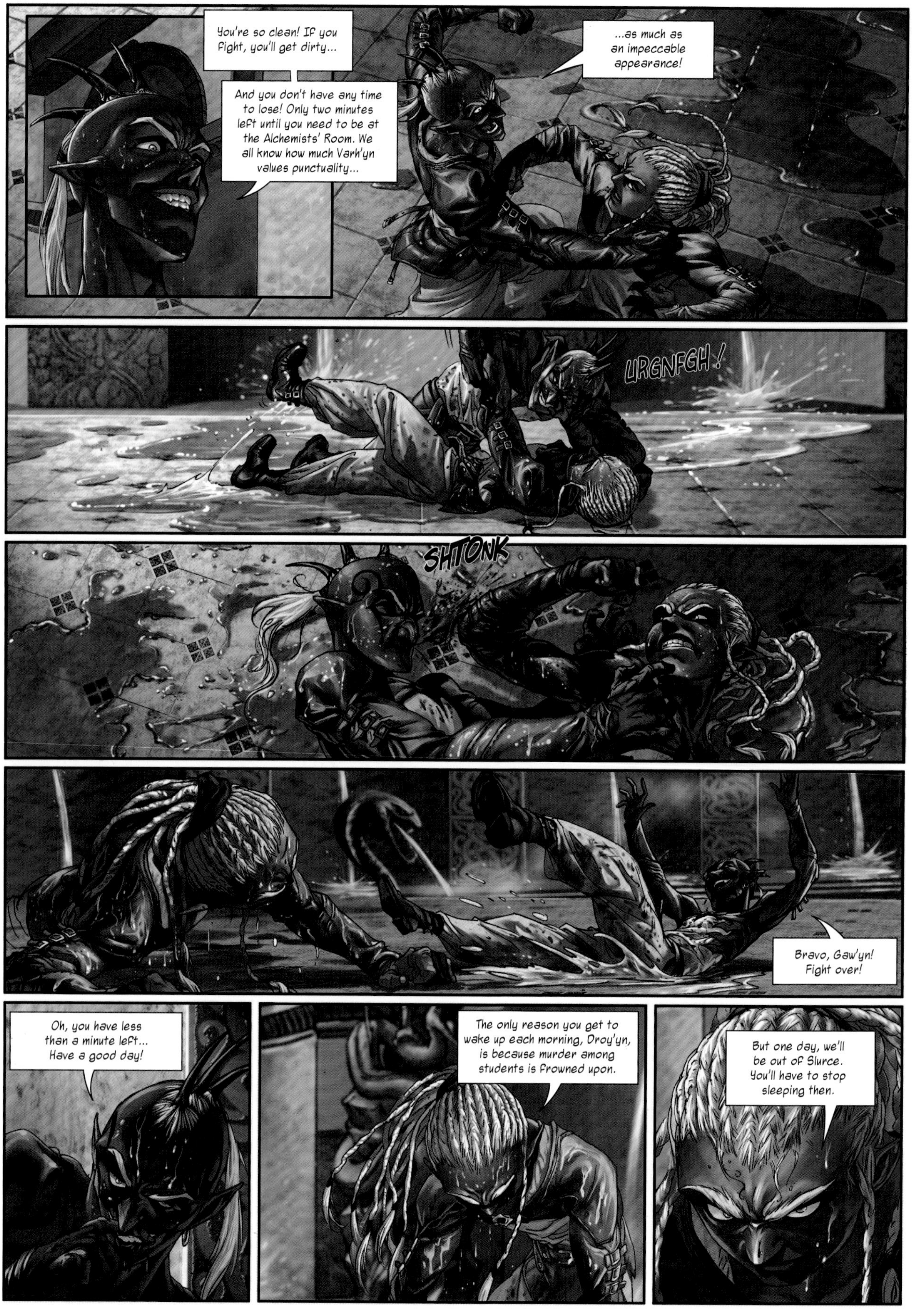

You're so clean! If you fight, you'll get dirty...
And you don't have any time to lose! Only two minutes left until you need to be at the Alchemists' Room. We all know how much Varh'yn values punctuality...
...as much as an impeccable appearance!
URGNFGH!
SHTONK
Bravo, Gaw'yn! Fight over!
Oh, you have less than a minute left... Have a good day!
The only reason you get to wake up each morning, Droy'yn, is because murder among students is frowned upon.
But one day, we'll be out of Slurce. You'll have to stop sleeping then.

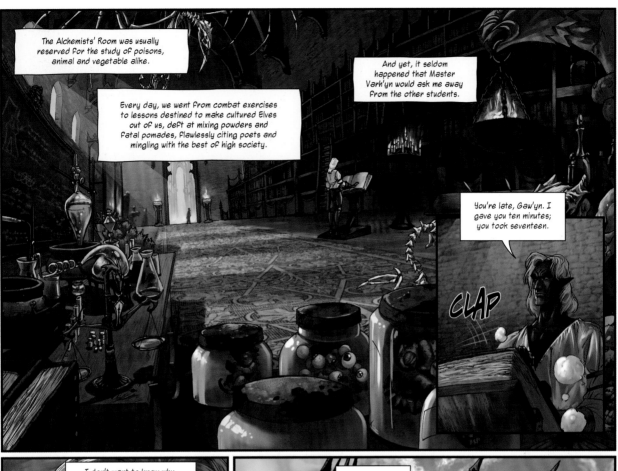

The Alchemists' Room was usually reserved for the study of poisons, animal and vegetable alike.

Every day, we went from combat exercises to lessons destined to make cultured Elves out of us, deft at mixing powders and fatal pomades, flawlessly citing poets and mingling with the best of high society.

And yet, it seldom happened that Master Varh'yn would ask me away from the other students.

You're late, Gaw'yn. I gave you ten minutes; you took seventeen.

CLAP

I don't want to know why. You will be whipped. Seven lashes, one for each minute you were late. I think your friend Oroy'yn will be thrilled to officiate.

He certainly will be, Master.

You can bring your punishment to his attention when we have finished here.

Since you are perhaps destined to become an Ar'thnen, you must know that there's a daily struggle to which you'll need to submit yourself.

Do you know about these plants?

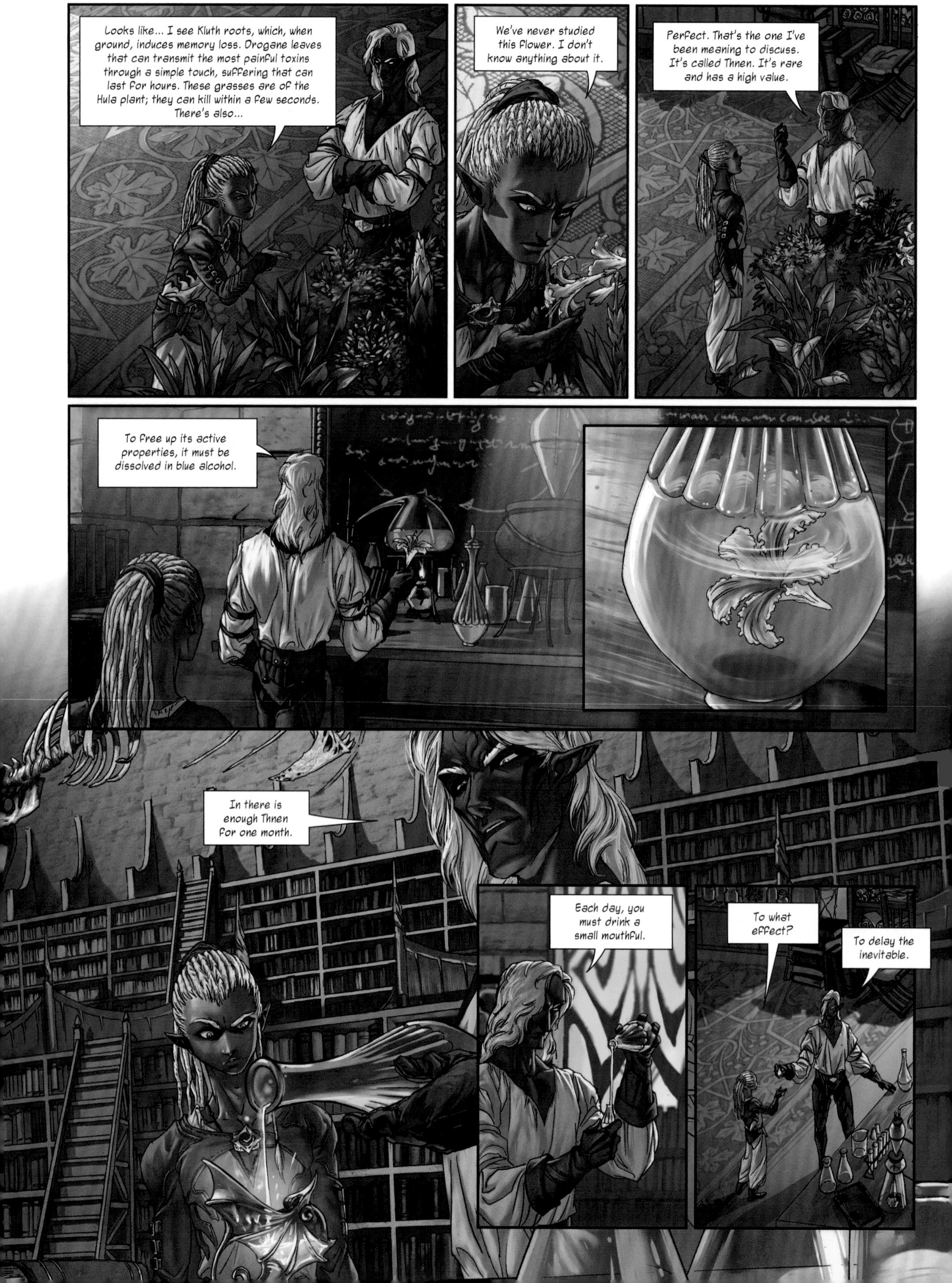

Looks like... I see Kluth roots, which, when ground, induces memory loss. Drogane leaves that can transmit the most painful toxins through a simple touch, suffering that can last for hours. These grasses are of the Hula plant; they can kill within a few seconds. There's also...
We've never studied this flower. I don't know anything about it.
Perfect. That's the one I've been meaning to discuss. It's called Thnen. It's rare and has a high value.
To free up its active properties, it must be dissolved in blue alcohol.
In there is enough Thnen for one month.
Each day, you must drink a small mouthful.
To what effect?
To delay the inevitable.

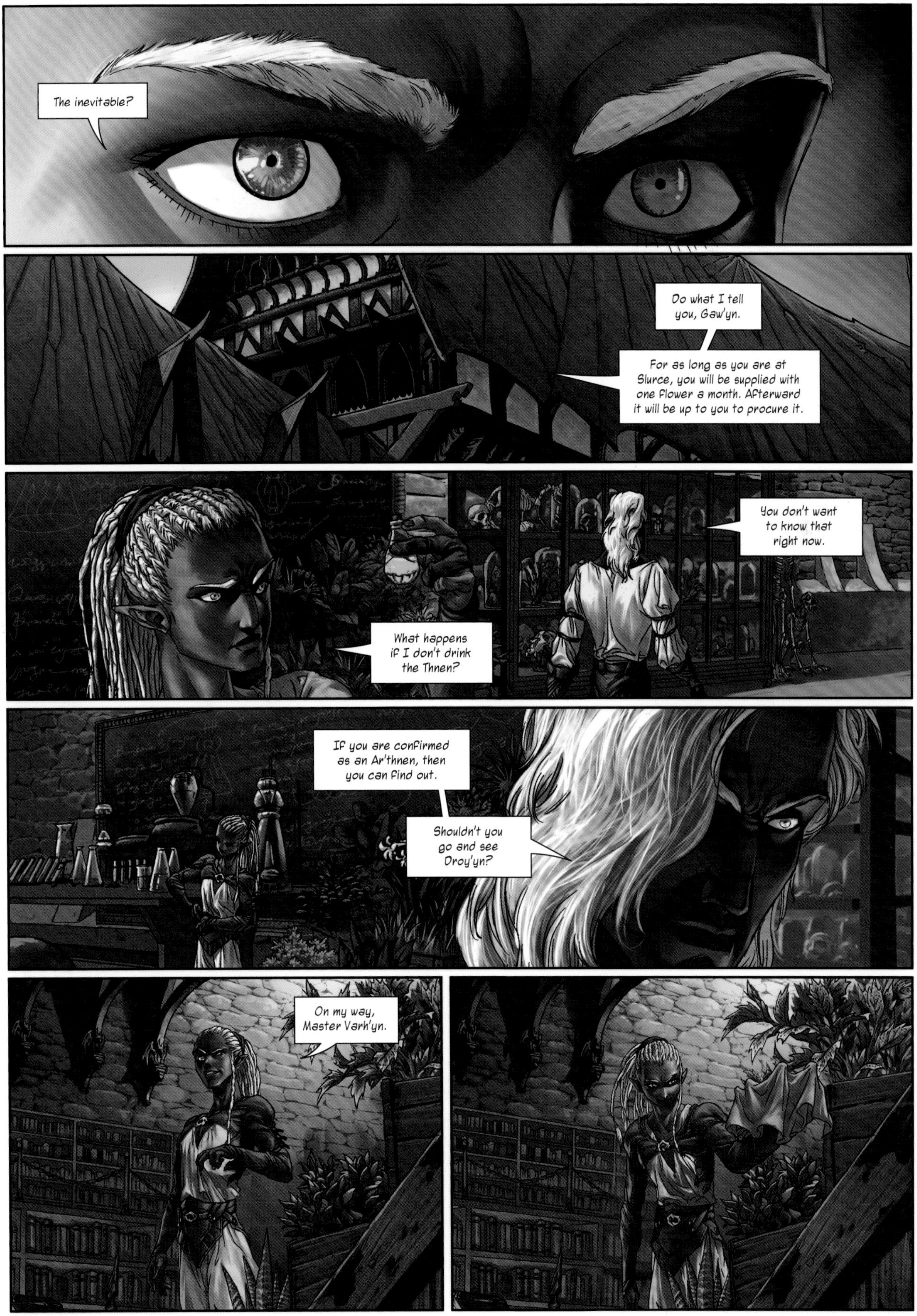
The inevitable?
Do what I tell you, Gaw'yn.
For as long as you are at Slurce, you will be supplied with one flower a month. Afterward it will be up to you to procure it.
You don't want to know that right now.
What happens if I don't drink the Thnen?
If you are confirmed as an Ar'thnen, then you can find out.
Shouldn't you go and see Droy'yn?
On my way, Master Varh'yn.

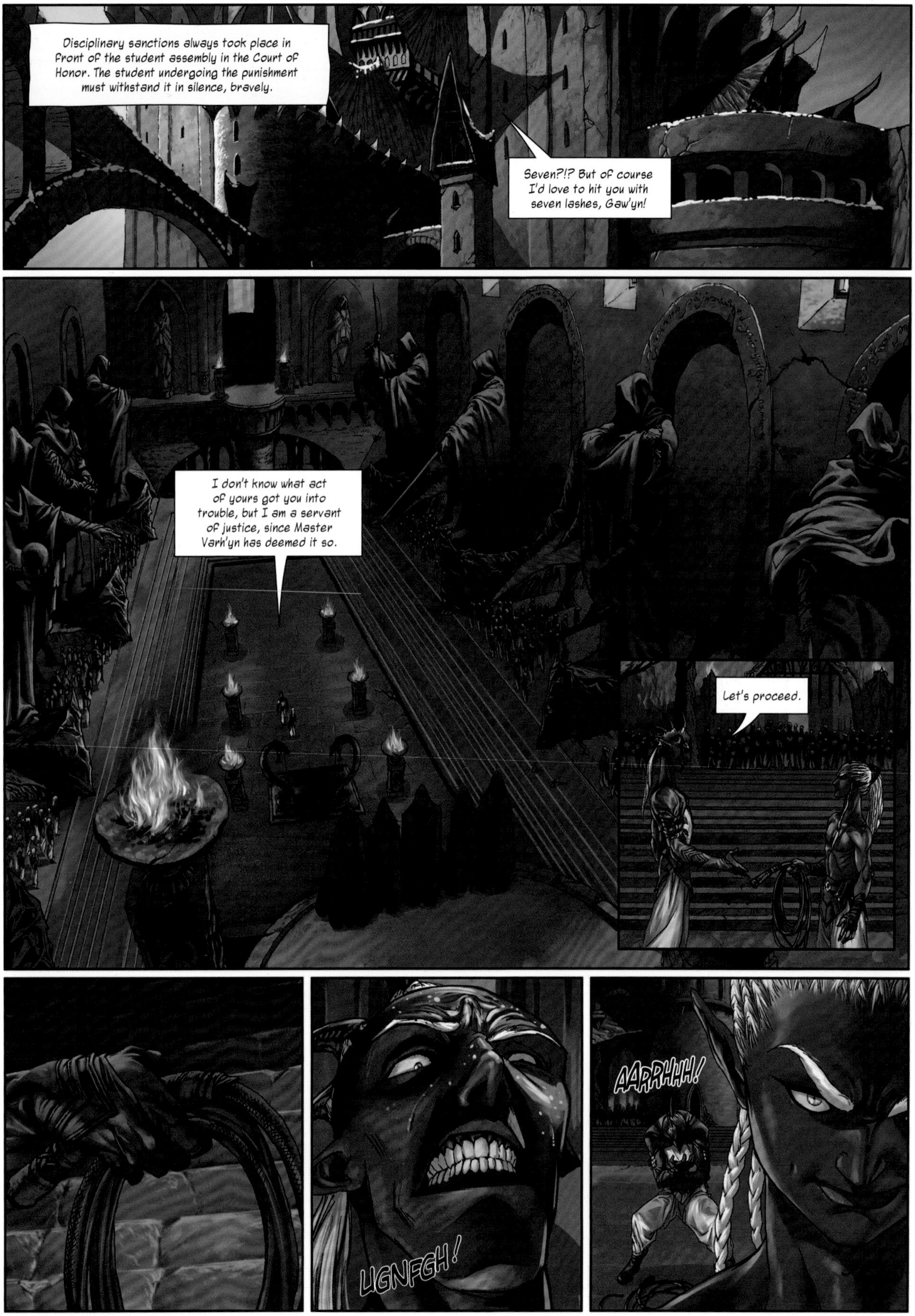
Disciplinary sanctions always took place in front of the student assembly in the Court of Honor. The student undergoing the punishment must withstand it in silence, bravely.
Seven?!? But of course I'd love to hit you with seven lashes, Gaw'yn!
I don't know what act of yours got you into trouble, but I am a servant of justice, since Master Varh'yn has deemed it so.
Let's proceed.
UGNFGH!
AARRHHH!

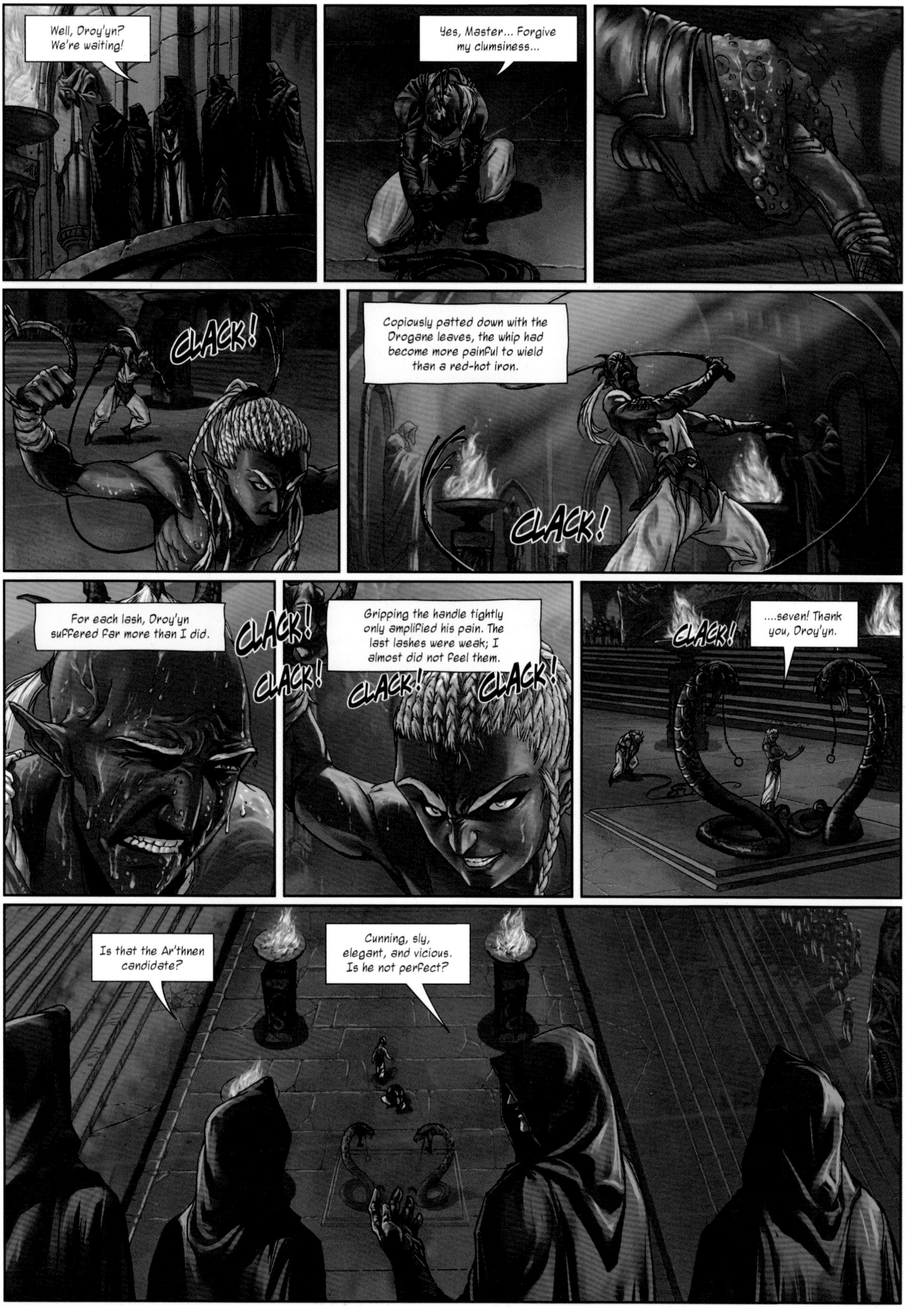
Well, Droy'yn? We're waiting!
Yes, Master... Forgive my clumsiness...
CLACK!
Copiously patted down with the Drogane leaves, the whip had become more painful to wield than a red-hot iron.
CLACK!
For each lash, Droy'yn suffered far more than I did.
CLACK!
CLACK!
Gripping the handle tightly only amplified his pain. The last lashes were weak; I almost did not feel them.
CLACK!
CLACK!
CLACK!
....seven! Thank you, Droy'yn.
Is that the Ar'thnen candidate?
Cunning, sly, elegant, and vicious. Is he not perfect?

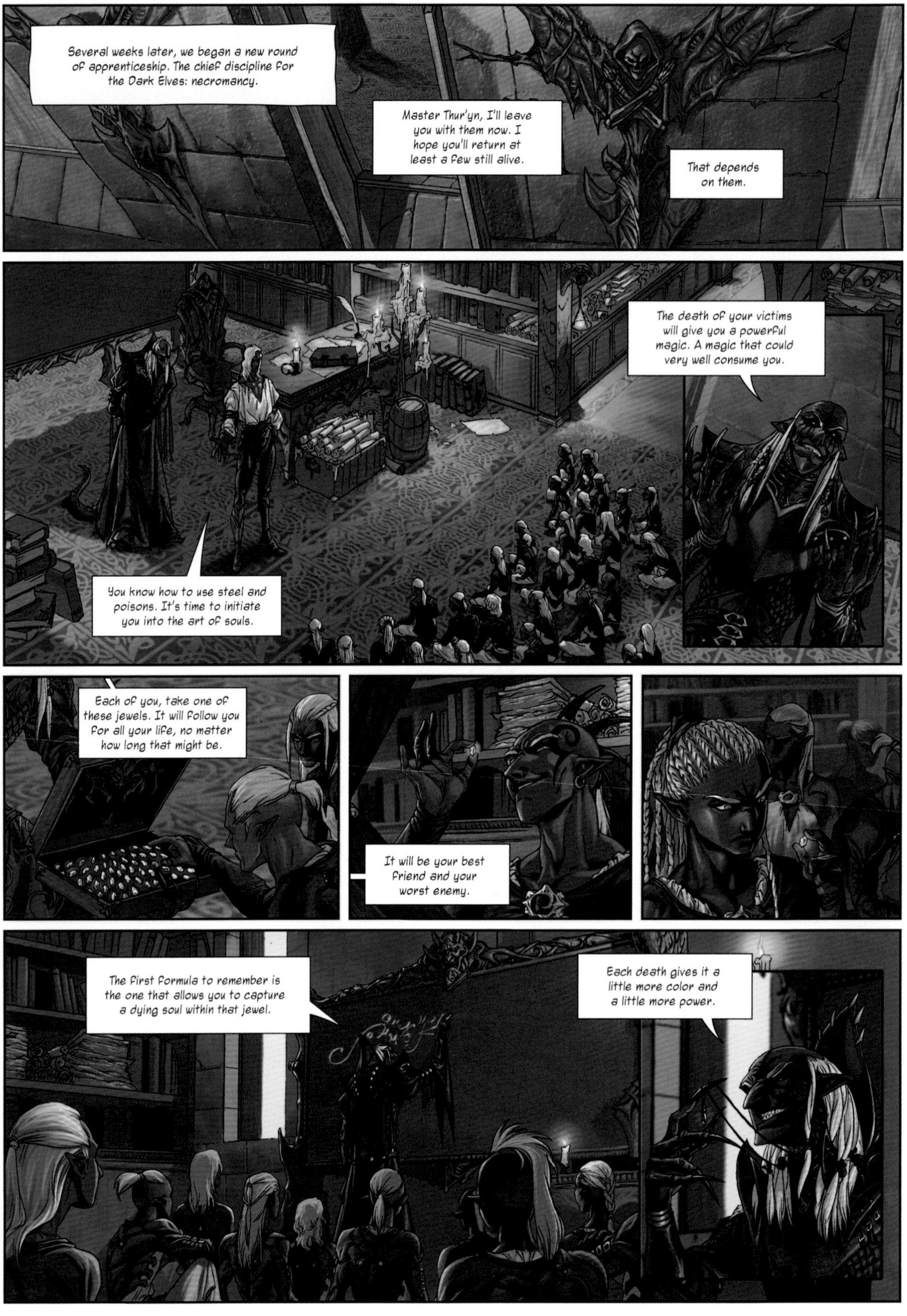
Several weeks later, we began a new round of apprenticeship. The chief discipline for the Dark Elves: necromancy.
Master Thur'yn, I'll leave you with them now. I hope you'll return at least a few still alive.
That depends on them.
The death of your victims will give you a powerful magic. A magic that could very well consume you.
You know how to use steel and poisons. It's time to initiate you into the art of souls.
Each of you, take one of these jewels. It will follow you for all your life, no matter how long that might be.
It will be your best friend and your worst enemy.
The first formula to remember is the one that allows you to capture a dying soul within that jewel.
Each death gives it a little more color and a little more power.

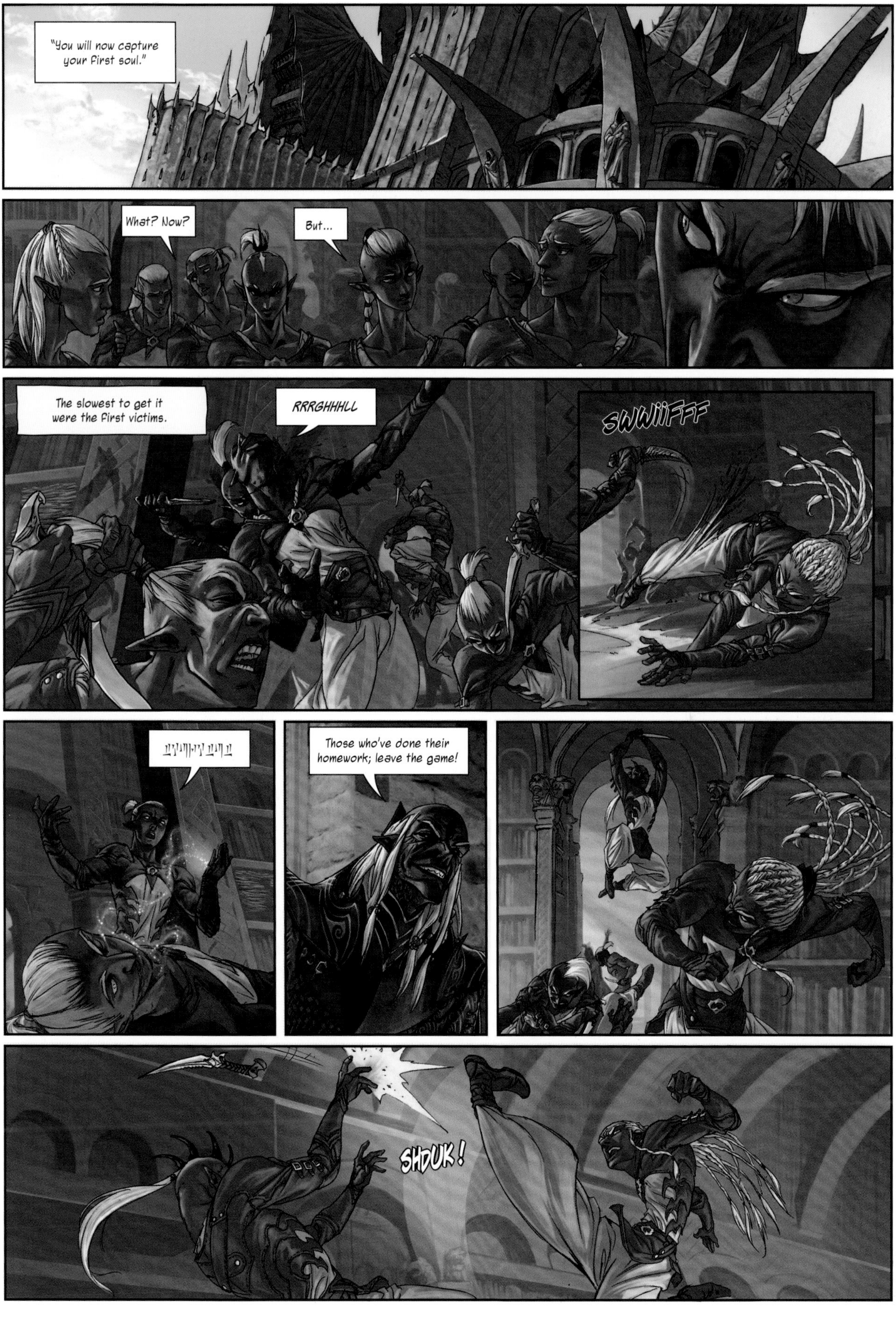
"You will now capture your first soul."
What? Now?
But...
The slowest to get it were the first victims.
RRRGHHHLL
SWWiiFFF
Those who've done their homework; leave the game!
SHDUK!

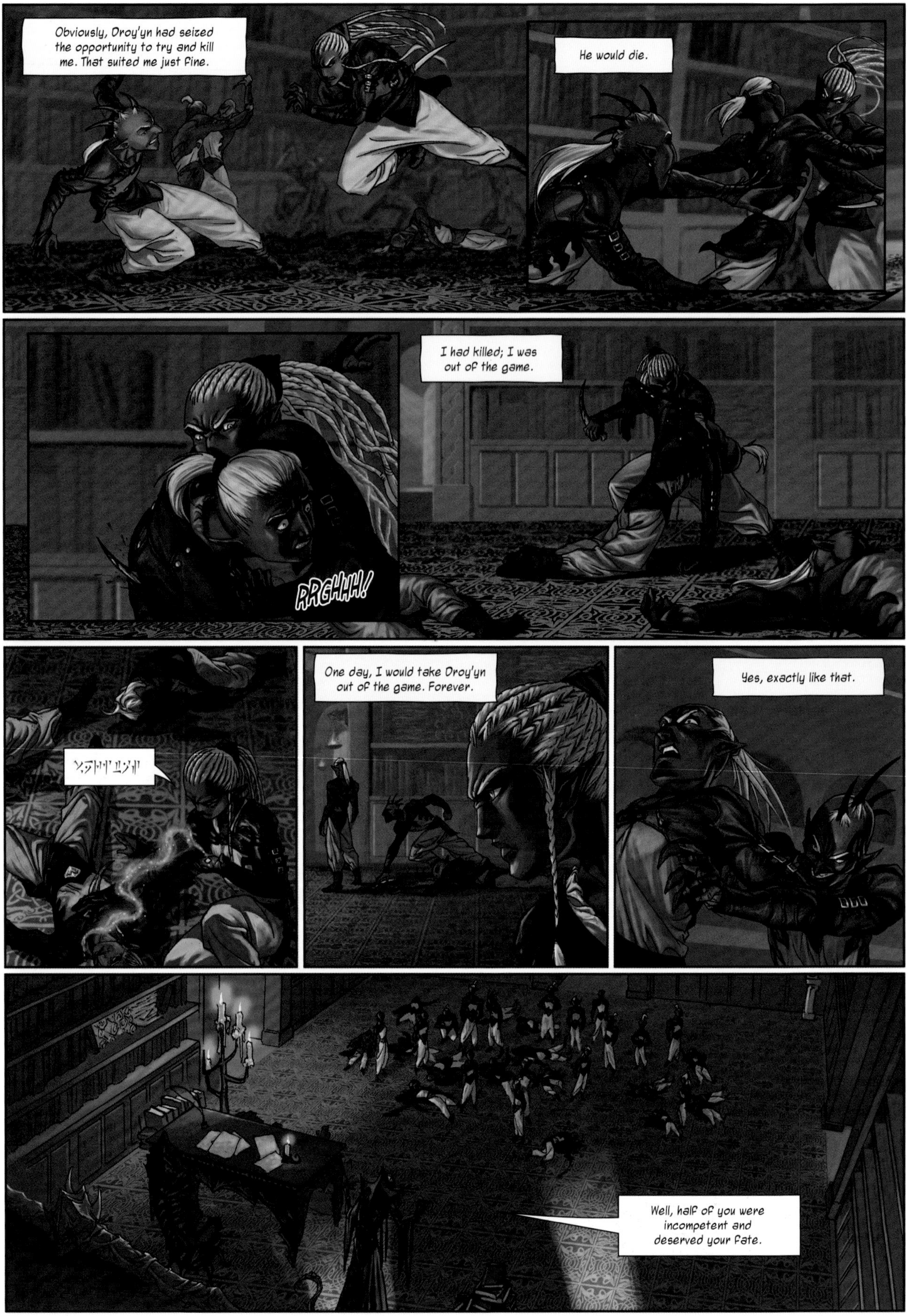
Obviously, Droy'yn had seized the opportunity to try and kill me. That suited me just fine.
He would die.
I had killed; I was out of the game.
RRGHHH!
One day, I would take Droy'yn out of the game. Forever.
Yes, exactly like that.
Well, half of you were incompetent and deserved your fate.

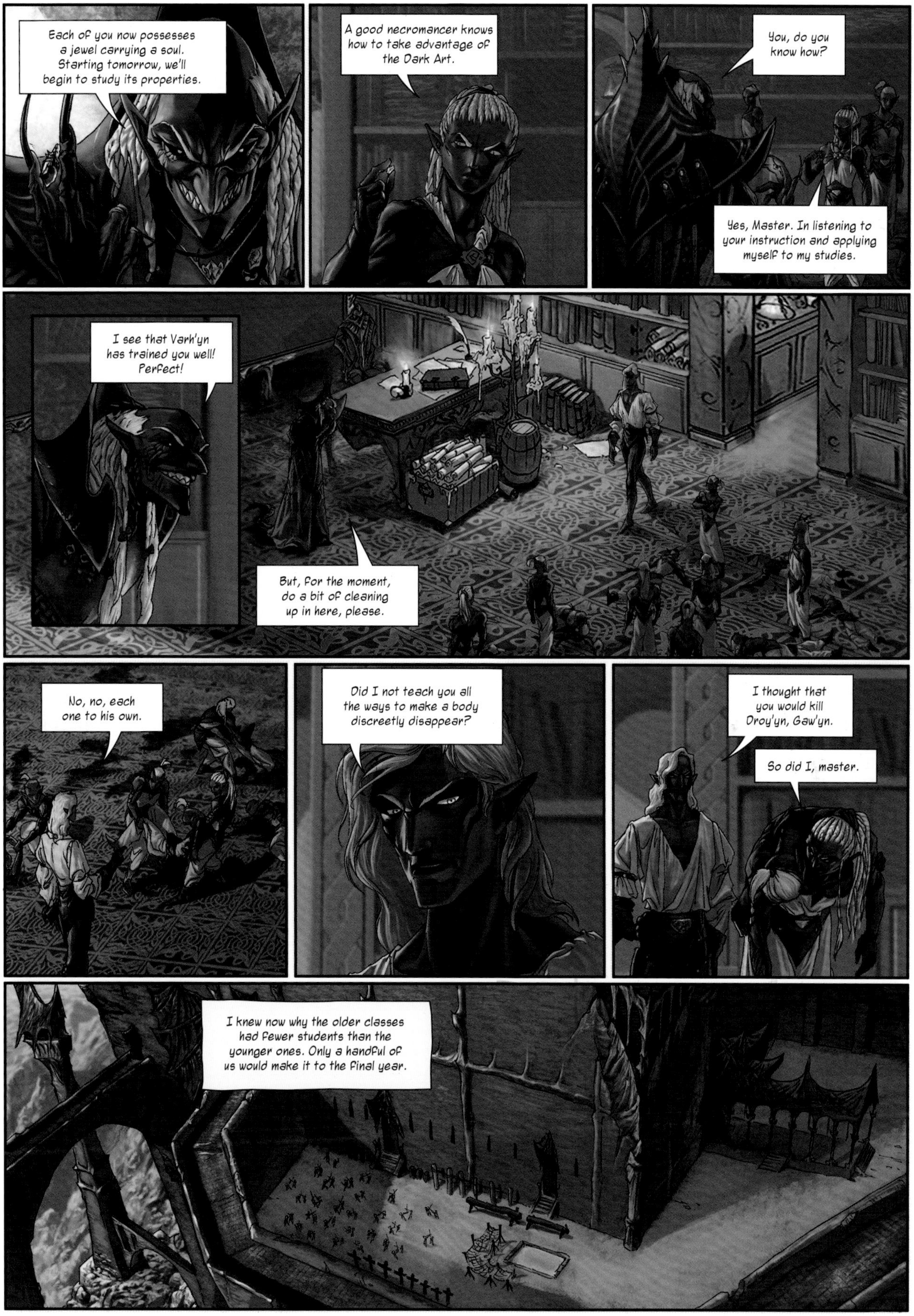
Each of you now possesses a jewel carrying a soul. Starting tomorrow, we'll begin to study its properties.
A good necromancer knows how to take advantage of the Dark Art.
You, do you know how?
Yes, Master. In listening to your instruction and applying myself to my studies.
I see that Varh'yn has trained you well! Perfect!
But, for the moment, do a bit of cleaning up in here, please.
No, no, each one to his own.
Did I not teach you all the ways to make a body discreetly disappear?
I thought that you would kill Droy'yn, Gaw'yn.
So did I, master.
I knew now why the older classes had fewer students than the younger ones. Only a handful of us would make it to the final year.

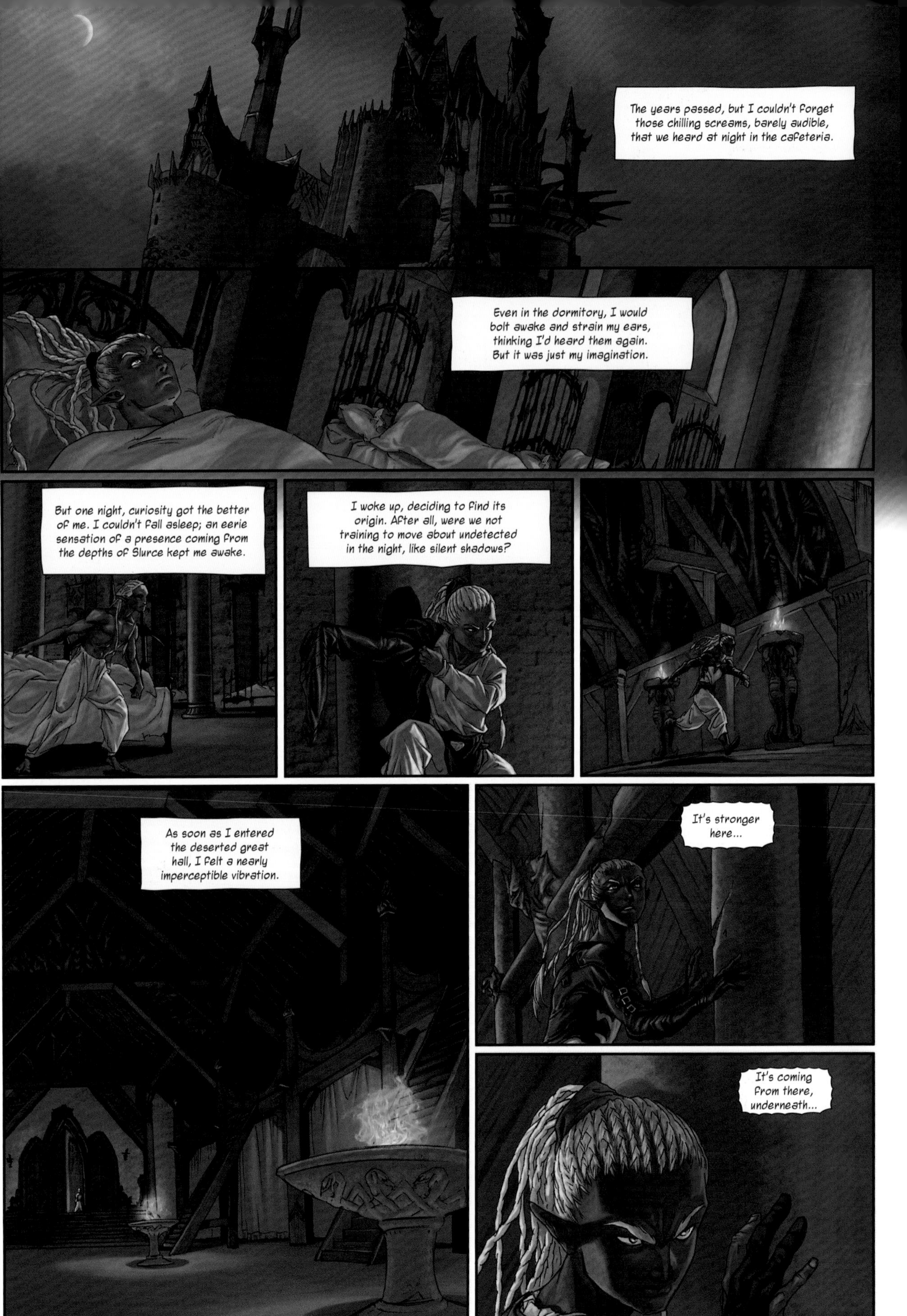

The years passed, but I couldn't forget those chilling screams, barely audible, that we heard at night in the cafeteria.
Even in the dormitory, I would bolt awake and strain my ears, thinking I'd heard them again. But it was just my imagination.
But one night, curiosity got the better of me. I couldn't fall asleep; an eerie sensation of a presence coming from the depths of Slurce kept me awake.
I woke up, deciding to find its origin. After all, were we not training to move about undetected in the night, like silent shadows?
As soon as I entered the deserted great hall, I felt a nearly imperceptible vibration.
It's stronger here...
It's coming from there, underneath...

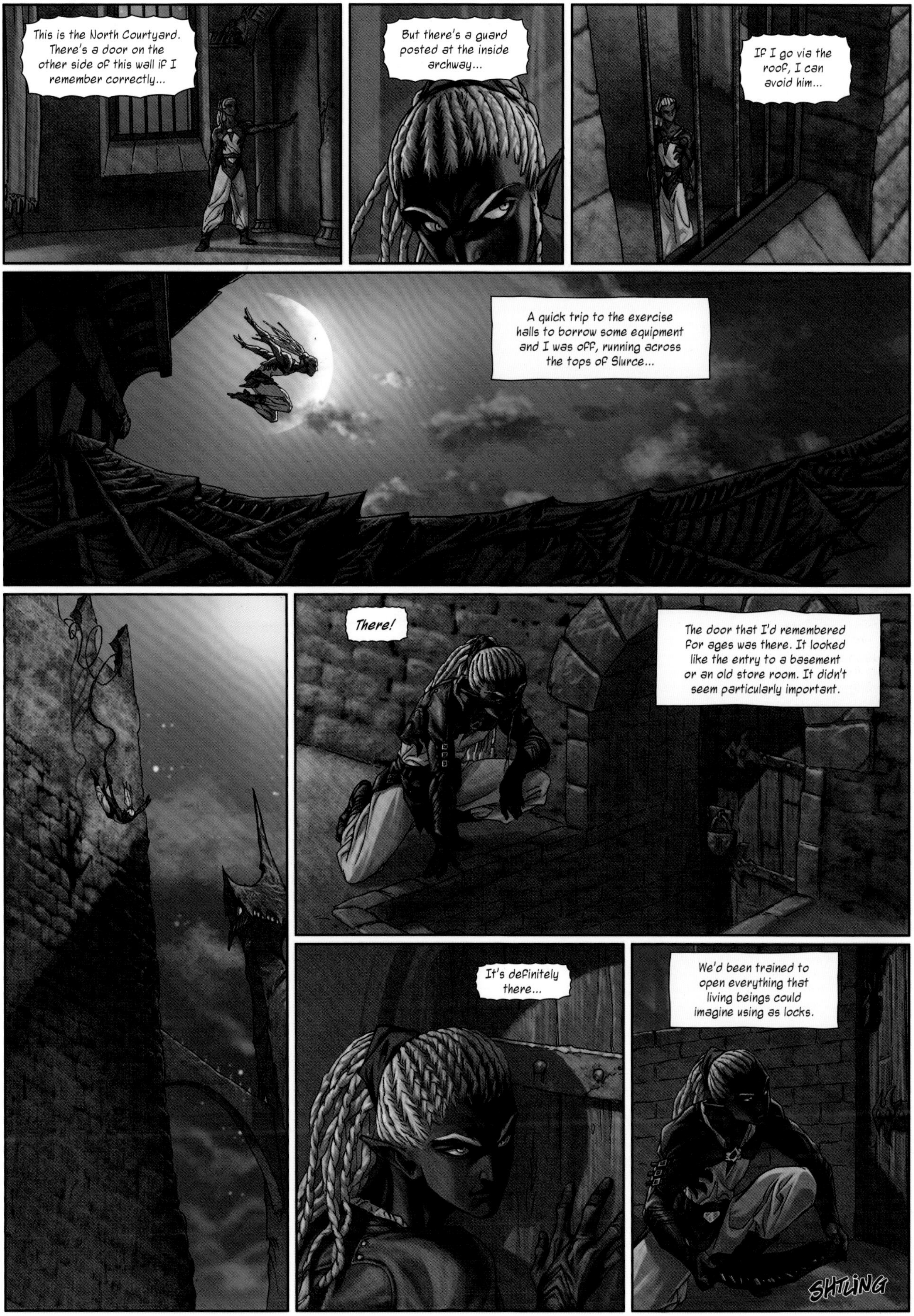
This is the North Courtyard. There's a door on the other side of this wall if I remember correctly...
But there's a guard posted at the inside archway...
If I go via the roof, I can avoid him...
A quick trip to the exercise halls to borrow some equipment and I was off, running across the tops of Slurce...
There!
The door that I'd remembered for ages was there. It looked like the entry to a basement or an old store room. It didn't seem particularly important.
It's definitely there...
We'd been trained to open everything that living beings could imagine using as locks.
SHTLING

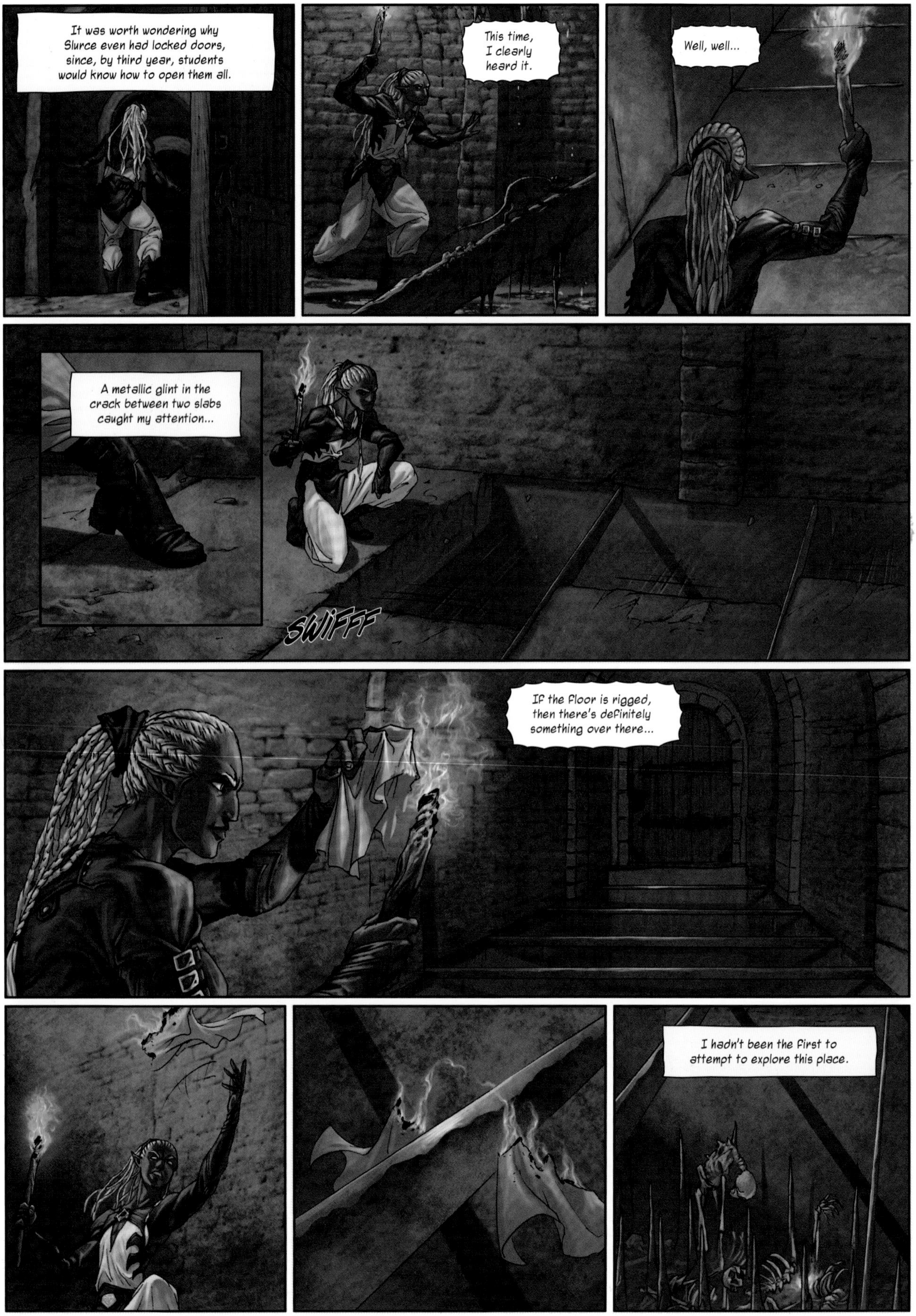
It was worth wondering why Slurce even had locked doors, since, by third year, students would know how to open them all.
This time, I clearly heard it.
Well, well...
A metallic glint in the crack between two slabs caught my attention...
SWIFFF
If the floor is rigged, then there's definitely something over there...
I hadn't been the first to attempt to explore this place.

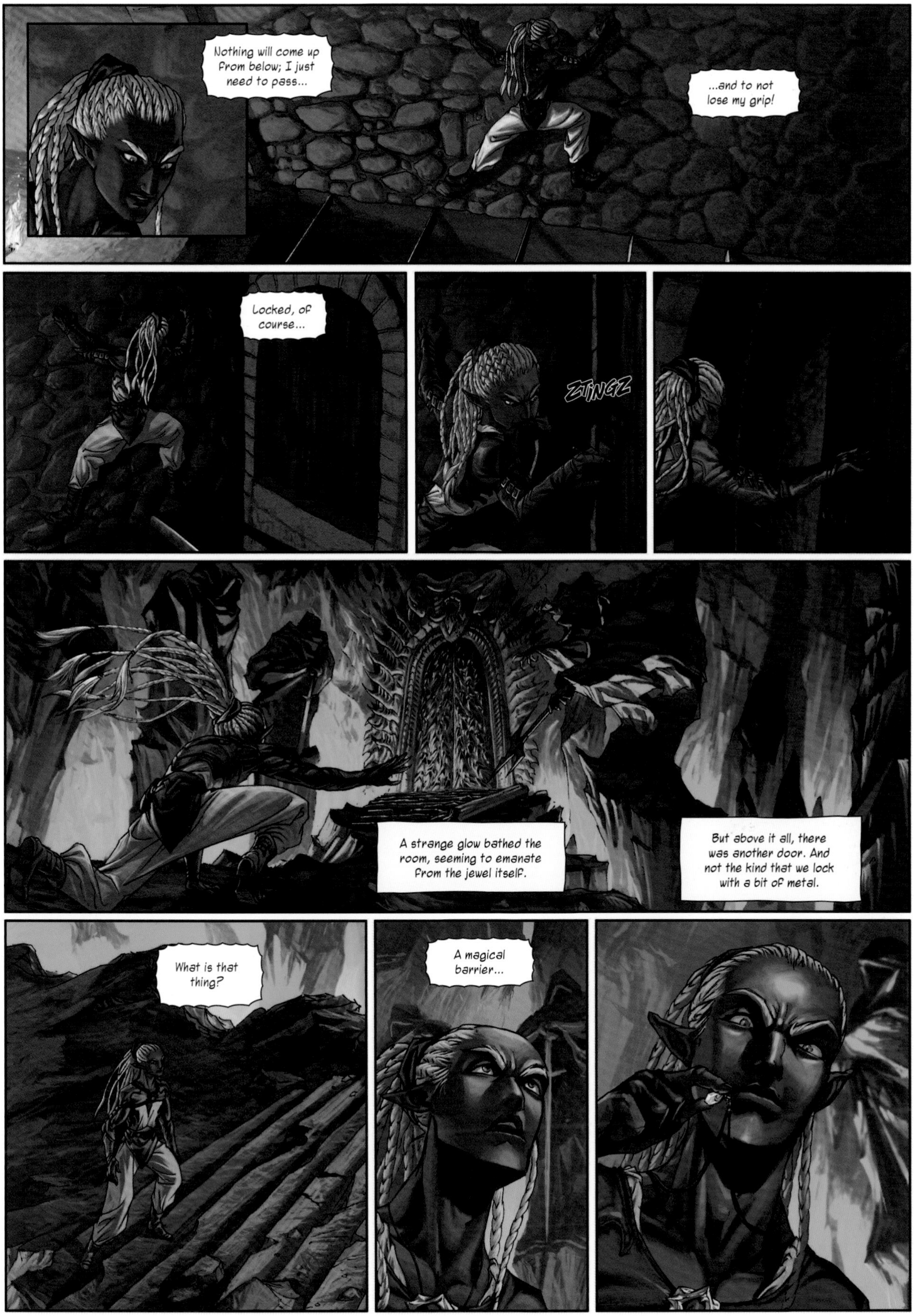
Nothing will come up from below; I just need to pass...
...and to not lose my grip!
Locked, of course...
ZTINGZ
A strange glow bathed the room, seeming to emanate from the jewel itself.
But above it all, there was another door. And not the kind that we lock with a bit of metal.
What is that thing?
A magical barrier...

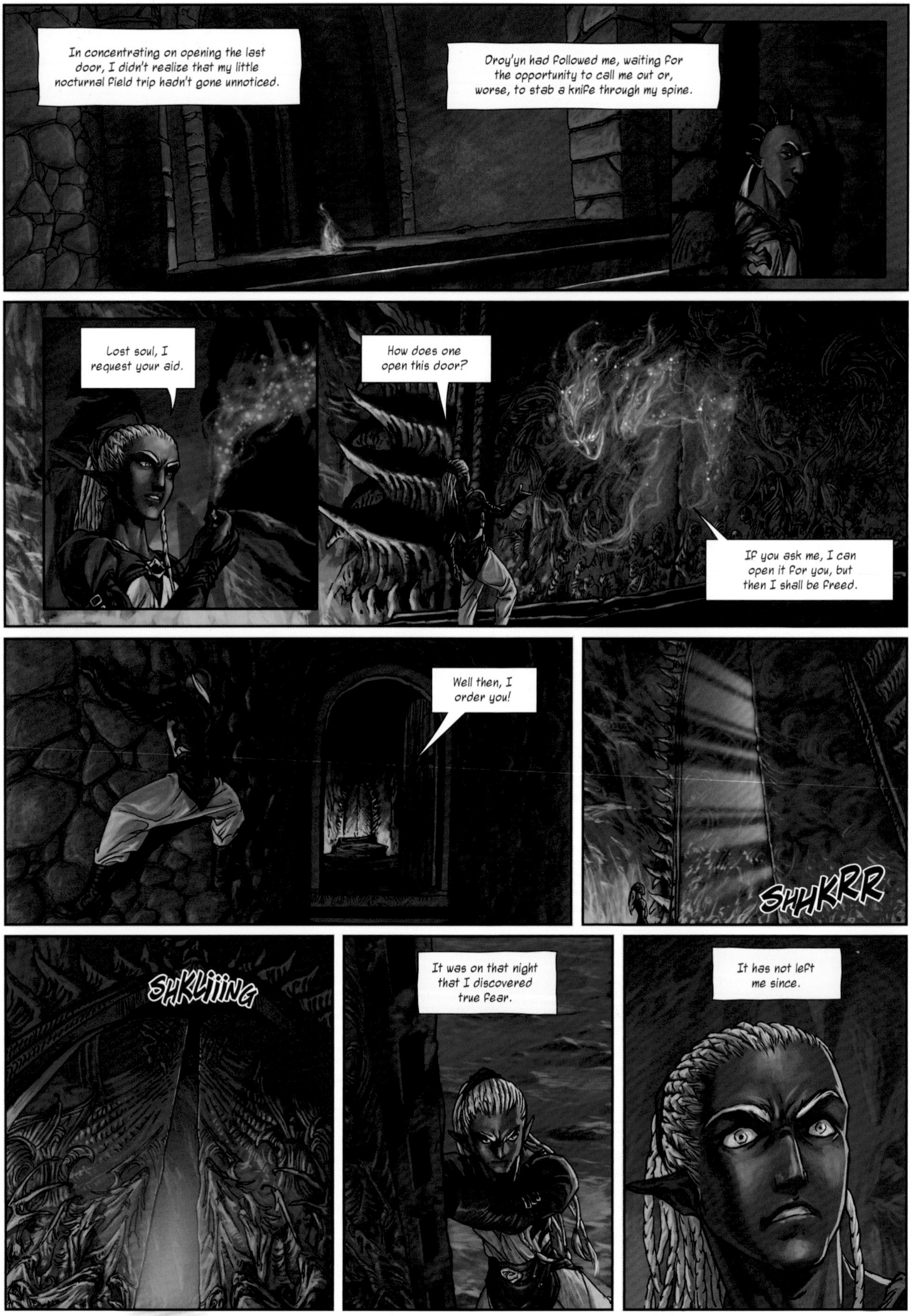
In concentrating on opening the last door, I didn't realize that my little nocturnal field trip hadn't gone unnoticed.
Oroy'yn had followed me, waiting for the opportunity to call me out or, worse, to stab a knife through my spine.
Lost soul, I request your aid.
How does one open this door?
If you ask me, I can open it for you, but then I shall be freed.
Well then, I order you!
SHYKRR
SHKLIIING
It was on that night that I discovered true fear.
It has not left me since.

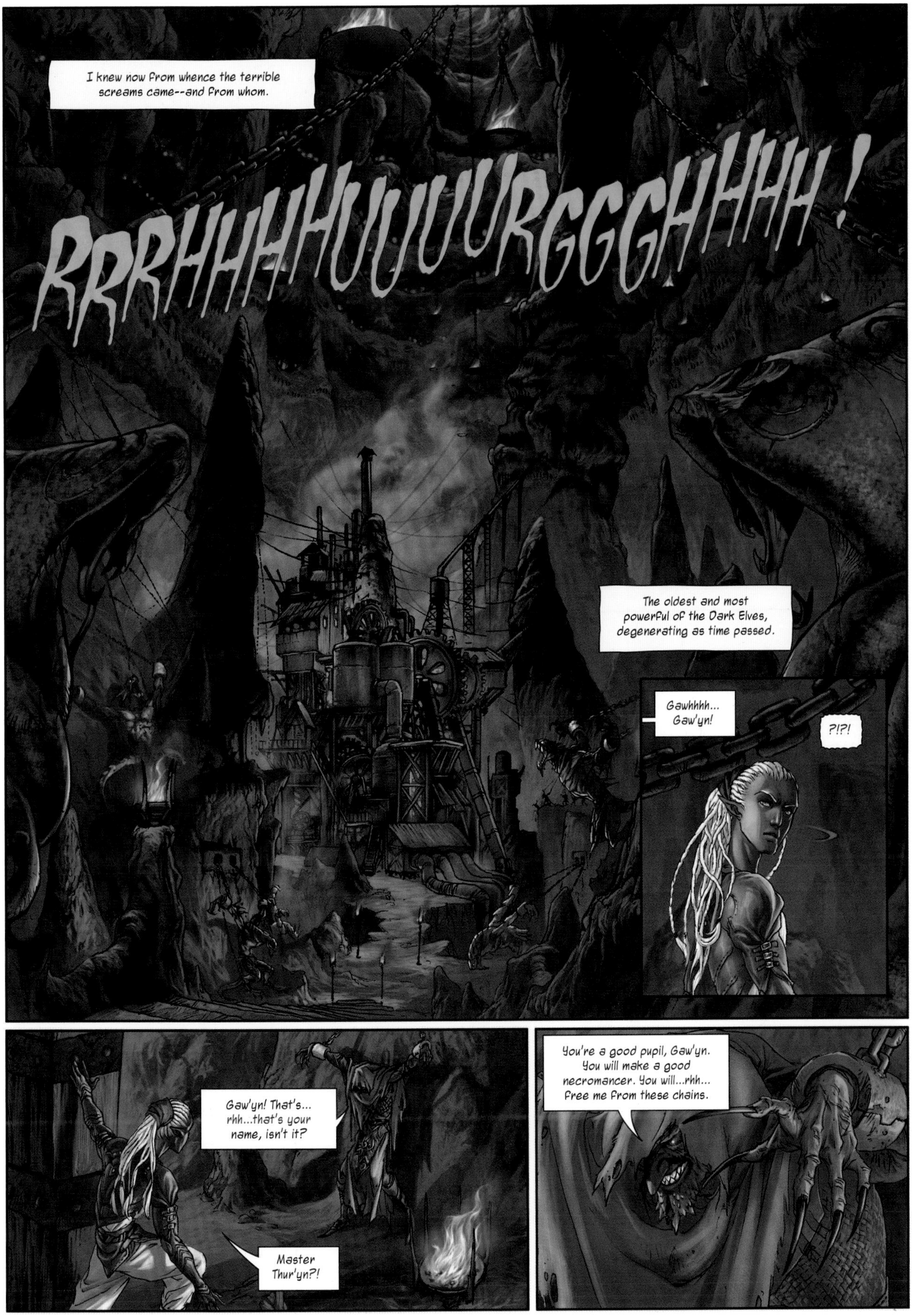

I knew now from whence the terrible screams came--and from whom.
RRRHHHHUUUURGGGHHHH!
The oldest and most powerful of the Dark Elves, degenerating as time passed.
Gawhhhh... Gaw'yn!
?!?!
Gaw'yn! That's... rhh...that's your name, isn't it?
Master Thur'yn?!
You're a good pupil, Gaw'yn. You will make a good necromancer. You will...rhh... free me from these chains.

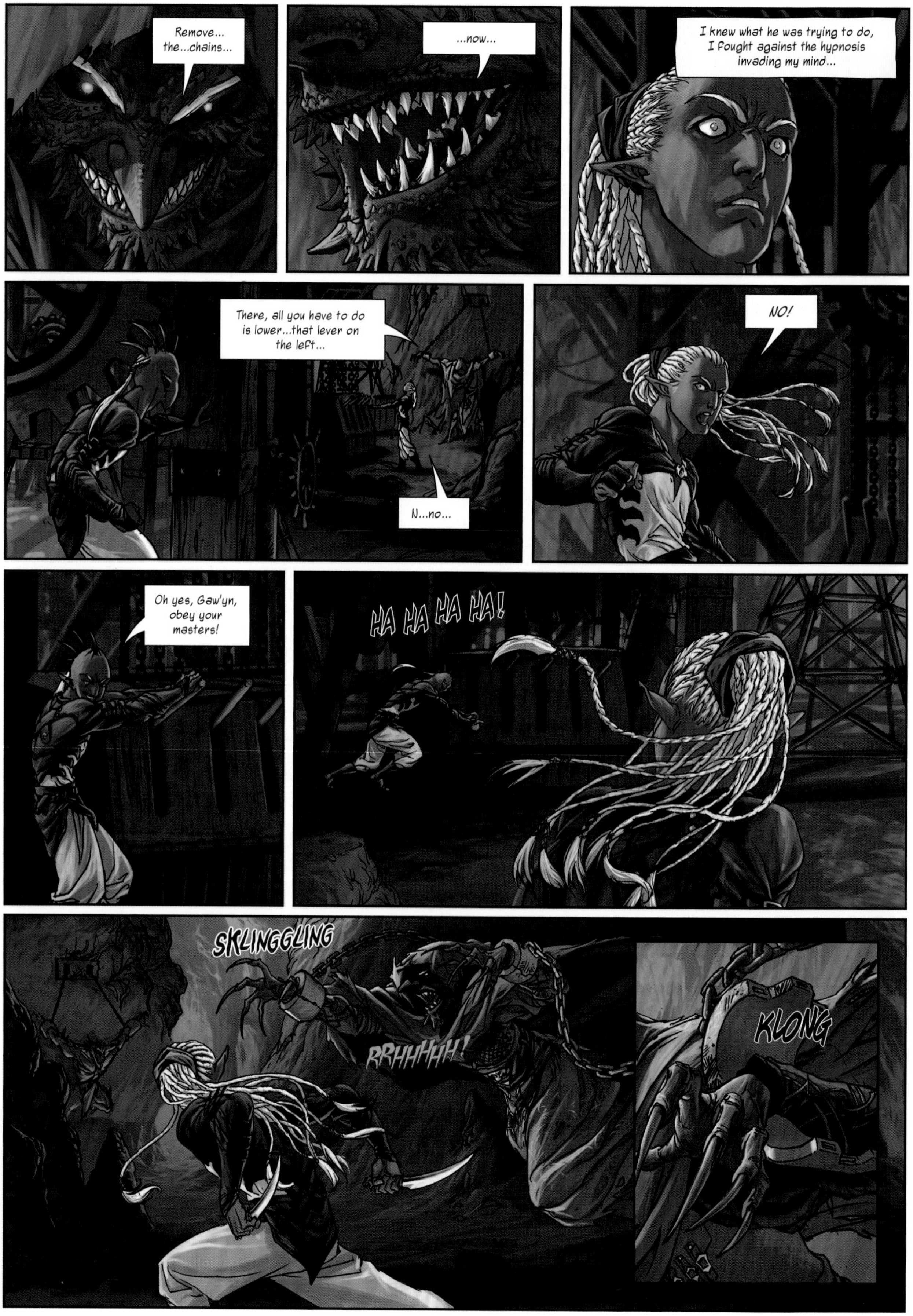
Remove... the...chains...
...now...
I knew what he was trying to do, I fought against the hypnosis invading my mind...
There, all you have to do is lower...that lever on the left...
N...no...
NO!
Oh yes, Gaw'yn, obey your masters!
HA HA HA HA!
SKLINGGLING
RRHHHHH!
KLONG

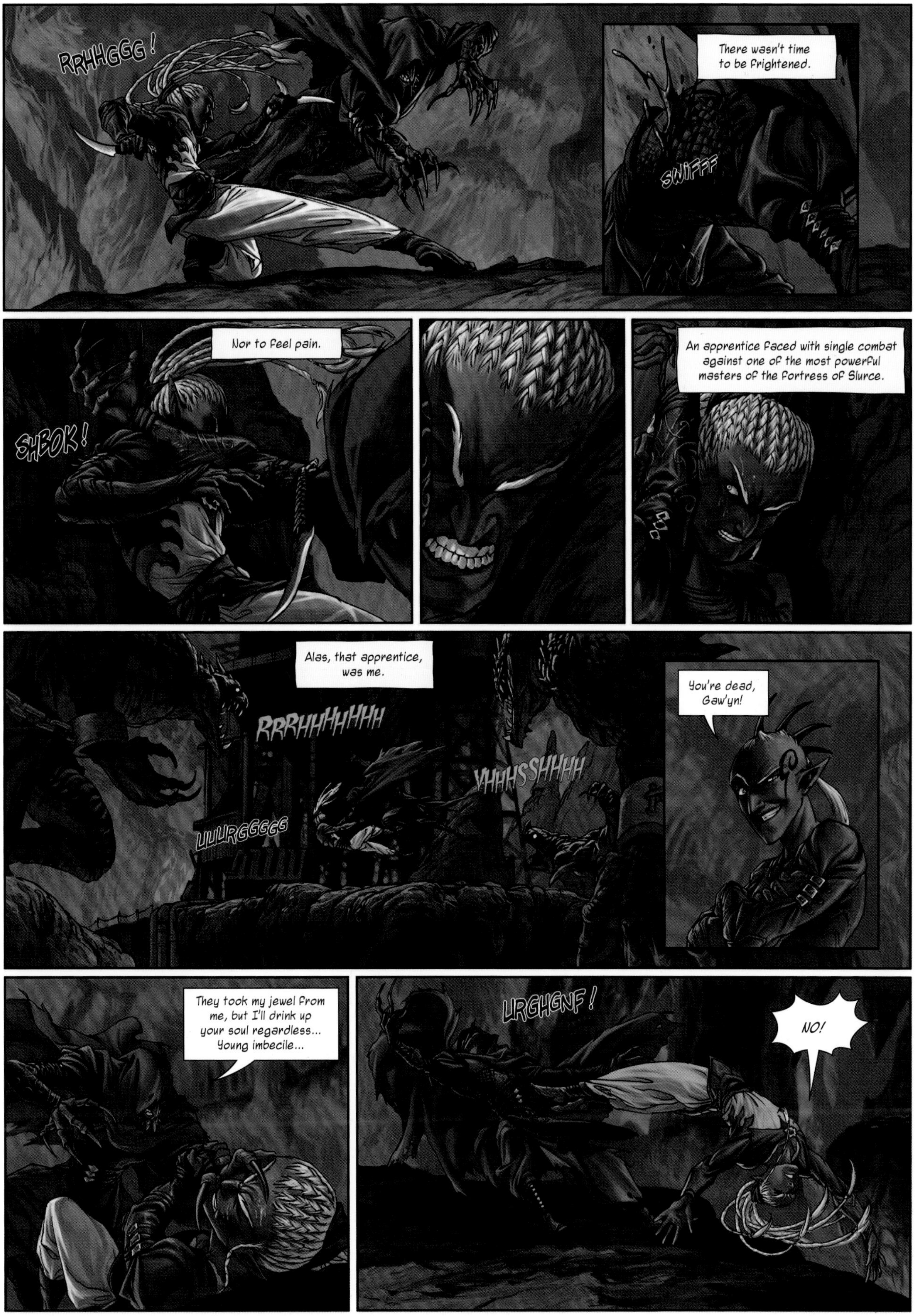
RRHHGGG!
There wasn't time to be frightened.
SWIFFF
Nor to feel pain.
SHBOK!
An apprentice faced with single combat against one of the most powerful masters of the Fortress of Slurce.
Alas, that apprentice, was me.
RRRHHHHHHH
YHHHSSHHH
UUURGGGGG
You're dead, Gaw'yn!
They took my jewel from me, but I'll drink up your soul regardless... Young imbecile...
URGHGNF!
NO!

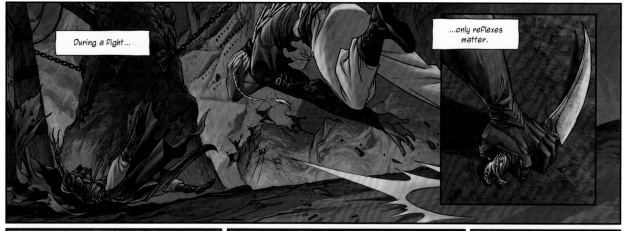

During a fight...

...only reflexes matter.

My body acted on its own.

All my energy racing toward a single goal...

SHLING

OH NO!

...to kill!

Alas, I no longer had one adversary...

TCHARK!

UUURRGGHHH

...but two.

GNF! SHTOK

EYYYH!

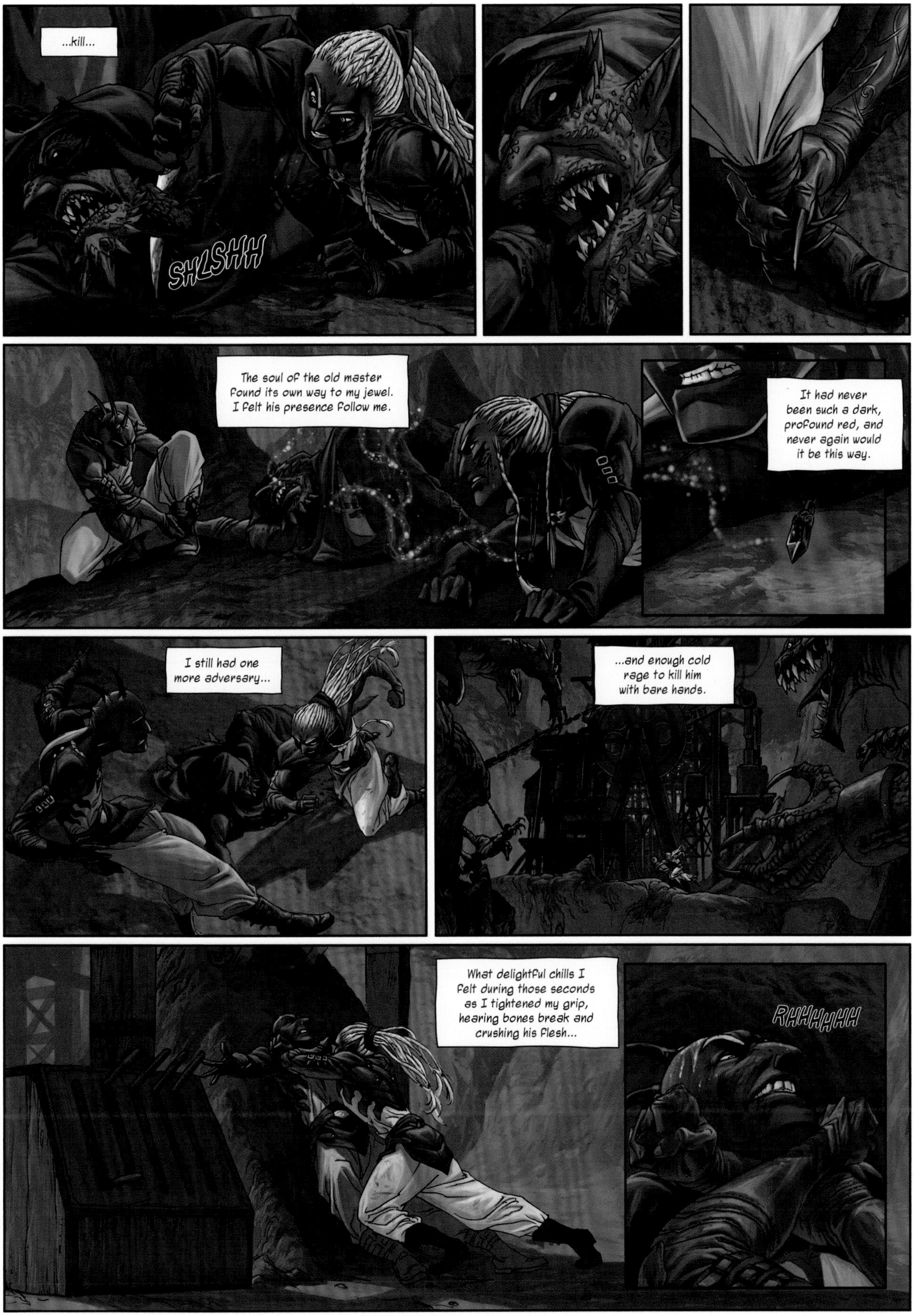
...kill...
SHLSHH
The soul of the old master found its own way to my jewel. I felt his presence follow me.
It had never been such a dark, profound red, and never again would it be this way.
I still had one more adversary...
...and enough cold rage to kill him with bare hands.
What delightful chills I felt during those seconds as I tightened my grip, hearing bones break and crushing his flesh...
RHHHHHH

GAW'YN! DROY'YN! STOP IMMEDIATELY!

UURRHHH!

RRGGHHRRR!

CLACK
CLACK
CLACK
BLONK

UUURRRHHHH!

RRHHEEERHHH

YAAARRRHHHGCKKK!

SHGLINK

SHKLING

Master Varh'yn!

The Murth'n Thuns are freed! I must close this door!

スシメゴ ゟ‛ワ ゾヺ‛ゔ‛ゔ

RRGGHHRRR!

UURRGGHHZZZ!

I was lucky to have escaped one of these monsters, and now more than 10 of them were trying to capture me.

RWWAAARGHH!

I barely managed.

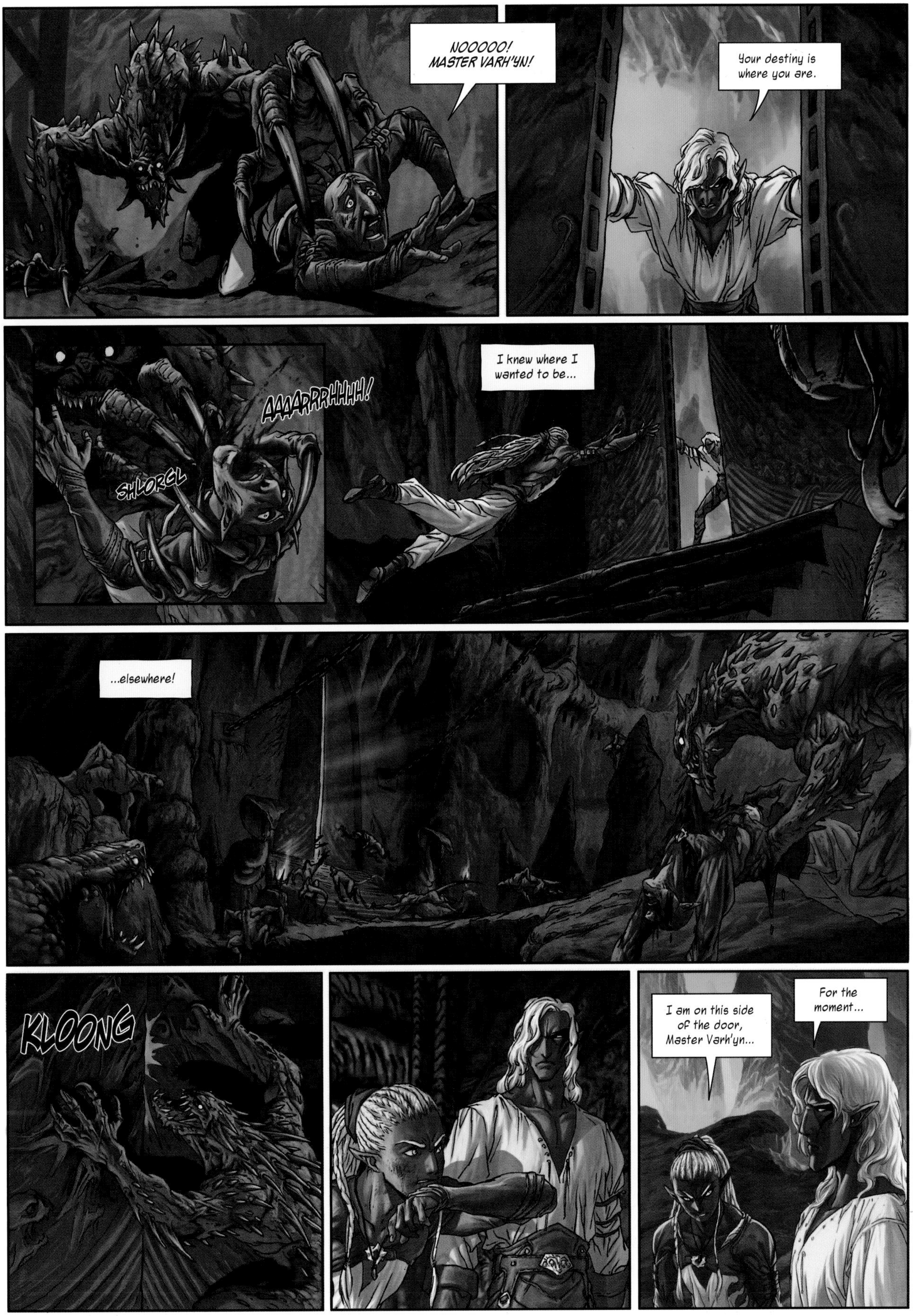
NOOOOO! MASTER VARH'YN!
Your destiny is where you are.
AAAARRHHHH!
SHLORGL
I knew where I wanted to be...
...elsewhere!
KLOONG
I am on this side of the door, Master Varh'yn...
For the moment...

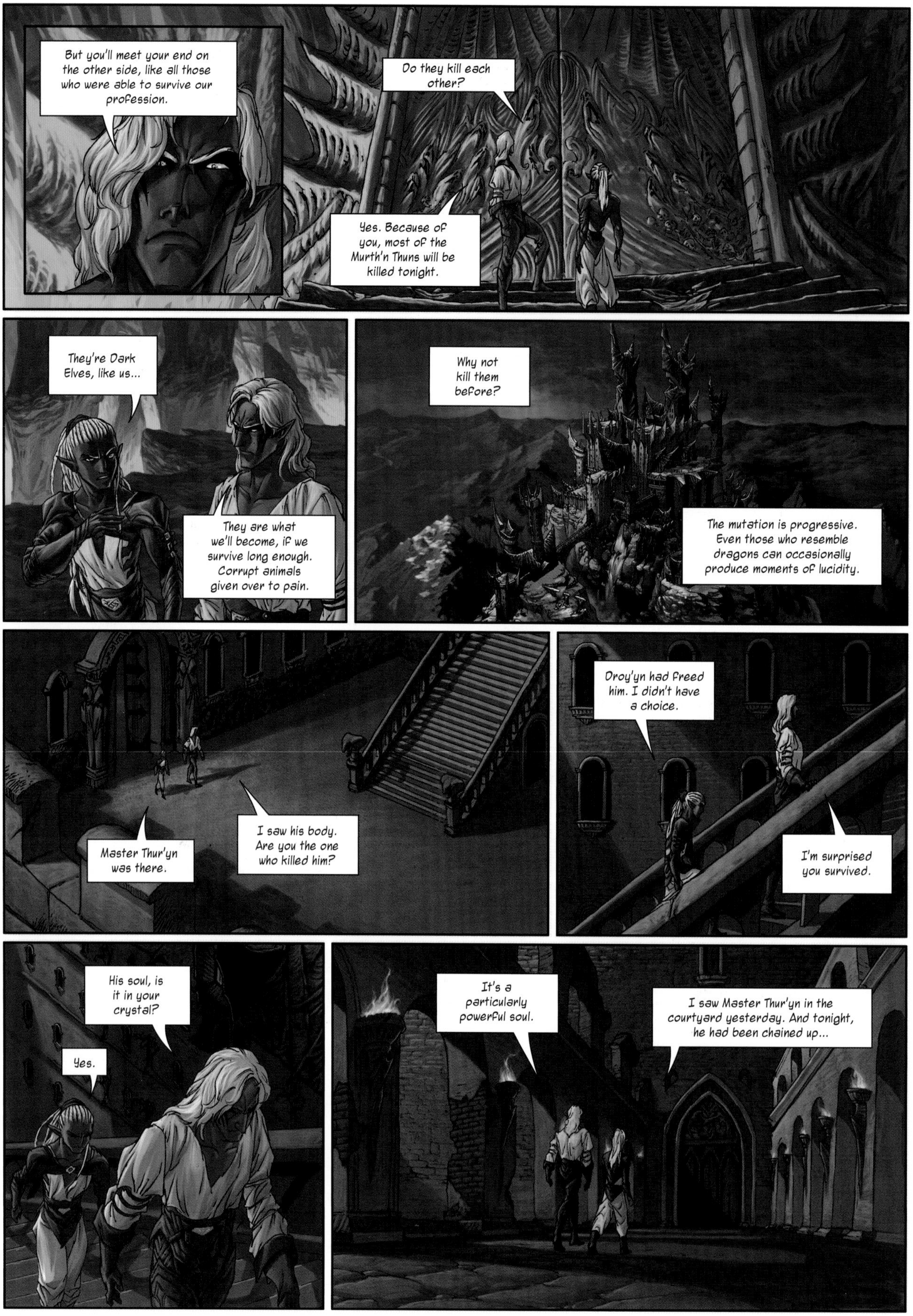
But you'll meet your end on the other side, like all those who were able to survive our profession.
Do they kill each other?
Yes. Because of you, most of the Murth'n Thuns will be killed tonight.
They're Dark Elves, like us...
They are what we'll become, if we survive long enough. Corrupt animals given over to pain.
Why not kill them before?
The mutation is progressive. Even those who resemble dragons can occasionally produce moments of lucidity.
Master Thur'yn was there.
I saw his body. Are you the one who killed him?
Droy'yn had freed him. I didn't have a choice.
I'm surprised you survived.
His soul, is it in your crystal?
Yes.
It's a particularly powerful soul.
I saw Master Thur'yn in the courtyard yesterday. And tonight, he had been chained up...

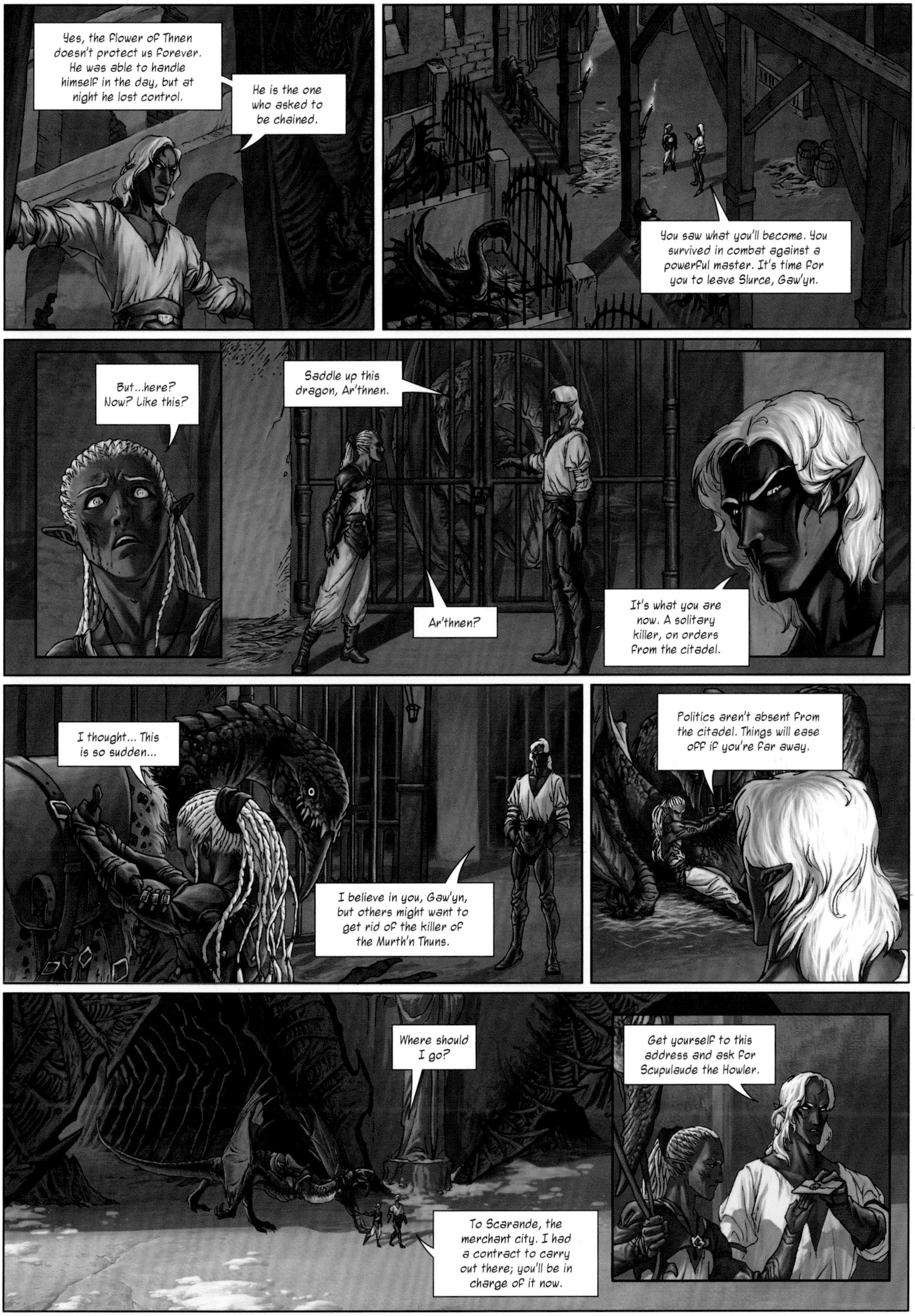
Yes, the flower of Thnen doesn't protect us forever. He was able to handle himself in the day, but at night he lost control.
He is the one who asked to be chained.
You saw what you'll become. You survived in combat against a powerful master. It's time for you to leave Slurce, Gaw'yn.
But...here? Now? Like this?
Saddle up this dragon, Ar'thnen.
Ar'thnen?
It's what you are now. A solitary killer, on orders from the citadel.
I thought... This is so sudden...
I believe in you, Gaw'yn, but others might want to get rid of the killer of the Murth'n Thuns.
Politics aren't absent from the citadel. Things will ease off if you're far away.
Where should I go?
To Scarande, the merchant city. I had a contract to carry out there; you'll be in charge of it now.
Get yourself to this address and ask for Scupulaude the Howler.

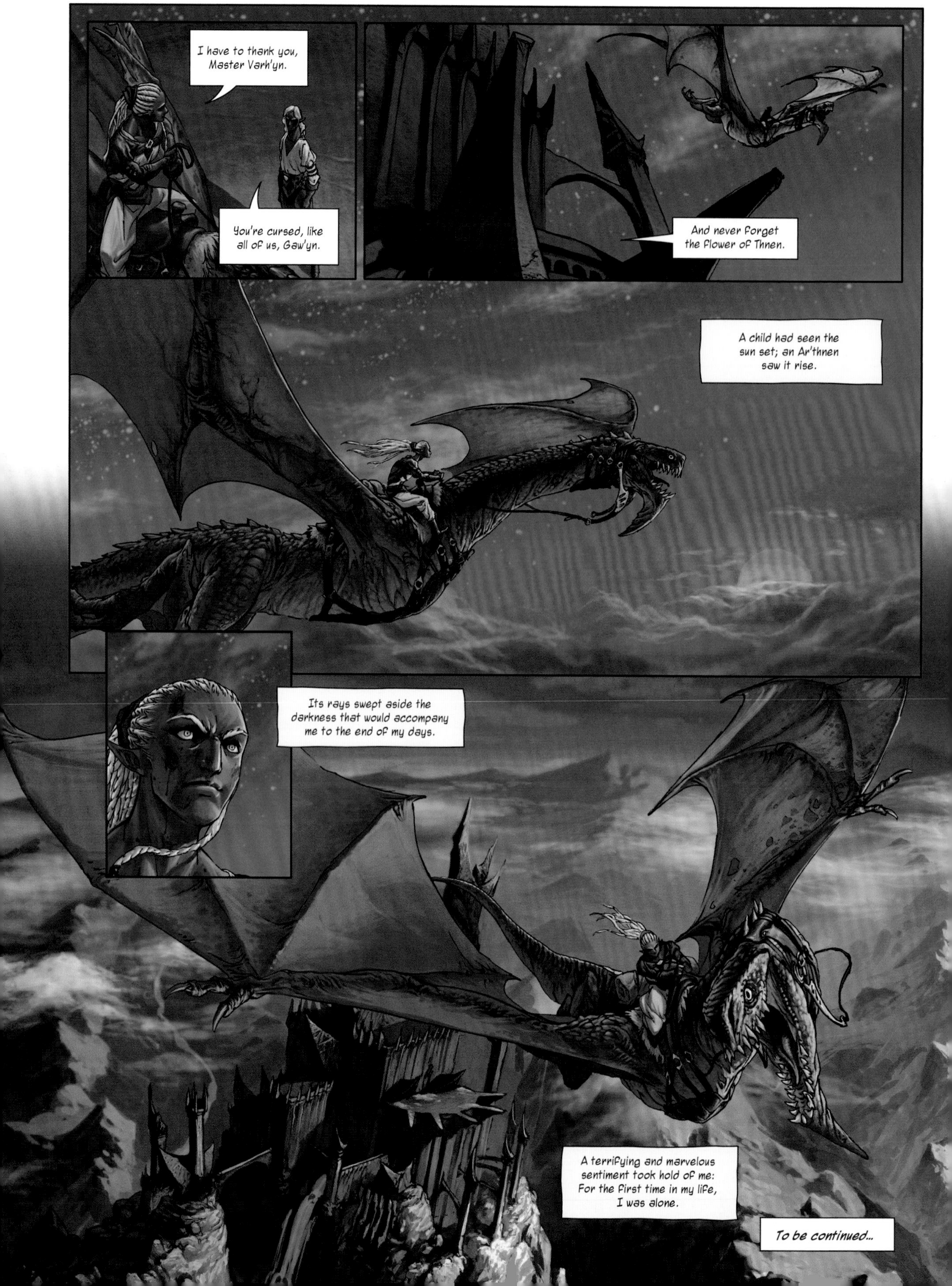
I have to thank you, Master Varh'yn.
You're cursed, like all of us, Gaw'yn.
And never forget the flower of Thnen.
A child had seen the sun set; an Ar'thnen saw it rise.
Its rays swept aside the darkness that would accompany me to the end of my days.
A terrifying and marvelous sentiment took hold of me: For the first time in my life, I was alone.
To be continued...

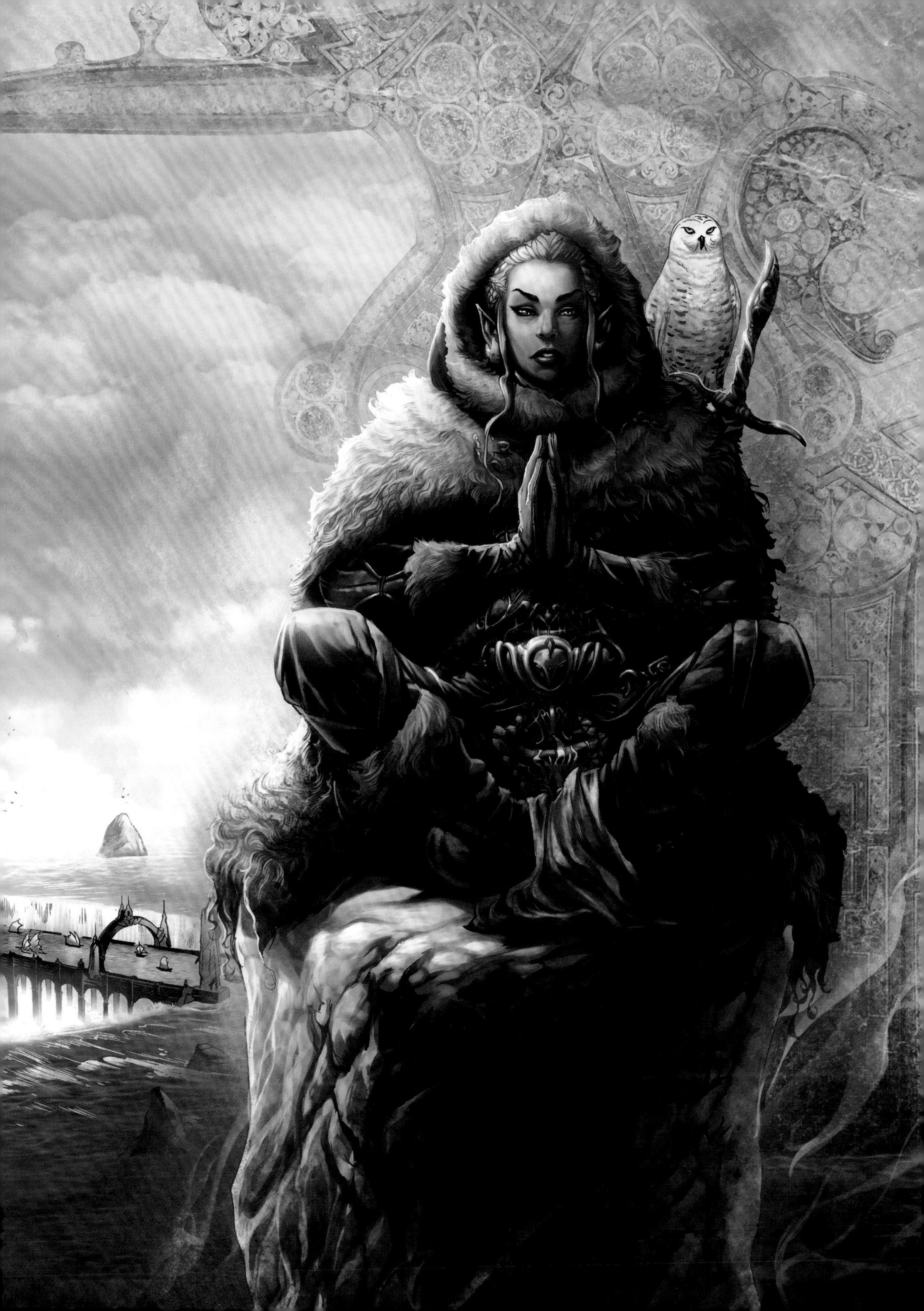

ELVES

PART 2:
"THE BLUE ELVES' MISSION"

WRITTEN BY JEAN-LUC ISTIN

ILLUSTRATED BY KYKO DUARTE

COLORS BY DIOGO SAITO

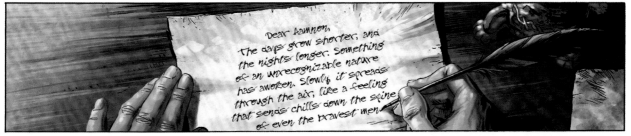

Dear Aamnen,
The days grow shorter, and the nights longer. Something of an unrecognizable nature has awoken. Slowly, it spreads through the air, like a feeling that sends chills down the spine of even the bravest men.

I do not know which orders to give my captains, for we do not have a clear explanation for the plague that has struck us.

It kills my men. We find their bodies in the cold glow of dawn.

The only concrete fact I have is that the number of deaths is growing.

Strangely, it is the strongest fighters who succumb first. My crew grows fearful.

With no further information, I've instated a curfew at night, for it was during night that the first disappearances occurred.

Is there a link between this and the excavation led by my protégé Leonan?

What he extracted from the ice floe is, to say the least, peculiar. I cannot ignore the striking coincidence between the arrival of these relics in Aspen and the start of these horrible murders.

I imagine, my friend, that you've already understood the reason for this message. I need your help, immediately. And I can count on only you.

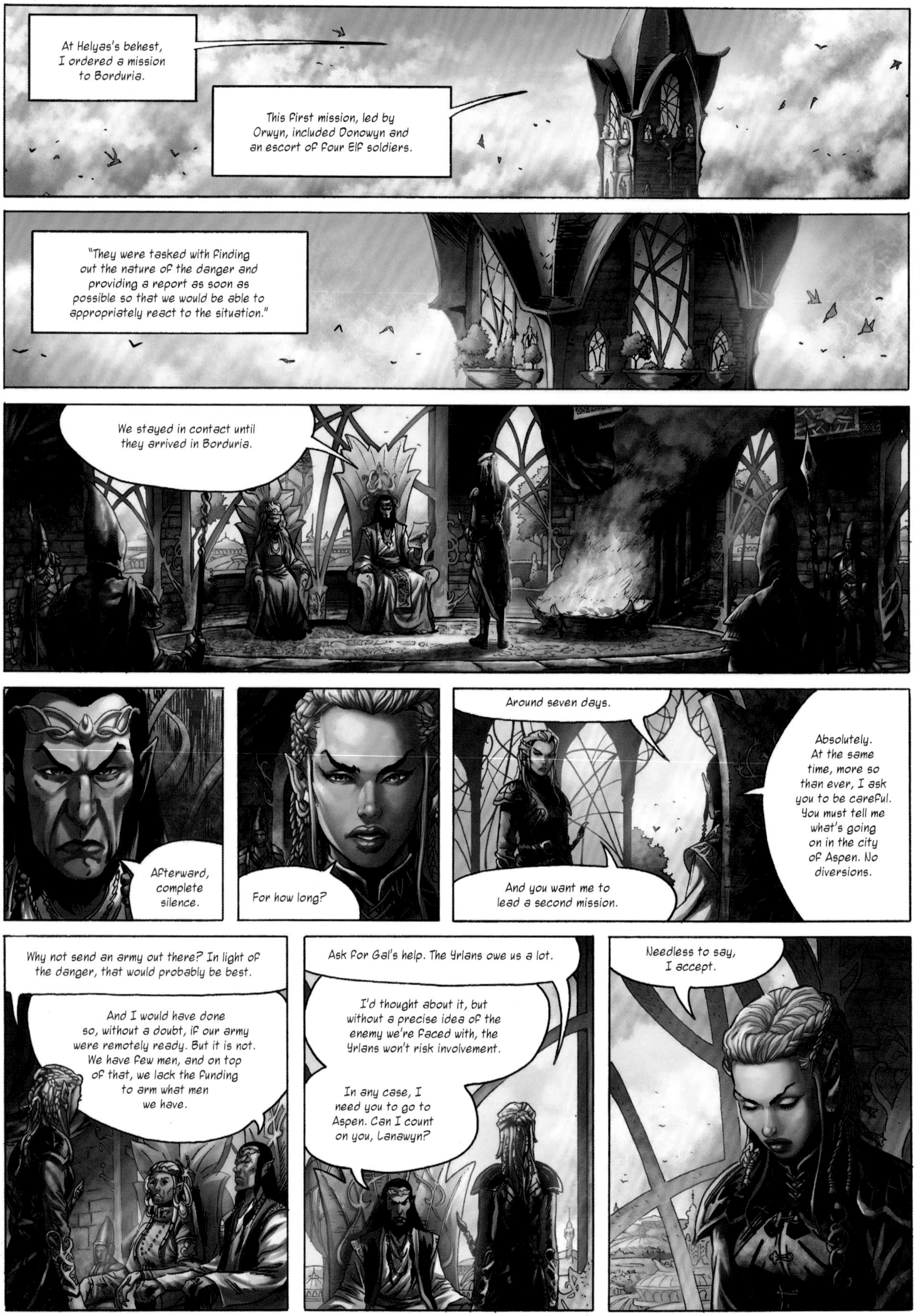
At Helyas's behest, I ordered a mission to Borduria.
This first mission, led by Orwyn, included Donowyn and an escort of four Elf soldiers.
"They were tasked with finding out the nature of the danger and providing a report as soon as possible so that we would be able to appropriately react to the situation."
We stayed in contact until they arrived in Borduria.
Afterward, complete silence.
For how long?
Around seven days.
And you want me to lead a second mission.
Absolutely. At the same time, more so than ever, I ask you to be careful. You must tell me what's going on in the city of Aspen. No diversions.
Why not send an army out there? In light of the danger, that would probably be best.
And I would have done so, without a doubt, if our army were remotely ready. But it is not. We have few men, and on top of that, we lack the funding to arm what men we have.
Ask for Gal's help. The Yrlans owe us a lot.
I'd thought about it, but without a precise idea of the enemy we're faced with, the Yrlans won't risk involvement.
In any case, I need you to go to Aspen. Can I count on you, Lanawyn?
Needless to say, I accept.

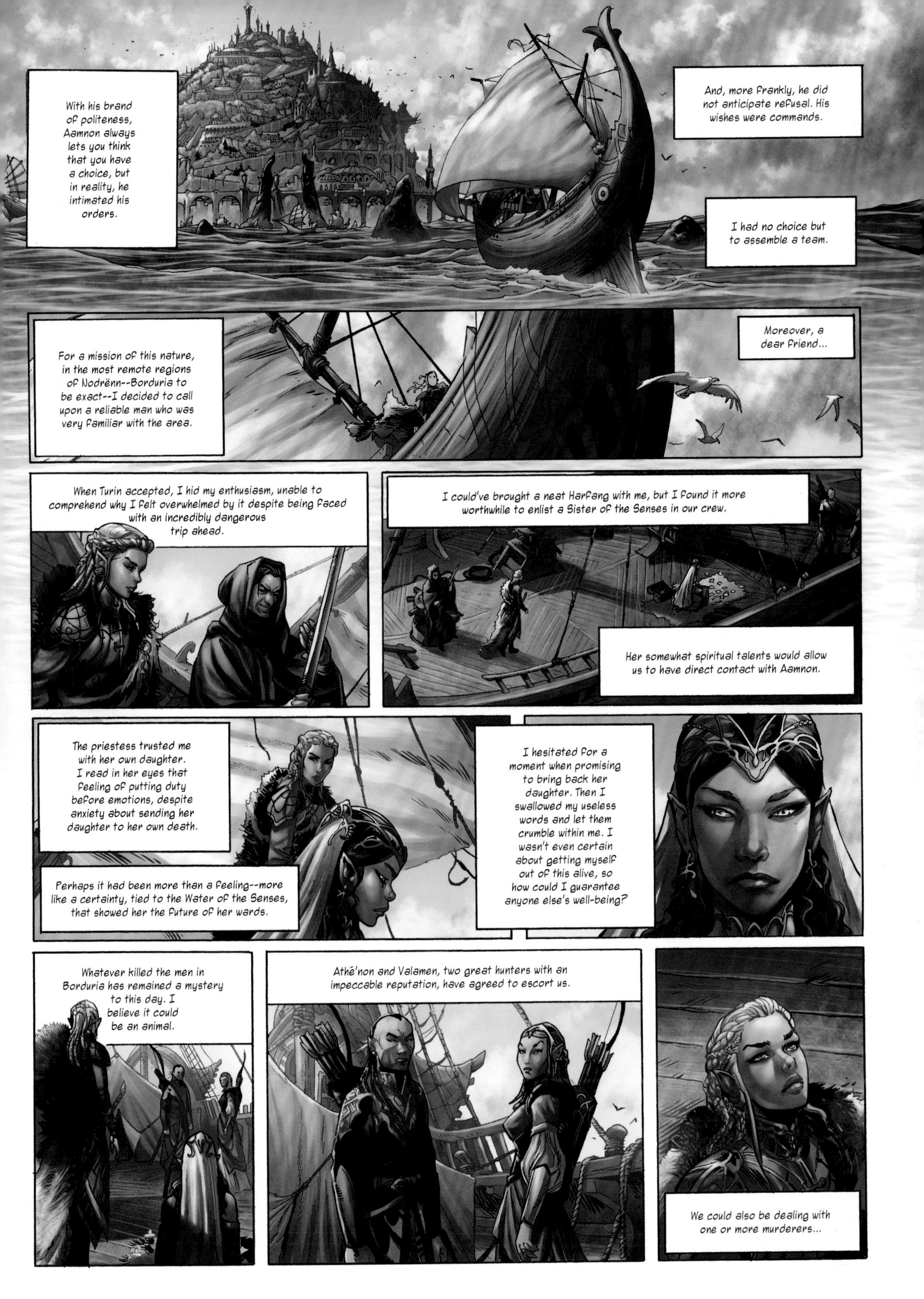
With his brand of politeness, Aamnon always lets you think that you have a choice, but in reality, he intimated his orders.
And, more frankly, he did not anticipate refusal. His wishes were commands.
I had no choice but to assemble a team.
For a mission of this nature, in the most remote regions of Nodrënn--Borduria to be exact--I decided to call upon a reliable man who was very familiar with the area.
Moreover, a dear friend...
When Turin accepted, I hid my enthusiasm, unable to comprehend why I felt overwhelmed by it despite being faced with an incredibly dangerous trip ahead.
I could've brought a neat Harfang with me, but I found it more worthwhile to enlist a Sister of the Senses in our crew.
Her somewhat spiritual talents would allow us to have direct contact with Aamnon.
The priestess trusted me with her own daughter. I read in her eyes that feeling of putting duty before emotions, despite anxiety about sending her daughter to her own death.
Perhaps it had been more than a feeling--more like a certainty, tied to the Water of the Senses, that showed her the future of her wards.
I hesitated for a moment when promising to bring back her daughter. Then I swallowed my useless words and let them crumble within me. I wasn't even certain about getting myself out of this alive, so how could I guarantee anyone else's well-being?
Whatever killed the men in Borduria has remained a mystery to this day. I believe it could be an animal.
Athé'non and Valamen, two great hunters with an impeccable reputation, have agreed to escort us.
We could also be dealing with one or more murderers...

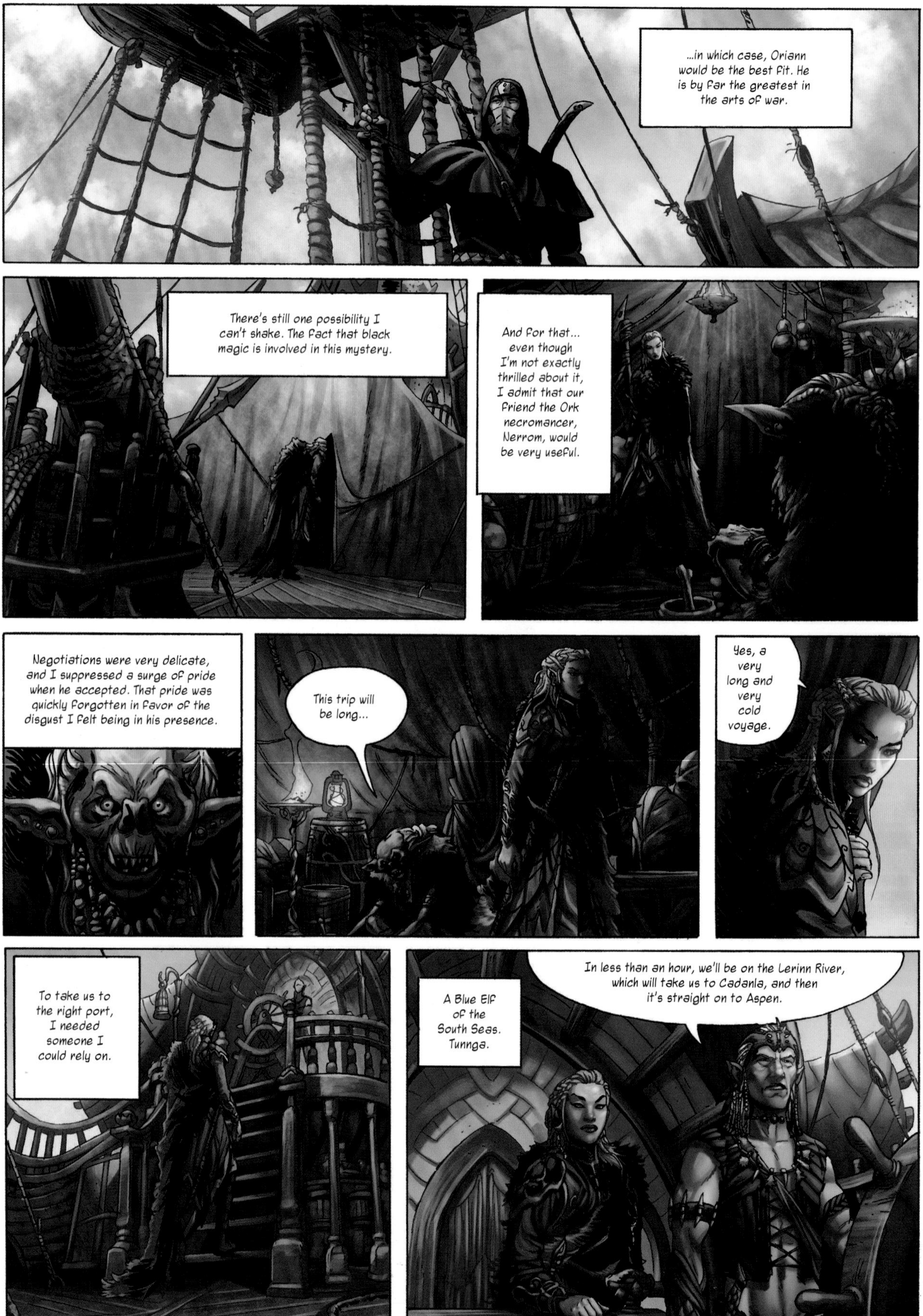
...in which case, Oriann would be the best fit. He is by far the greatest in the arts of war.
There's still one possibility I can't shake. The fact that black magic is involved in this mystery.
And for that... even though I'm not exactly thrilled about it, I admit that our friend the Ork necromancer, Nerrom, would be very useful.
Negotiations were very delicate, and I suppressed a surge of pride when he accepted. That pride was quickly forgotten in favor of the disgust I felt being in his presence.
This trip will be long...
Yes, a very long and very cold voyage.
To take us to the right port, I needed someone I could rely on.
A Blue Elf of the South Seas. Tunnga.
In less than an hour, we'll be on the Lerinn River, which will take us to Cadanla, and then it's straight on to Aspen.

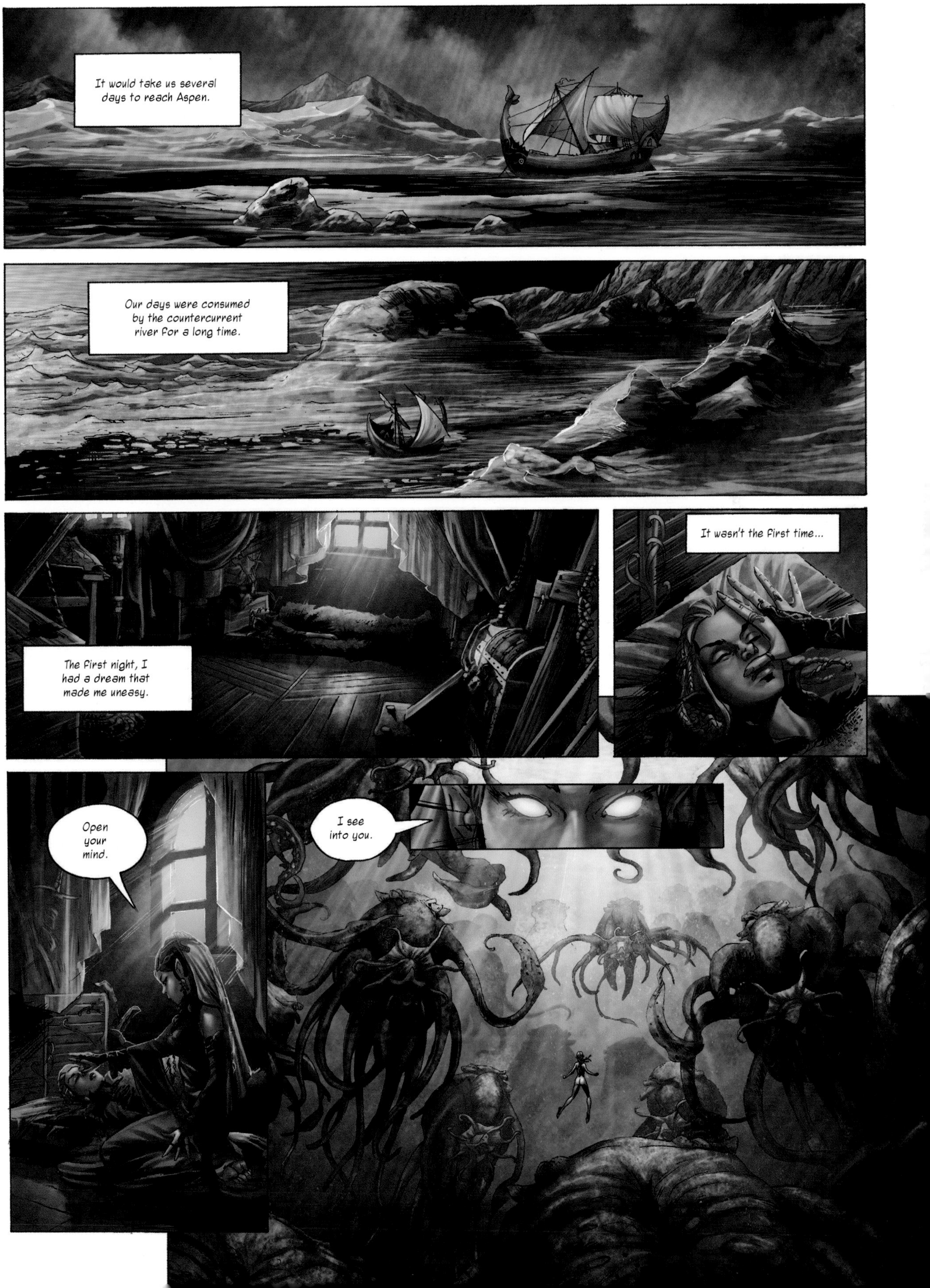

It would take us several days to reach Aspen.
Our days were consumed by the countercurrent river for a long time.
The first night, I had a dream that made me uneasy.
It wasn't the first time...
Open your mind.
I see into you.

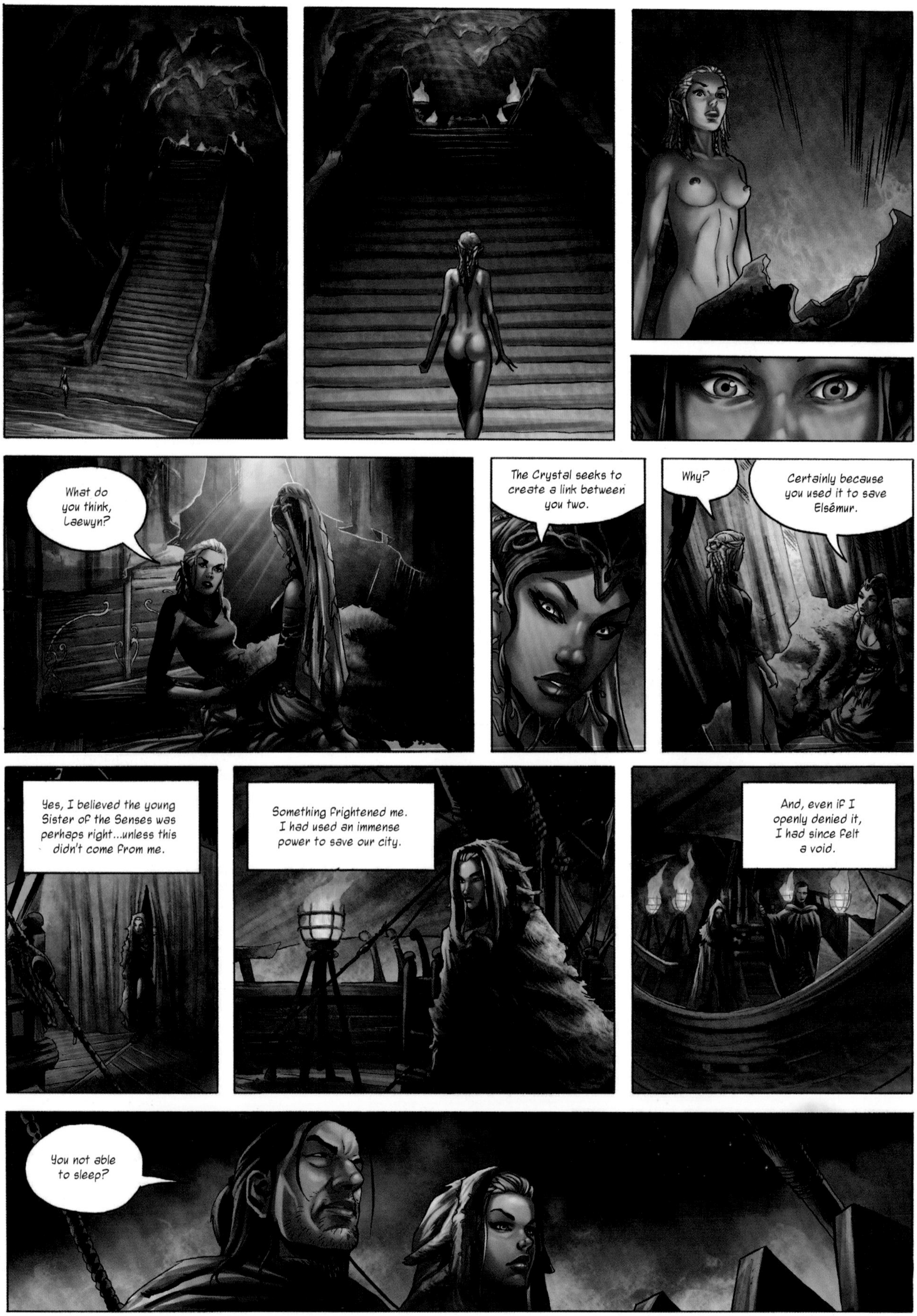
What do you think, Laewyn?
The Crystal seeks to create a link between you two.
Why?
Certainly because you used it to save Elsêmur.
Yes, I believed the young Sister of the Senses was perhaps right...unless this didn't come from me.
Something frightened me. I had used an immense power to save our city.
And, even if I openly denied it, I had since felt a void.
You not able to sleep?

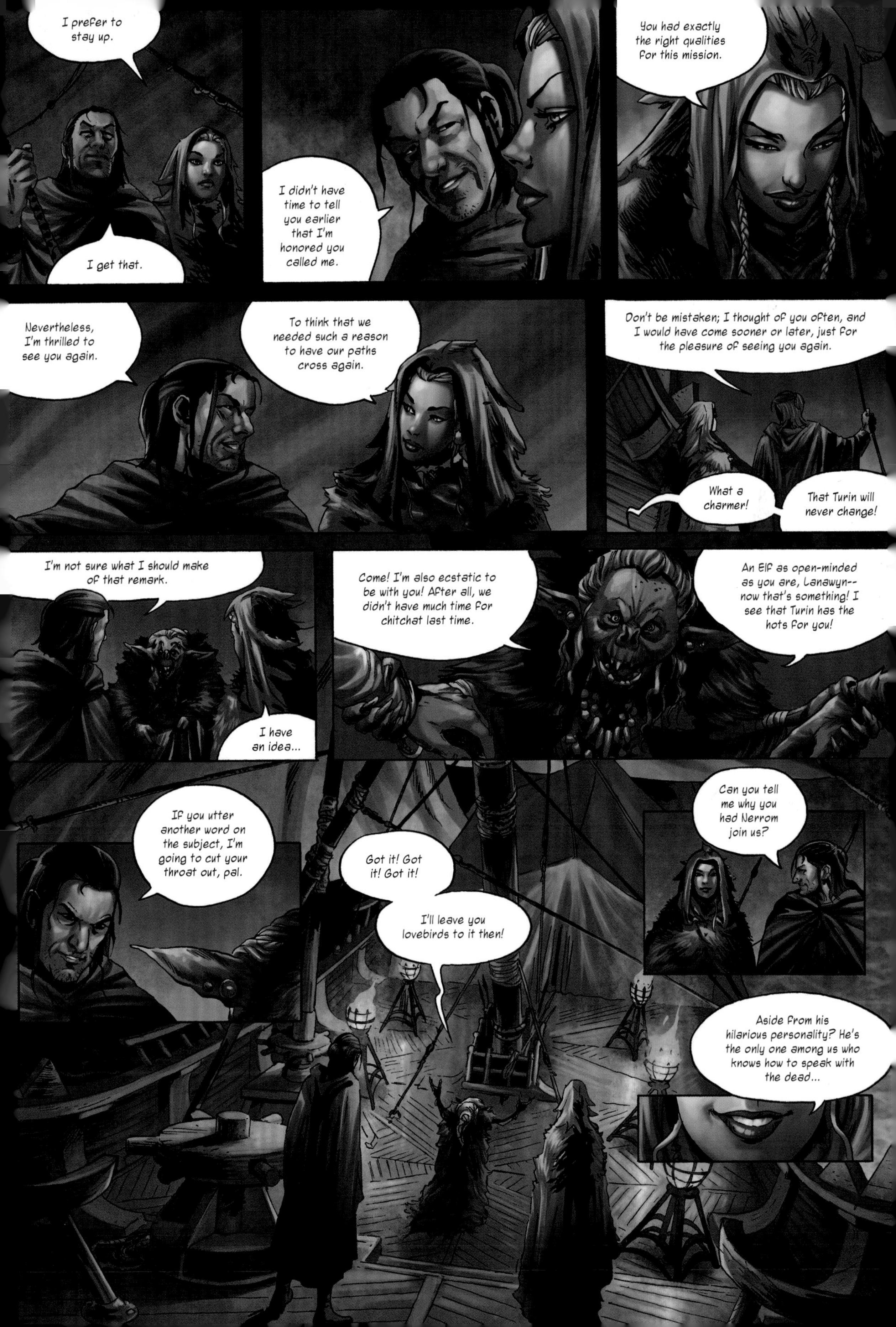

I prefer to stay up.
I get that.
I didn't have time to tell you earlier that I'm honored you called me.
You had exactly the right qualities for this mission.
Nevertheless, I'm thrilled to see you again.
To think that we needed such a reason to have our paths cross again.
Don't be mistaken; I thought of you often, and I would have come sooner or later, just for the pleasure of seeing you again.
What a charmer!
That Turin will never change!
I'm not sure what I should make of that remark.
I have an idea...
Come! I'm also ecstatic to be with you! After all, we didn't have much time for chitchat last time.
An Elf as open-minded as you are, Lanawyn-- now that's something! I see that Turin has the hots for you!
If you utter another word on the subject, I'm going to cut your throat out, pal.
Got it! Got it! Got it!
I'll leave you lovebirds to it then!
Can you tell me why you had Nerrom join us?
Aside from his hilarious personality? He's the only one among us who knows how to speak with the dead...

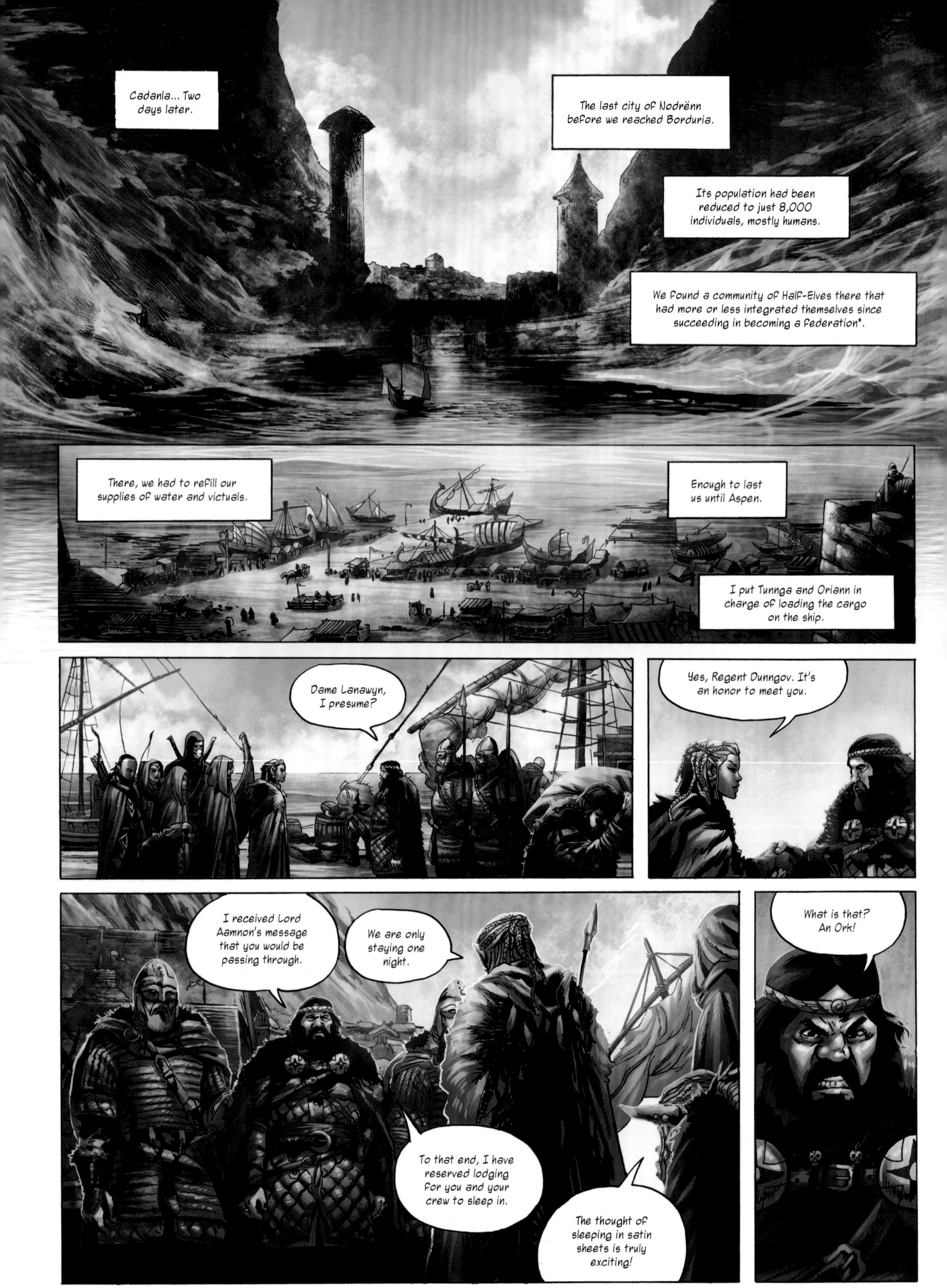
Cadanla... Two days later.
The last city of Nodrënn before we reached Borduria.
Its population had been reduced to just 8,000 individuals, mostly humans.
We found a community of Half-Elves there that had more or less integrated themselves since succeeding in becoming a federation*.
There, we had to refill our supplies of water and victuals.
Enough to last us until Aspen.
I put Tunnga and Oriann in charge of loading the cargo on the ship.
Dame Lanawyn, I presume?
Yes, Regent Dunngov. It's an honor to meet you.
I received Lord Aamnon's message that you would be passing through.
We are only staying one night.
To that end, I have reserved lodging for you and your crew to sleep in.
The thought of sleeping in satin sheets is truly exciting!
What is that? An Ork!

*See Elves, Vol. 2

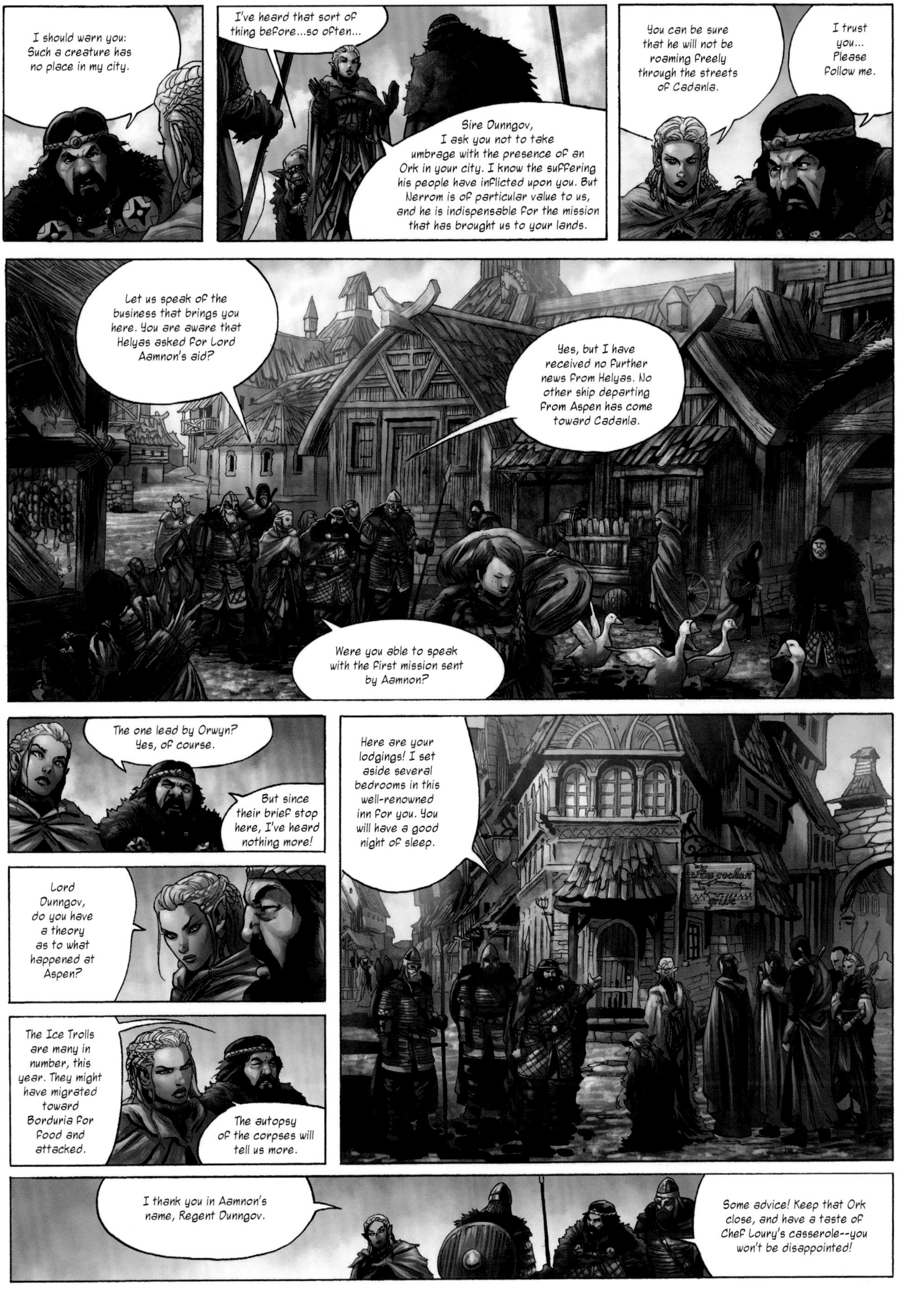
I should warn you: Such a creature has no place in my city.
I've heard that sort of thing before...so often...
Sire Dunngov, I ask you not to take umbrage with the presence of an Ork in your city. I know the suffering his people have inflicted upon you. But Nerrom is of particular value to us, and he is indispensable for the mission that has brought us to your lands.
You can be sure that he will not be roaming freely through the streets of Cadanla.
I trust you... Please follow me.
Let us speak of the business that brings you here. You are aware that Helyas asked for Lord Aamnon's aid?
Yes, but I have received no further news from Helyas. No other ship departing from Aspen has come toward Cadanla.
Were you able to speak with the first mission sent by Aamnon?
The one lead by Orwyn? Yes, of course.
But since their brief stop here, I've heard nothing more!
Lord Dunngov, do you have a theory as to what happened at Aspen?
The Ice Trolls are many in number, this year. They might have migrated toward Borduria for food and attacked.
The autopsy of the corpses will tell us more.
Here are your lodgings! I set aside several bedrooms in this well-renowned inn for you. You will have a good night of sleep.
I thank you in Aamnon's name, Regent Dunngov.
Some advice! Keep that Ork close, and have a taste of Chef Loury's casserole--you won't be disappointed!

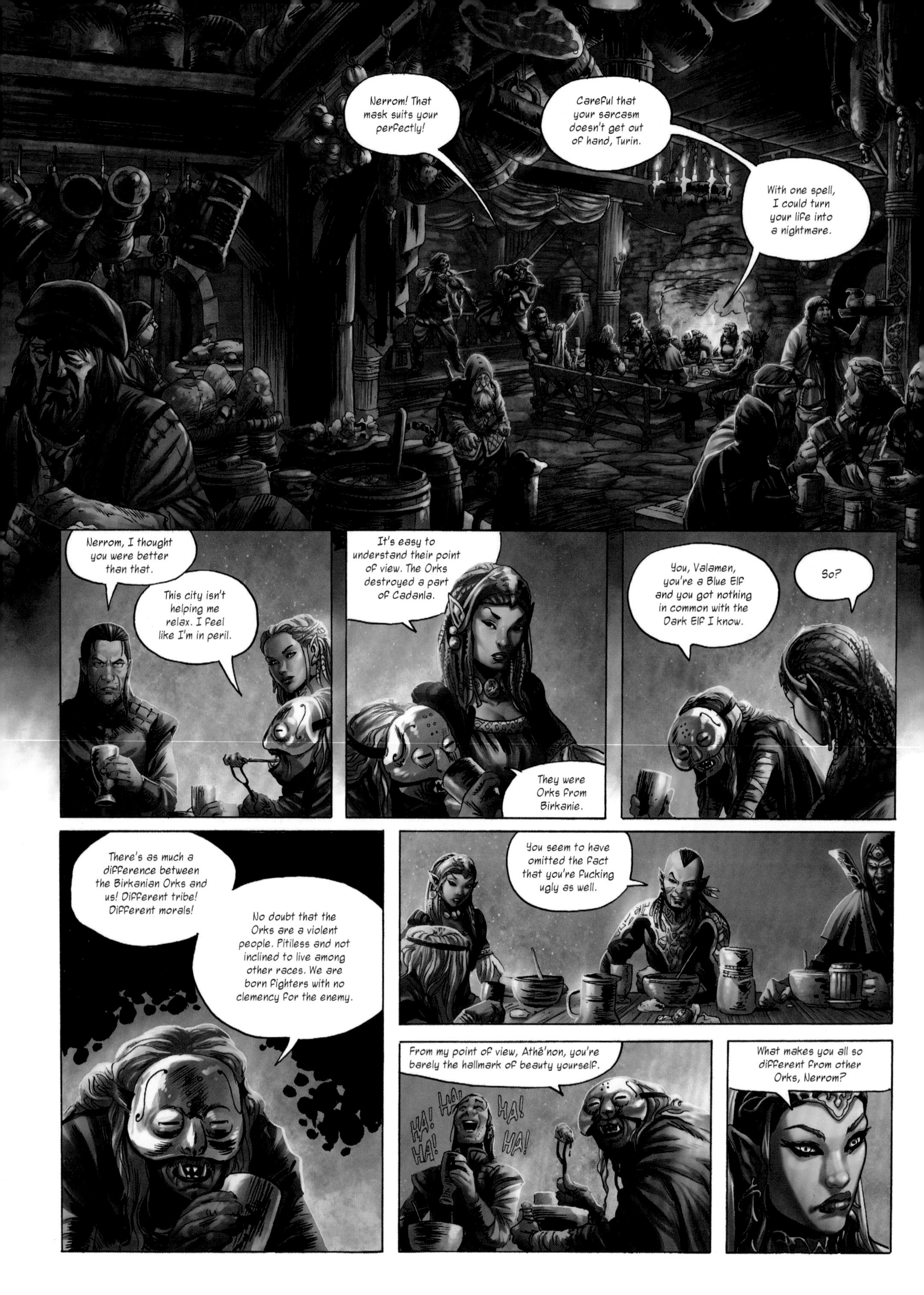
Nerrom! That mask suits your perfectly!
Careful that your sarcasm doesn't get out of hand, Turin.
With one spell, I could turn your life into a nightmare.
Nerrom, I thought you were better than that.
This city isn't helping me relax. I feel like I'm in peril.
It's easy to understand their point of view. The Orks destroyed a part of Cadanla.
They were Orks from Birkanie.
You, Valamen, you're a Blue Elf and you got nothing in common with the Dark Elf I know.
So?
There's as much a difference between the Birkanian Orks and us! Different tribe! Different morals!
No doubt that the Orks are a violent people. Pitiless and not inclined to live among other races. We are born fighters with no clemency for the enemy.
You seem to have omitted the fact that you're fucking ugly as well.
From my point of view, Athê'non, you're barely the hallmark of beauty yourself.
HA! HA! HA! HA! HA! HA!
What makes you all so different from other Orks, Nerrom?

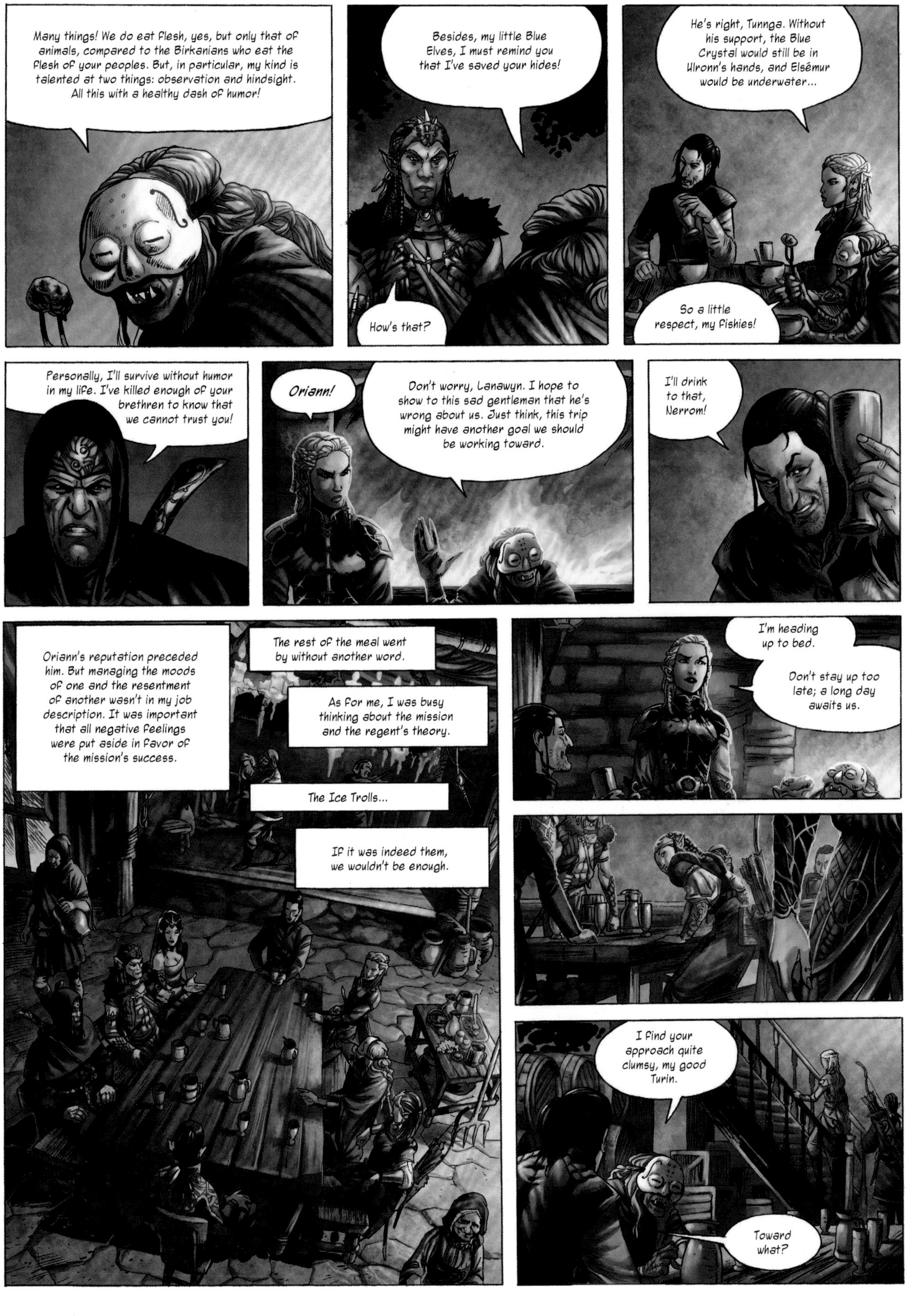
Many things! We do eat flesh, yes, but only that of animals, compared to the Birkanians who eat the flesh of your peoples. But, in particular, my kind is talented at two things: observation and hindsight. All this with a healthy dash of humor!
Besides, my little Blue Elves, I must remind you that I've saved your hides!
How's that?
He's right, Tunnga. Without his support, the Blue Crystal would still be in Ulronn's hands, and Elsêmur would be underwater...
So a little respect, my fishies!
Personally, I'll survive without humor in my life. I've killed enough of your brethren to know that we cannot trust you!
Oriann!
Don't worry, Lanawyn. I hope to show to this sad gentleman that he's wrong about us. Just think, this trip might have another goal we should be working toward.
I'll drink to that, Nerrom!
Oriann's reputation preceded him. But managing the moods of one and the resentment of another wasn't in my job description. It was important that all negative feelings were put aside in favor of the mission's success.
The rest of the meal went by without another word.
As for me, I was busy thinking about the mission and the regent's theory.
The Ice Trolls...
If it was indeed them, we wouldn't be enough.
I'm heading up to bed.
Don't stay up too late; a long day awaits us.
I find your approach quite clumsy, my good Turin.
Toward what?

Toward the young Elf.

Clumsy with a touch of fear!

On the contrary, I'm patient.

Why's that?

When you wait, doubt and hope play games with your mind, making you wonder and anticipate all the more. When the moment finally does come, it is that much sweeter for the time spent.

Turin, the adventurer of love! Who would have thought?

HA! HA! HA!

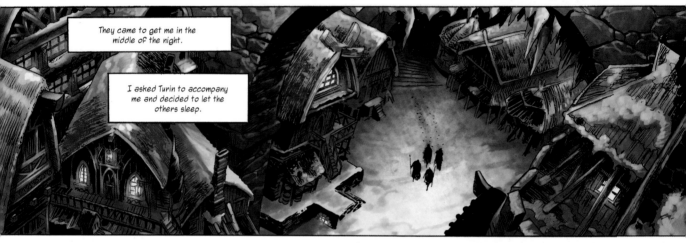

They came to get me in the middle of the night.

I asked Turin to accompany me and decided to let the others sleep.

Ounngov was waiting for us on the ramparts above the North Gate. His face lined, his expression grave.

I could sense his sweat from under his clothes.

He was afraid.

He pointed out something to me, over yonder.

Who is it?

No idea. But one thing is for sure. He's from the North!

Why is he keeping his distance?

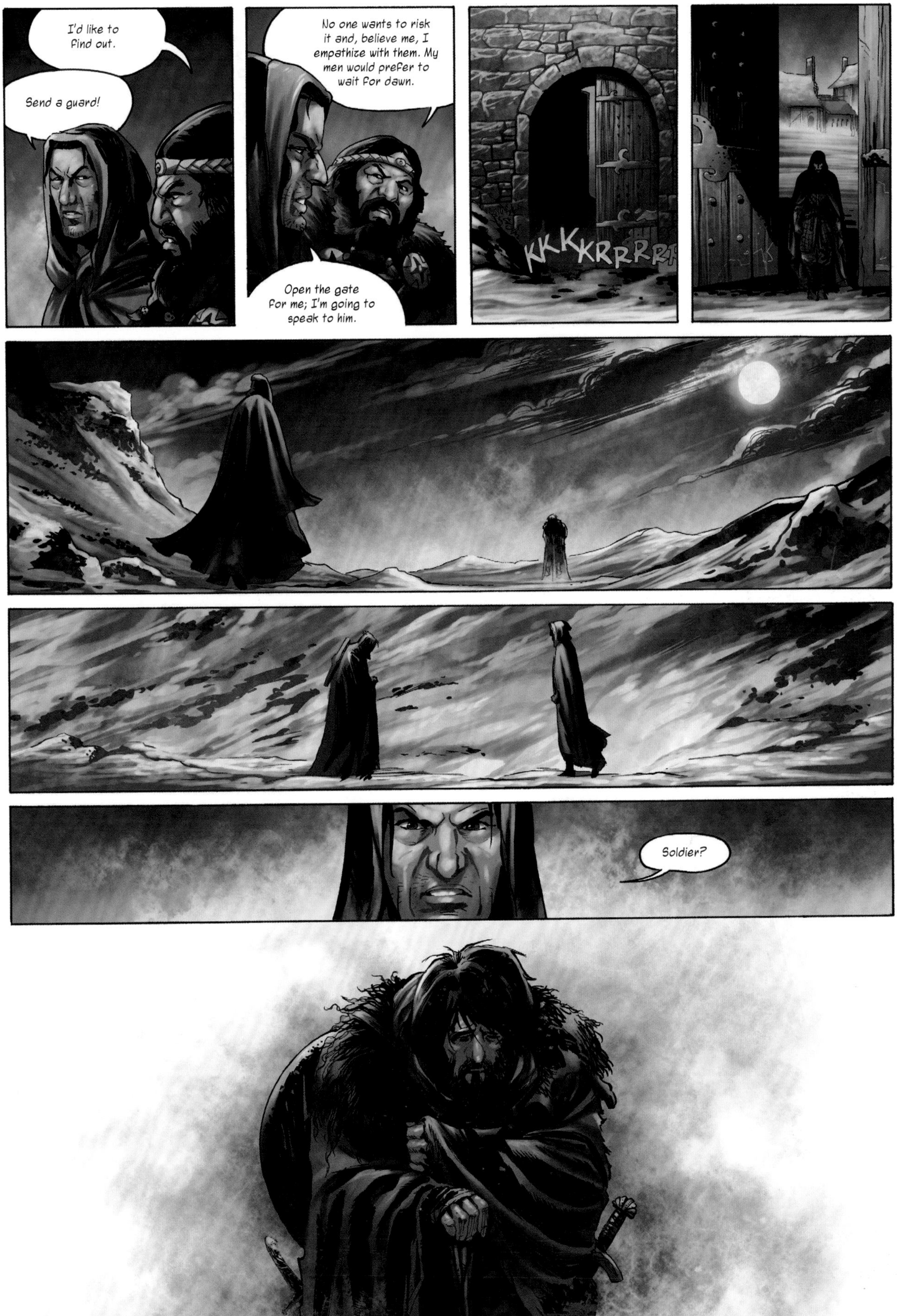
I'd like to find out.
Send a guard!
No one wants to risk it and, believe me, I empathize with them. My men would prefer to wait for dawn.
Open the gate for me; I'm going to speak to him.
KKKKRRRRR
Soldier?

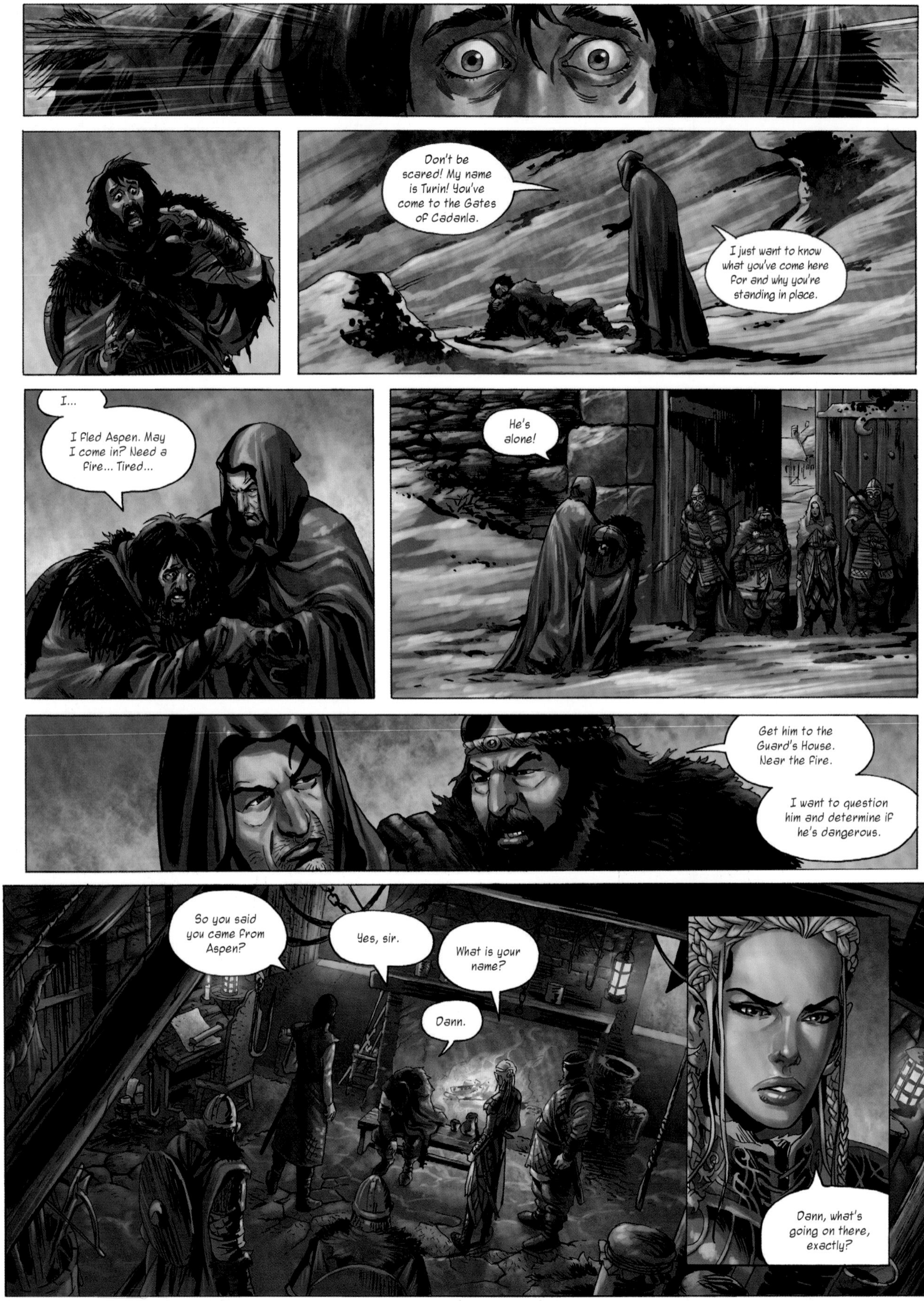

Don't be scared! My name is Turin! You've come to the Gates of Cadanla.
I just want to know what you've come here for and why you're standing in place.
I...
I fled Aspen. May I come in? Need a fire... Tired...
He's alone!
Get him to the Guard's House. Near the fire.
I want to question him and determine if he's dangerous.
So you said you came from Aspen?
Yes, sir.
What is your name?
Dann.
Dann, what's going on there, exactly?

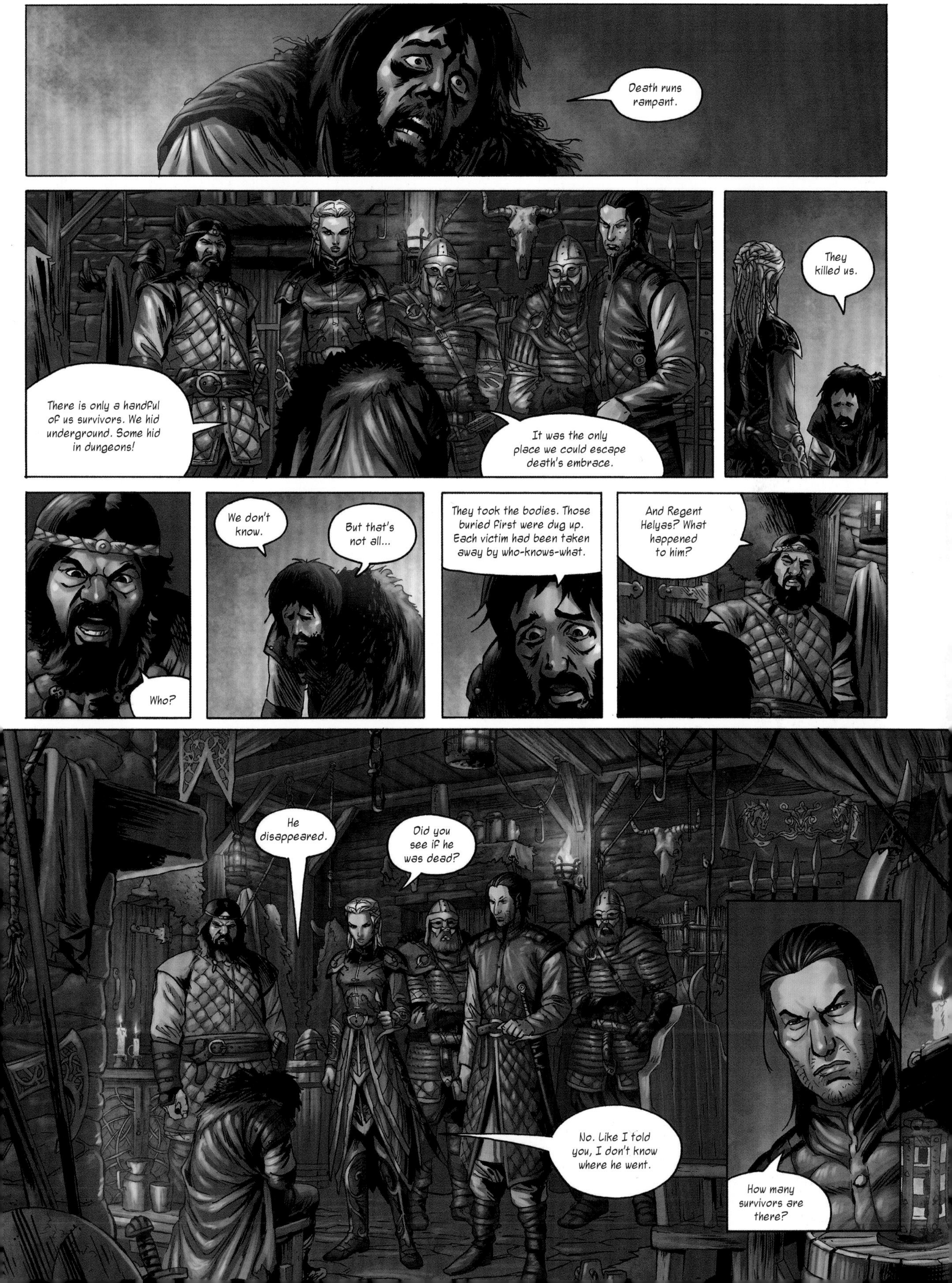
Death runs rampant.
There is only a handful of us survivors. We hid underground. Some hid in dungeons!
It was the only place we could escape death's embrace.
They killed us.
Who?
We don't know.
But that's not all...
They took the bodies. Those buried first were dug up. Each victim had been taken away by who-knows-what.
And Regent Helyas? What happened to him?
He disappeared.
Did you see if he was dead?
No. Like I told you, I don't know where he went.
How many survivors are there?

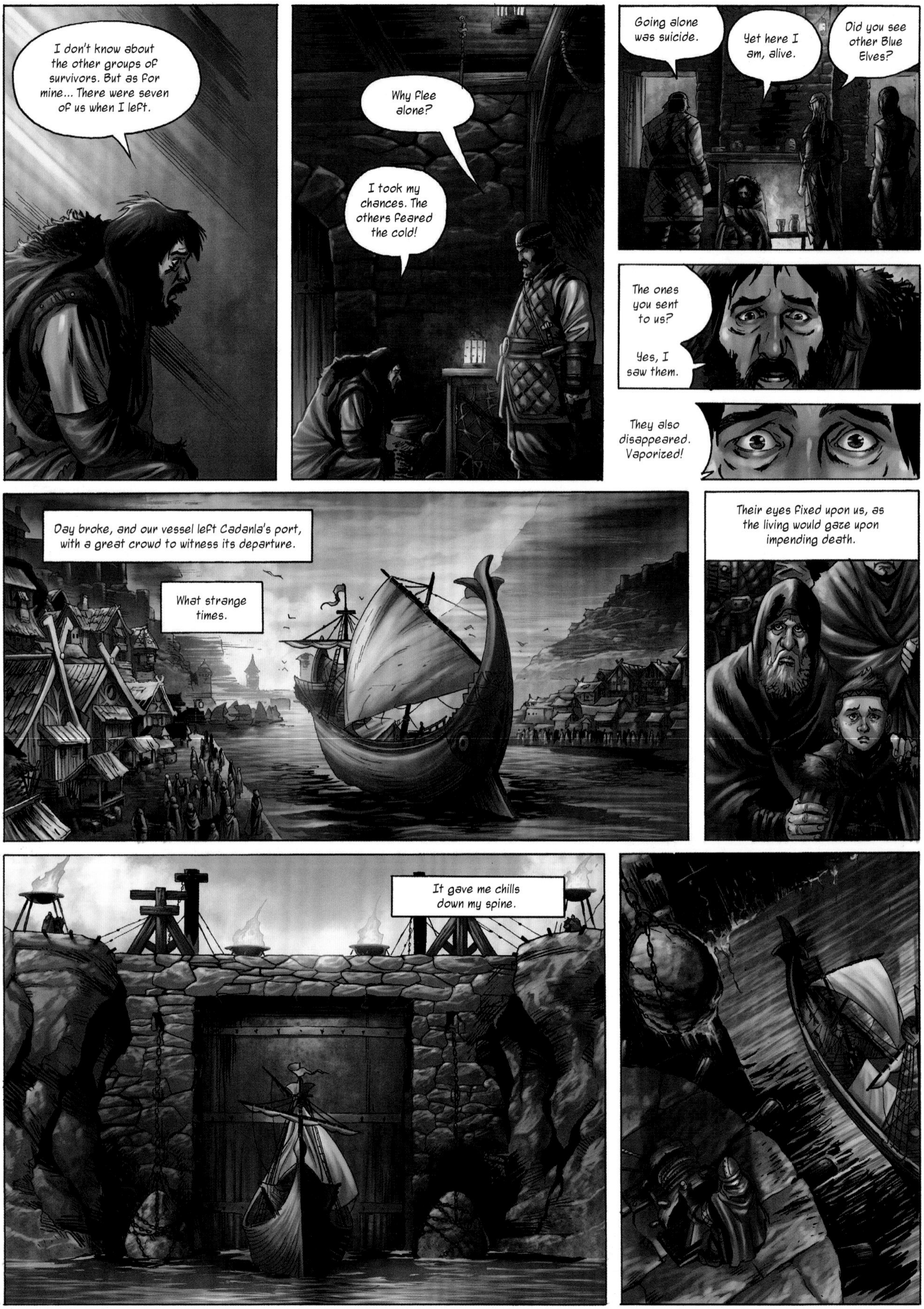
I don't know about the other groups of survivors. But as for mine... There were seven of us when I left.
Why flee alone?
I took my chances. The others feared the cold!
Going alone was suicide.
Yet here I am, alive.
Did you see other Blue Elves?
The ones you sent to us?
Yes, I saw them.
They also disappeared. Vaporized!
Day broke, and our vessel left Cadanla's port, with a great crowd to witness its departure.
What strange times.
Their eyes fixed upon us, as the living would gaze upon impending death.
It gave me chills down my spine.

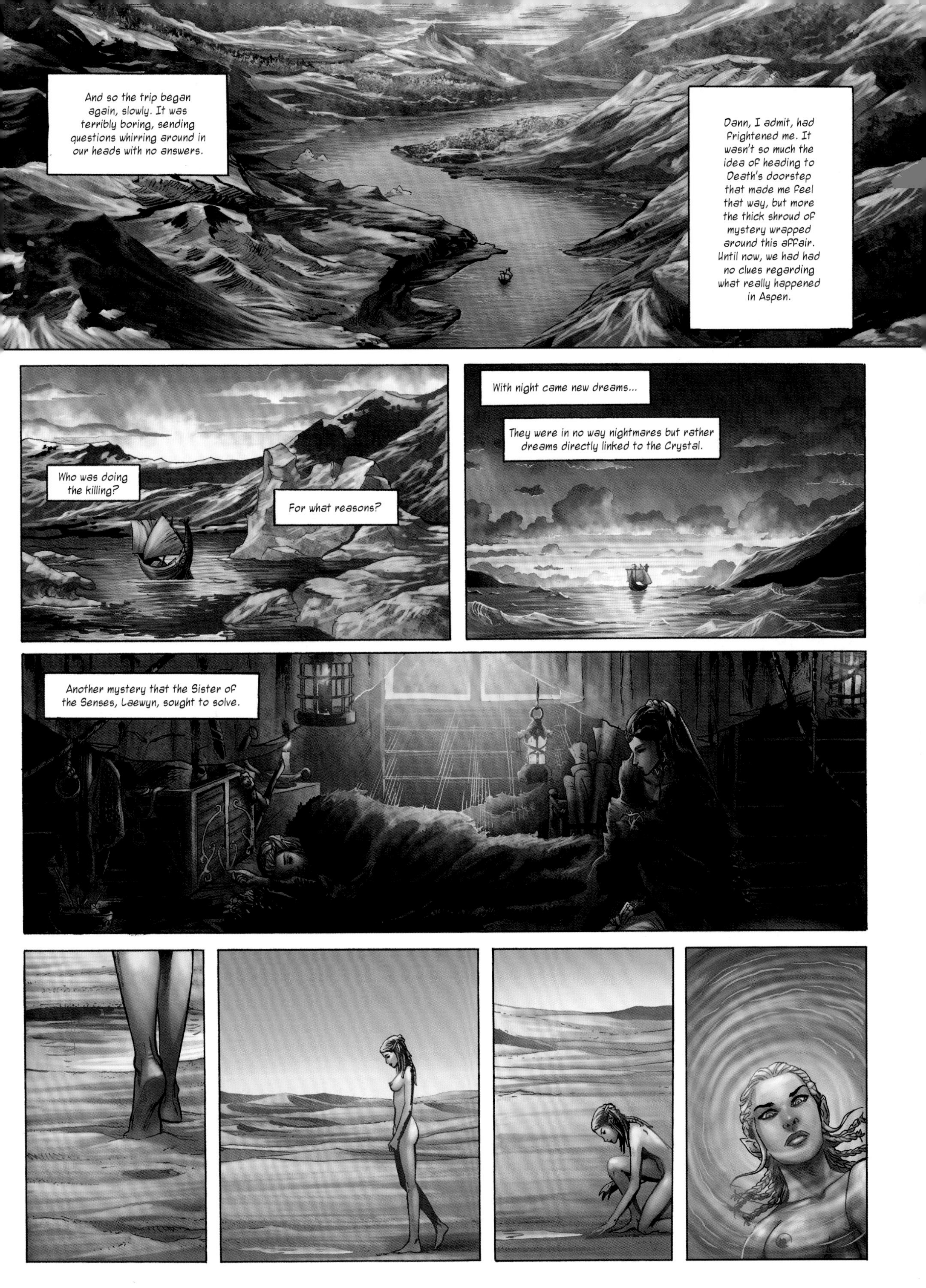
And so the trip began again, slowly. It was terribly boring, sending questions whirring around in our heads with no answers.
Dann, I admit, had frightened me. It wasn't so much the idea of heading to Death's doorstep that made me feel that way, but more the thick shroud of mystery wrapped around this affair. Until now, we had had no clues regarding what really happened in Aspen.
Who was doing the killing?
For what reasons?
With night came new dreams...
They were in no way nightmares but rather dreams directly linked to the Crystal.
Another mystery that the Sister of the Senses, Laewyn, sought to solve.

Lift your hand, would you?

You understand?

Do you understand what this means?

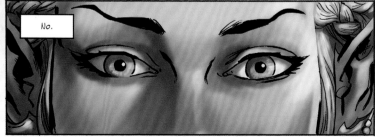

No.

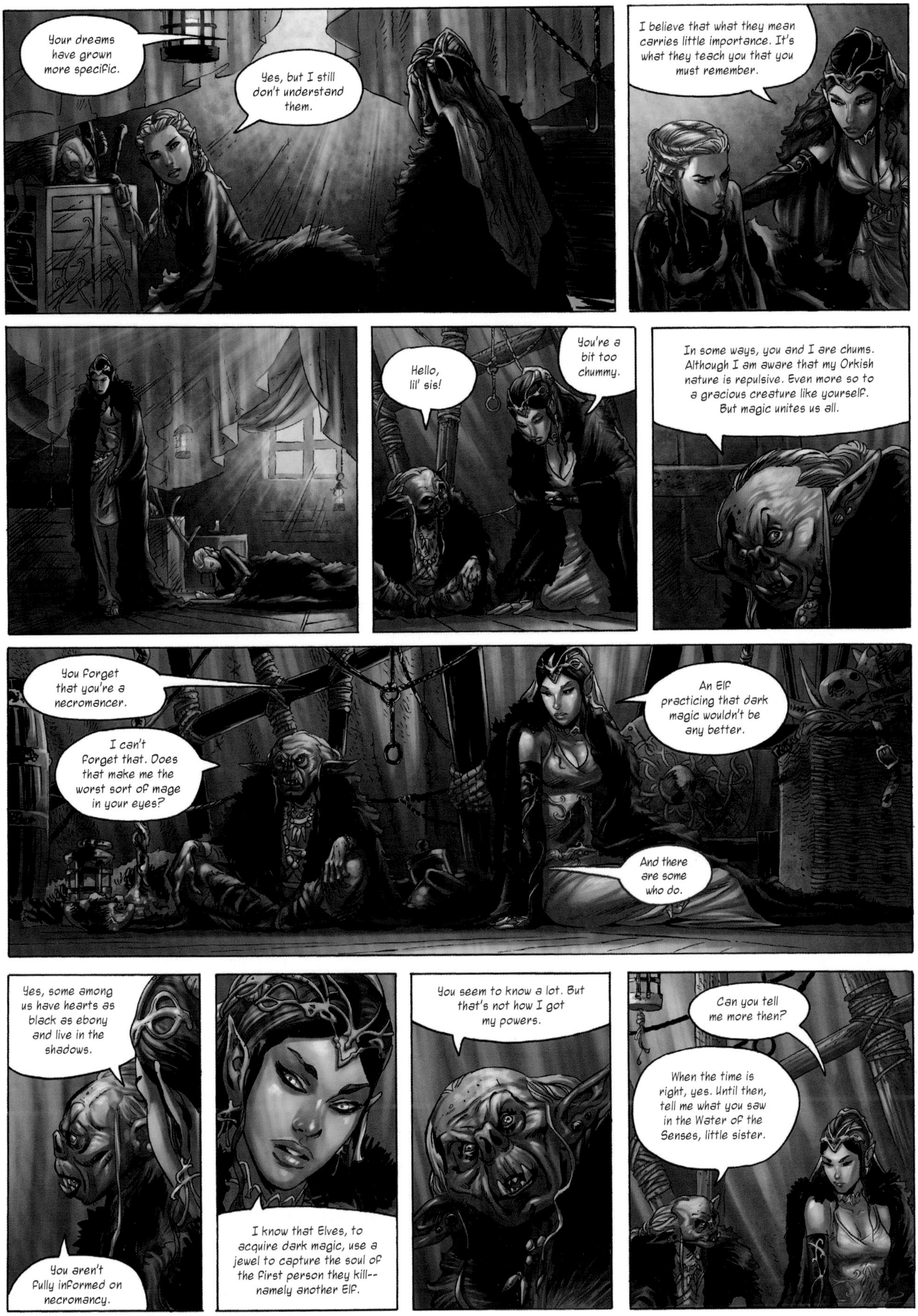
Your dreams have grown more specific.
Yes, but I still don't understand them.
I believe that what they mean carries little importance. It's what they teach you that you must remember.
Hello, lil' sis!
You're a bit too chummy.
In some ways, you and I are chums. Although I am aware that my Orkish nature is repulsive. Even more so to a gracious creature like yourself. But magic unites us all.
You forget that you're a necromancer.
An Elf practicing that dark magic wouldn't be any better.
I can't forget that. Does that make me the worst sort of mage in your eyes?
And there are some who do.
Yes, some among us have hearts as black as ebony and live in the shadows.
You aren't fully informed on necromancy.
I know that Elves, to acquire dark magic, use a jewel to capture the soul of the first person they kill-- namely another Elf.
You seem to know a lot. But that's not how I got my powers.
Can you tell me more then?
When the time is right, yes. Until then, tell me what you saw in the Water of the Senses, little sister.

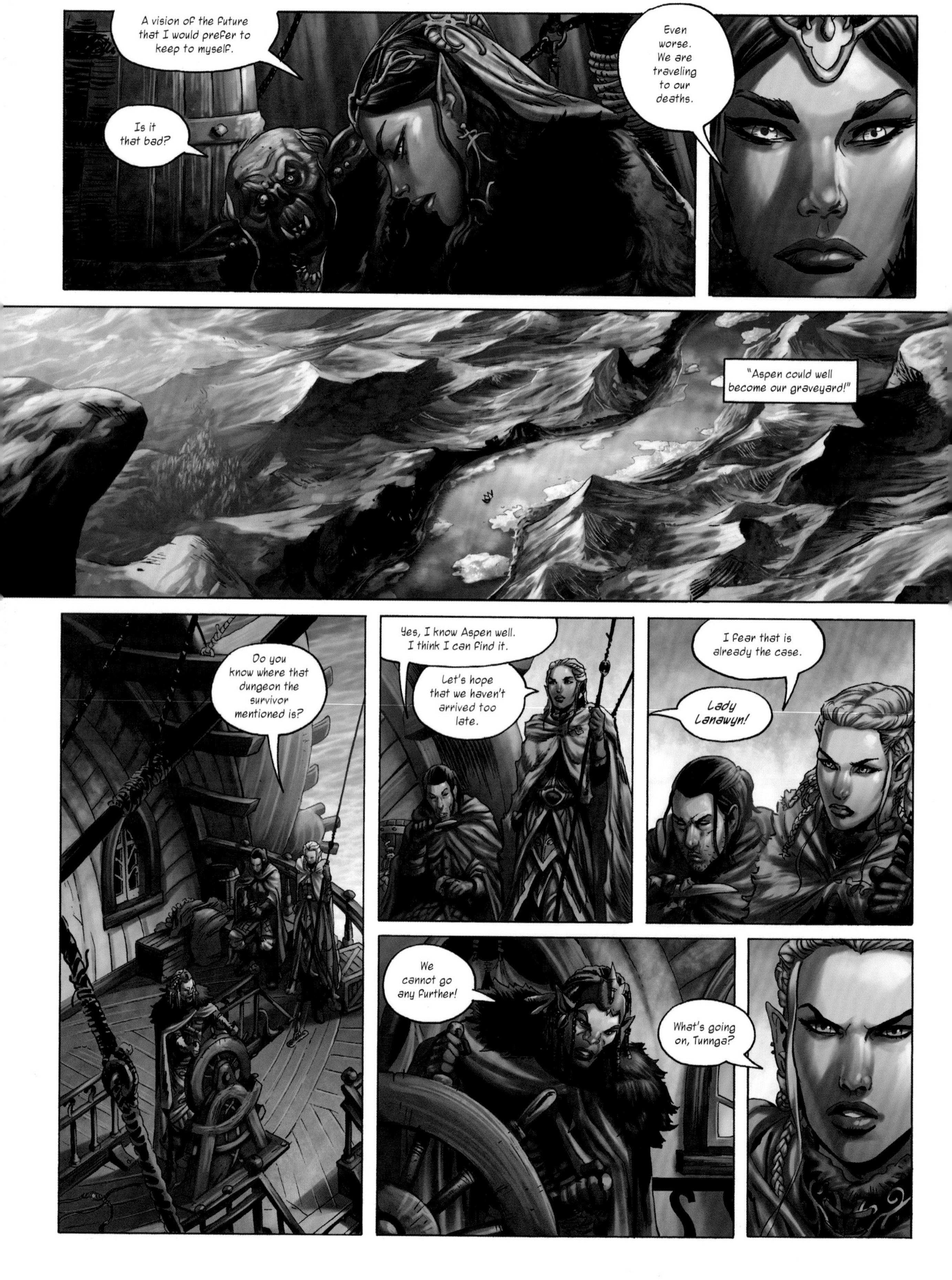
A vision of the future that I would prefer to keep to myself.
Is it that bad?
Even worse. We are traveling to our deaths.
"Aspen could well become our graveyard!"
Do you know where that dungeon the survivor mentioned is?
Yes, I know Aspen well. I think I can find it.
Let's hope that we haven't arrived too late.
I fear that is already the case.
Lady Lanawyn!
We cannot go any further!
What's going on, Tunnga?

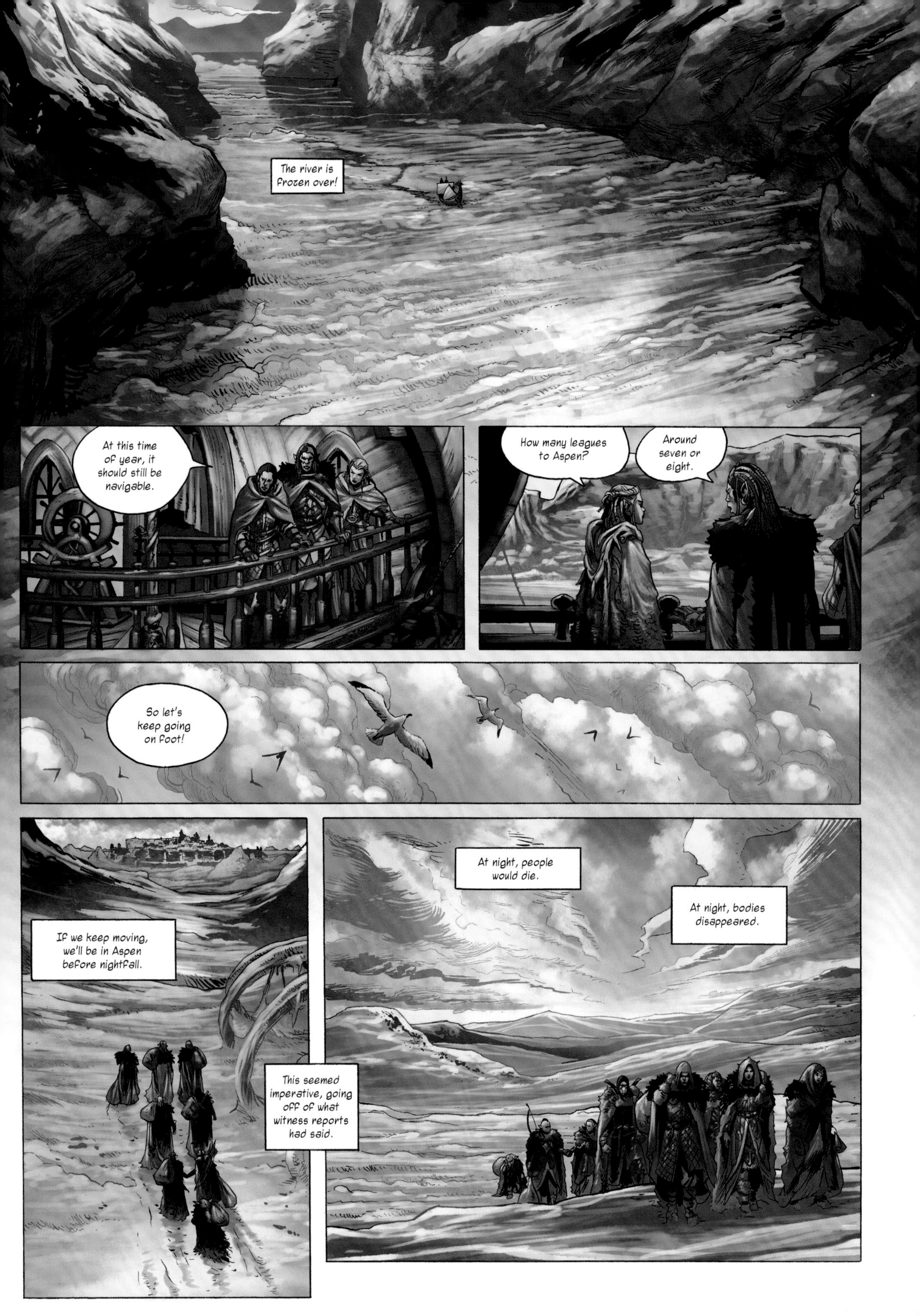
The river is frozen over!
At this time of year, it should still be navigable.
How many leagues to Aspen?
Around seven or eight.
So let's keep going on foot!
If we keep moving, we'll be in Aspen before nightfall.
This seemed imperative, going off of what witness reports had said.
At night, people would die.
At night, bodies disappeared.

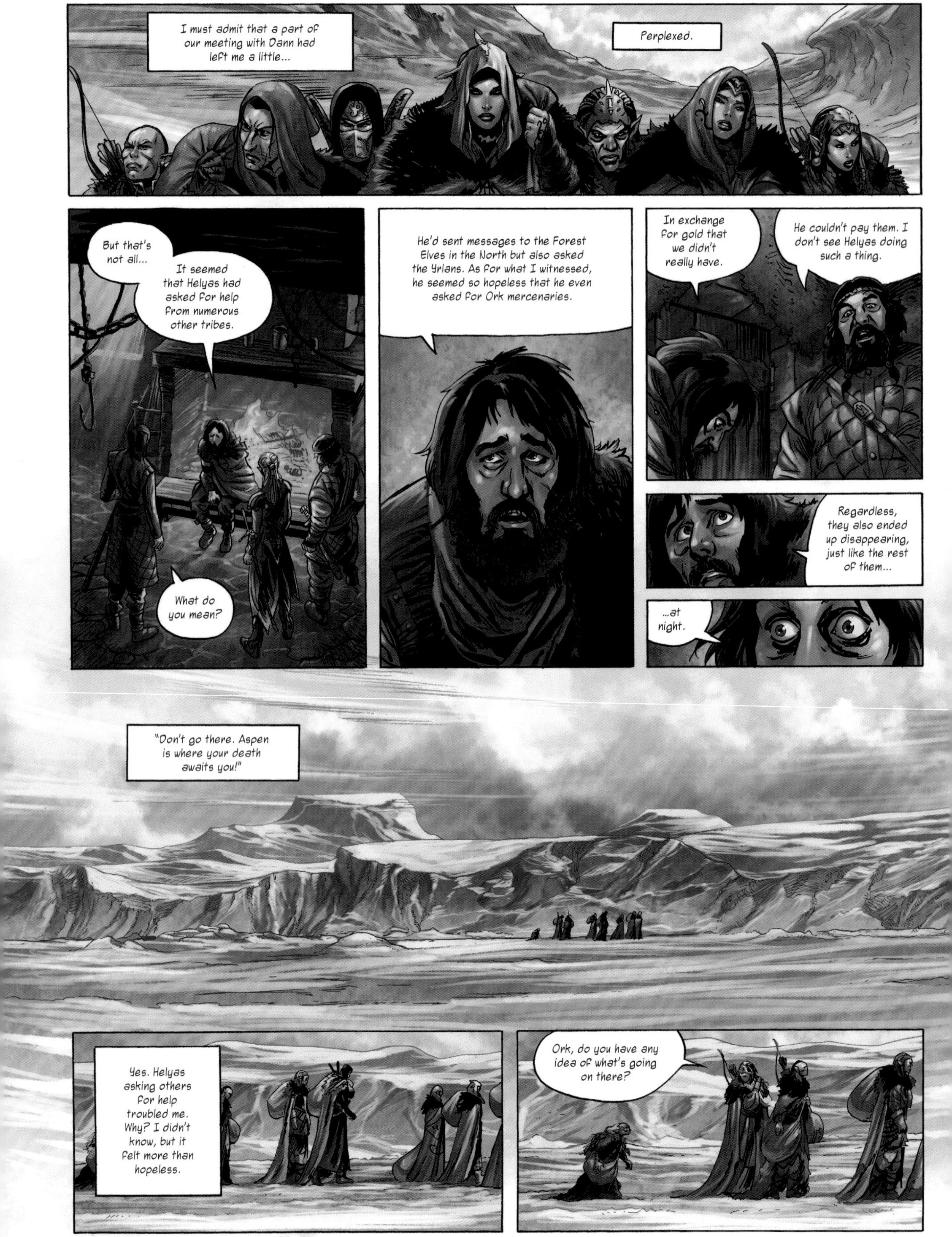
I must admit that a part of our meeting with Dann had left me a little...
Perplexed.
But that's not all...
It seemed that Helyas had asked for help from numerous other tribes.
What do you mean?
He'd sent messages to the Forest Elves in the North but also asked the Yrlans. As for what I witnessed, he seemed so hopeless that he even asked for Ork mercenaries.
In exchange for gold that we didn't really have.
He couldn't pay them. I don't see Helyas doing such a thing.
Regardless, they also ended up disappearing, just like the rest of them...
...at night.
"Don't go there. Aspen is where your death awaits you!"
Yes. Helyas asking others for help troubled me. Why? I didn't know, but it felt more than hopeless.
Ork, do you have any idea of what's going on there?

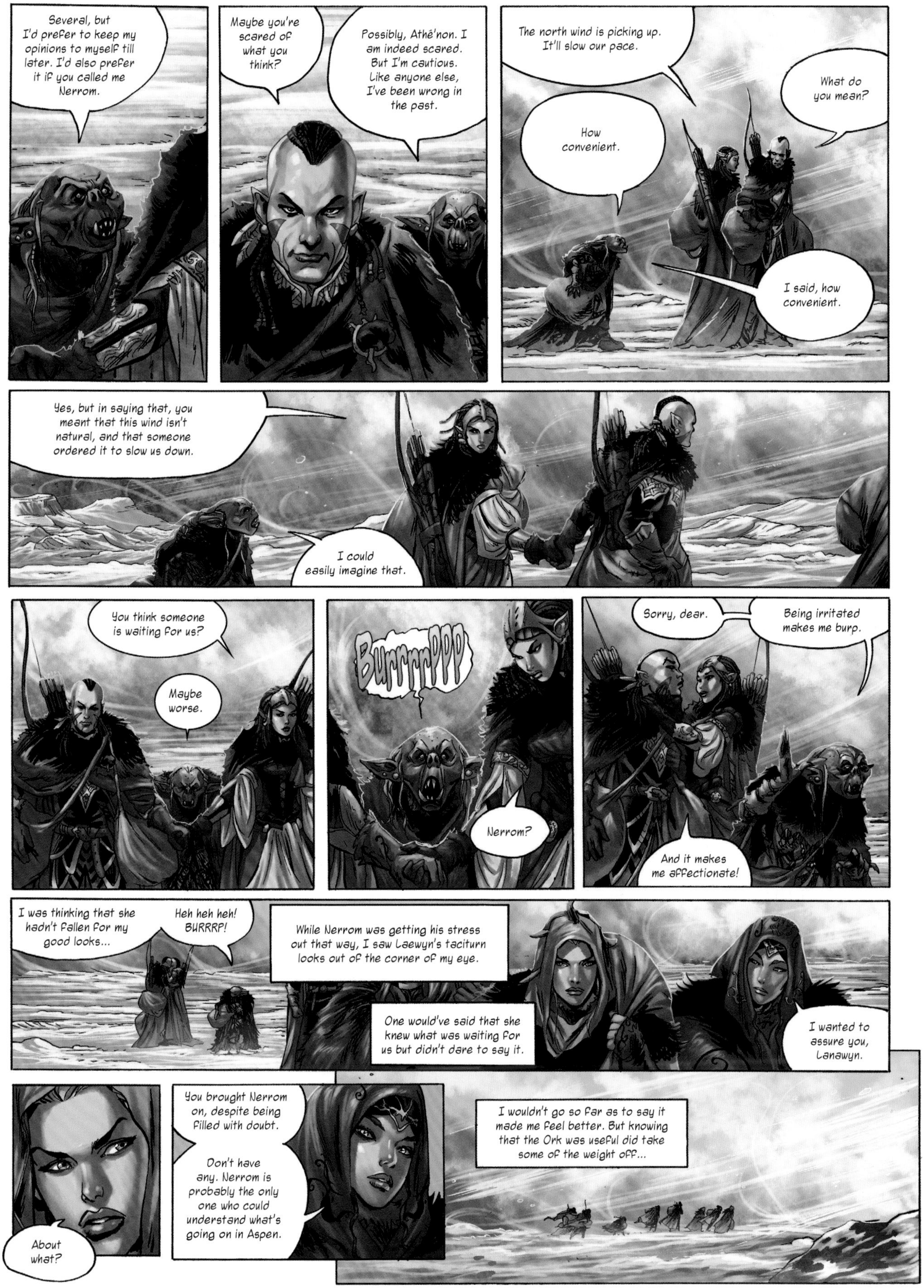

Several, but I'd prefer to keep my opinions to myself till later. I'd also prefer it if you called me Nerrom.
Maybe you're scared of what you think?
Possibly, Athé'non. I am indeed scared. But I'm cautious. Like anyone else, I've been wrong in the past.
The north wind is picking up. It'll slow our pace.
How convenient.
What do you mean?
I said, how convenient.
Yes, but in saying that, you meant that this wind isn't natural, and that someone ordered it to slow us down.
I could easily imagine that.
You think someone is waiting for us?
Maybe worse.
BURRRRPPP
Nerrom?
Sorry, dear.
Being irritated makes me burp.
And it makes me affectionate!
I was thinking that she hadn't fallen for my good looks...
Heh heh heh! BURRRP!
While Nerrom was getting his stress out that way, I saw Laewyn's taciturn looks out of the corner of my eye.
One would've said that she knew what was waiting for us but didn't dare to say it.
I wanted to assure you, Lanawyn.
About what?
You brought Nerrom on, despite being filled with doubt.
Don't have any. Nerrom is probably the only one who could understand what's going on in Aspen.
I wouldn't go so far as to say it made me feel better. But knowing that the Ork was useful did take some of the weight off...

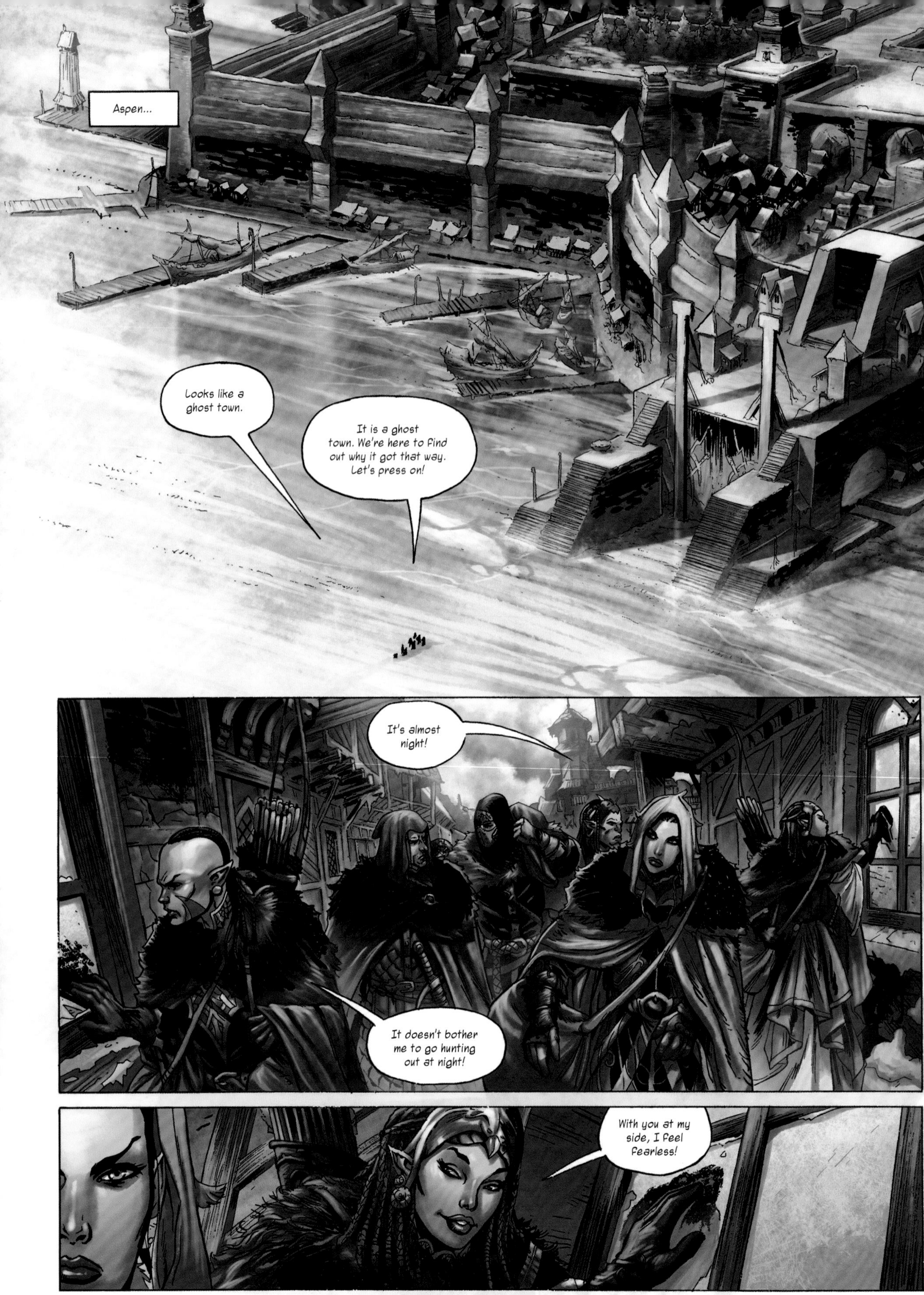
Aspen...
Looks like a ghost town.
It is a ghost town. We're here to find out why it got that way. Let's press on!
It's almost night!
It doesn't bother me to go hunting out at night!
With you at my side, I feel fearless!

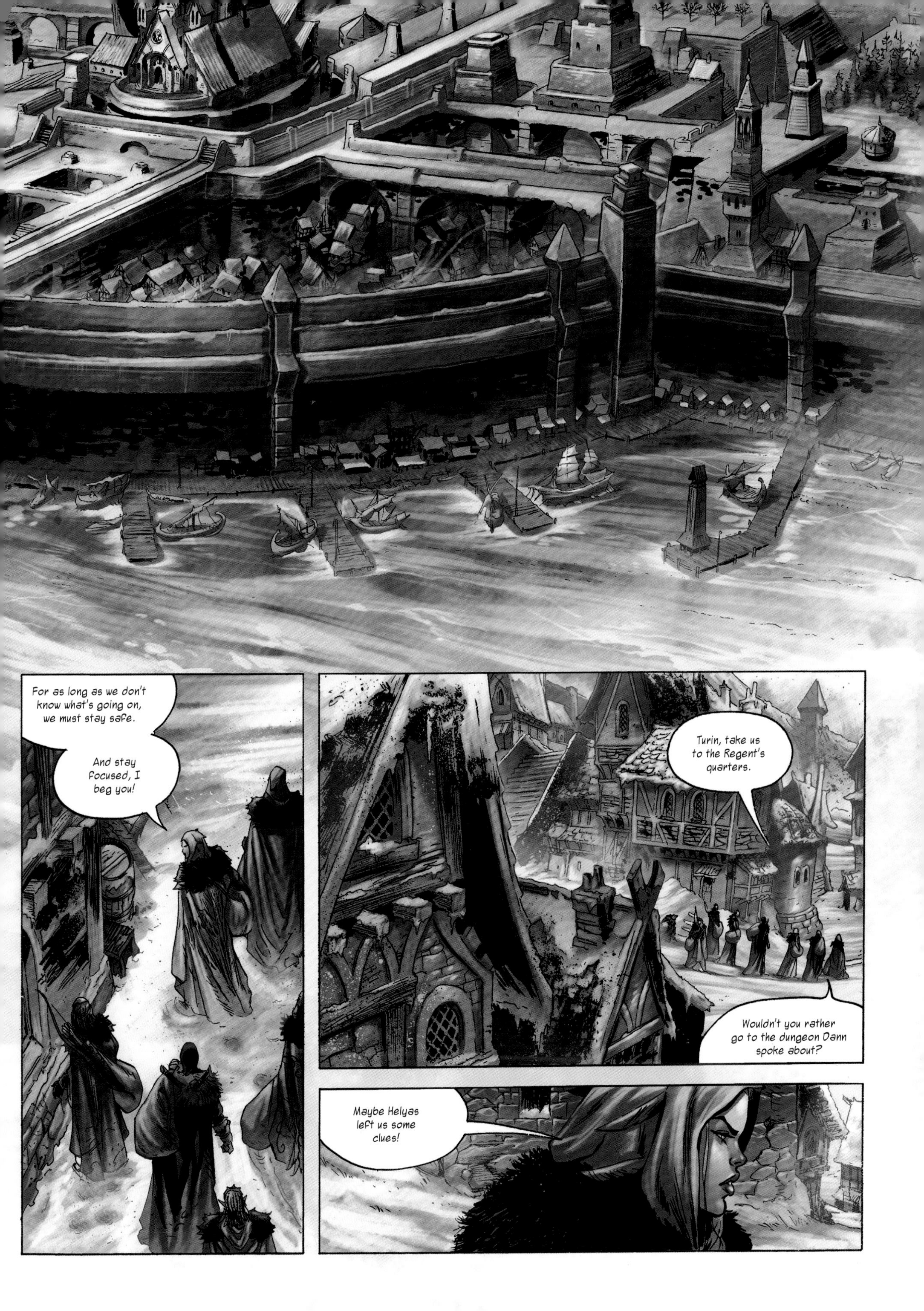
For as long as we don't know what's going on, we must stay safe.
And stay focused, I beg you!
Turin, take us to the Regent's quarters.
Wouldn't you rather go to the dungeon Dann spoke about?
Maybe Helyas left us some clues!

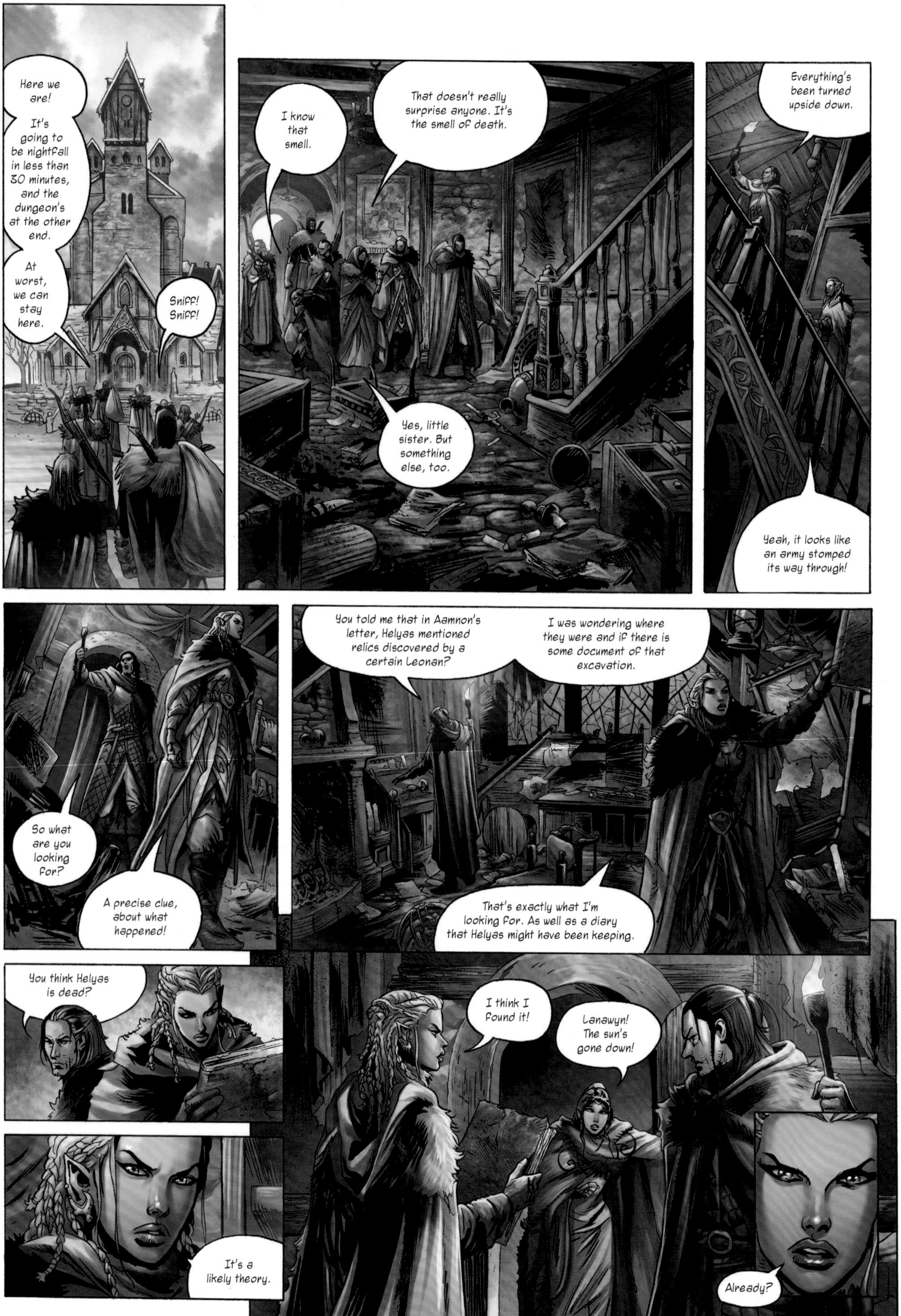
Here we are!
It's going to be nightfall in less than 30 minutes, and the dungeon's at the other end.
At worst, we can stay here.
Sniff! Sniff!
I know that smell.
That doesn't really surprise anyone. It's the smell of death.
Yes, little sister. But something else, too.
Everything's been turned upside down.
Yeah, it looks like an army stomped its way through!
So what are you looking for?
A precise clue, about what happened!
You told me that in Aamnon's letter, Helyas mentioned relics discovered by a certain Leonan?
I was wondering where they were and if there is some document of that excavation.
That's exactly what I'm looking for. As well as a diary that Helyas might have been keeping.
You think Helyas is dead?
It's a likely theory.
I think I found it!
Lanawyn! The sun's gone down!
Already?

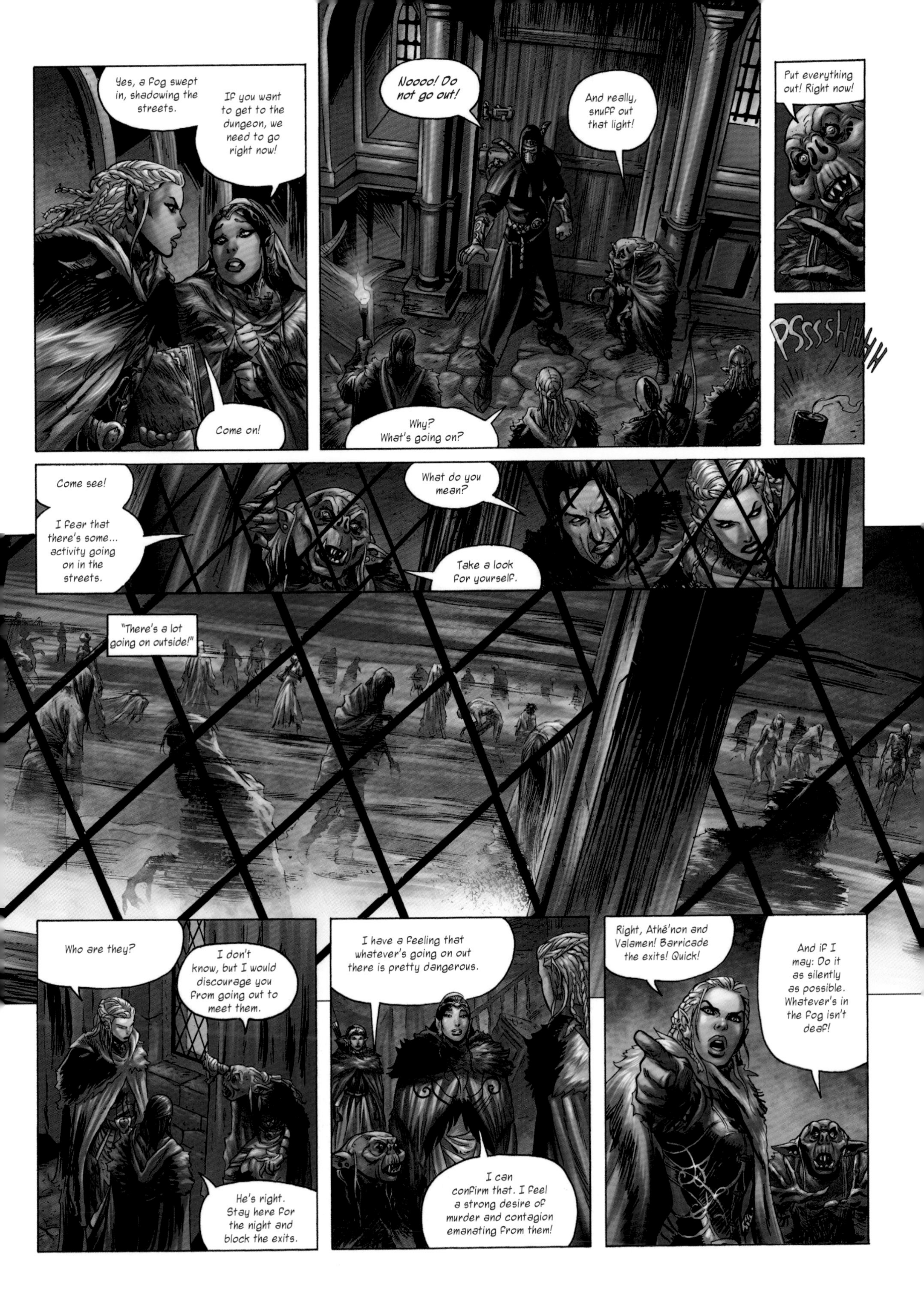

Yes, a fog swept in, shadowing the streets.
If you want to get to the dungeon, we need to go right now!
Come on!
Noooo! Do not go out!
And really, snuff out that light!
Why? What's going on?
Put everything out! Right now!
PSSSSHHHH
Come see!
I fear that there's some... activity going on in the streets.
What do you mean?
Take a look for yourself.
"There's a lot going on outside!"
Who are they?
I don't know, but I would discourage you from going out to meet them.
He's right. Stay here for the night and block the exits.
I have a feeling that whatever's going on out there is pretty dangerous.
I can confirm that. I feel a strong desire of murder and contagion emanating from them!
Right, Athé'non and Valamen! Barricade the exits! Quick!
And if I may: Do it as silently as possible. Whatever's in the fog isn't deaf!

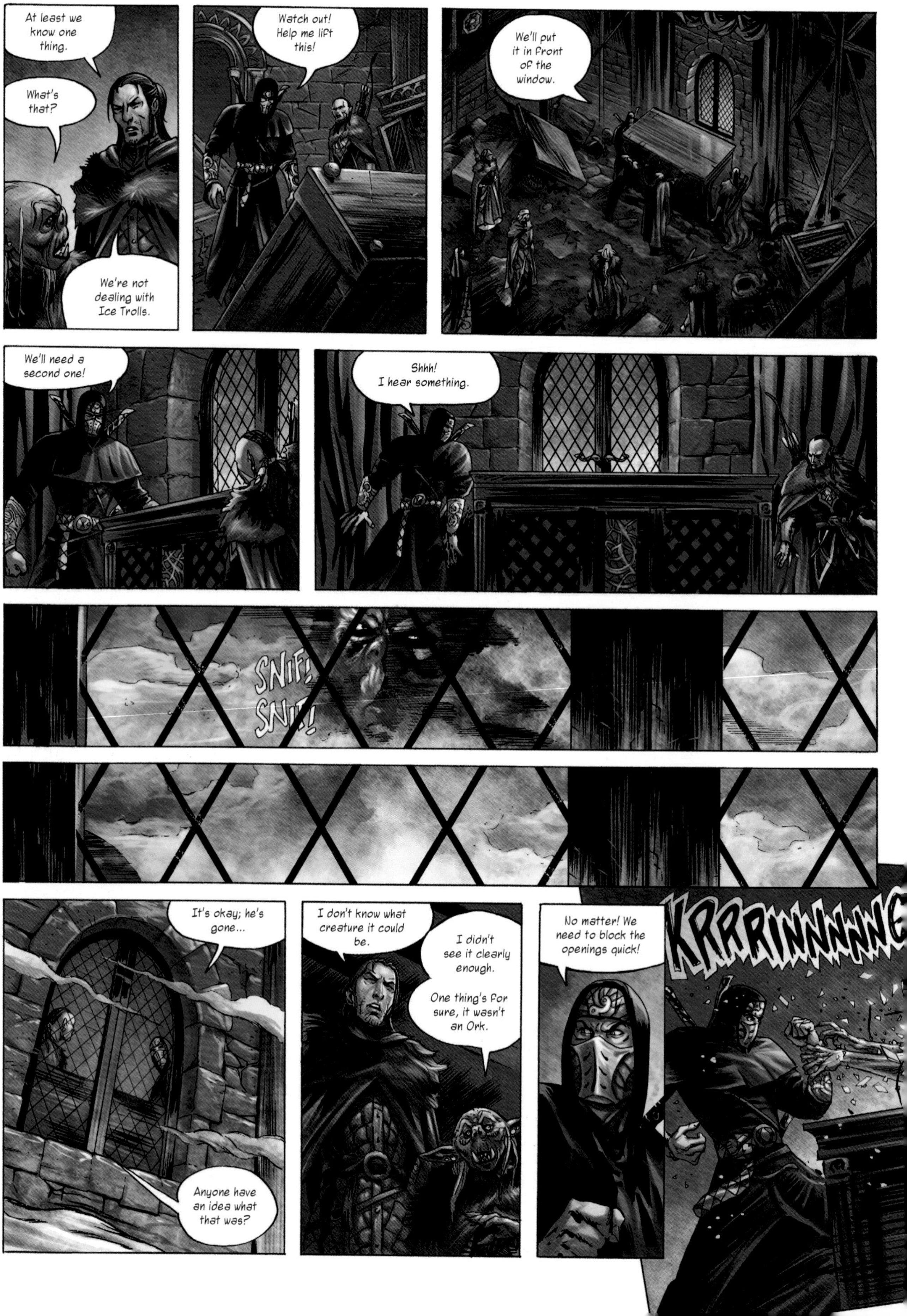
At least we know one thing.
What's that?
We're not dealing with Ice Trolls.
Watch out! Help me lift this!
We'll put it in front of the window.
We'll need a second one!
Shhh! I hear something.
SNIF! SNIF!
It's okay; he's gone...
Anyone have an idea what that was?
I don't know what creature it could be.
I didn't see it clearly enough.
One thing's for sure, it wasn't an Ork.
No matter! We need to block the openings quick!
KRRRINNNNNG

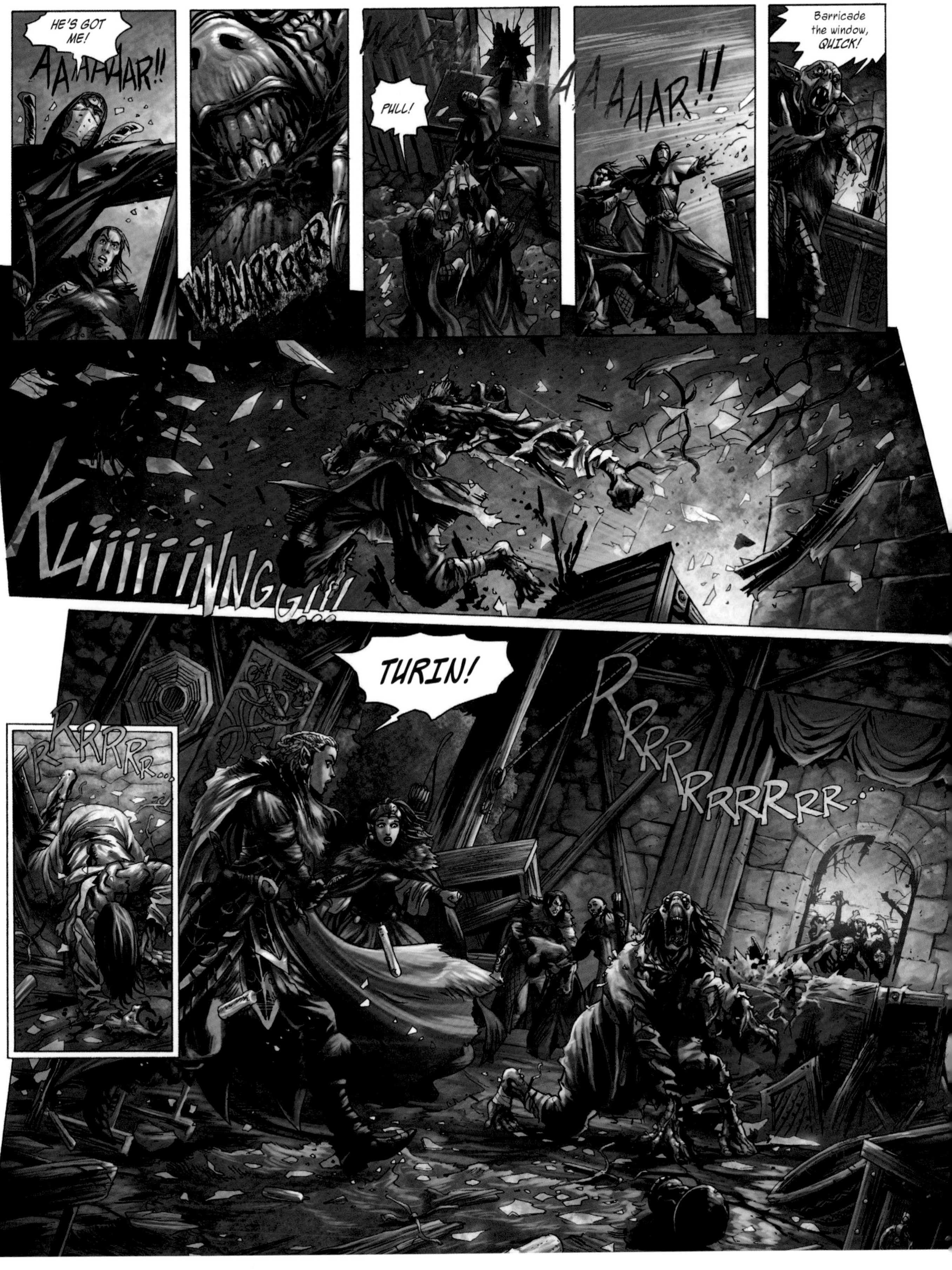
HE'S GOT ME!
AAHHHAR!!
WANRRRRR
PULL!
AAAAAR!!
Barricade the window, QUICK!
KLIIIIIINNGG!!!
TURIN!
RRRRRRR...
RRRRRRRRRR...

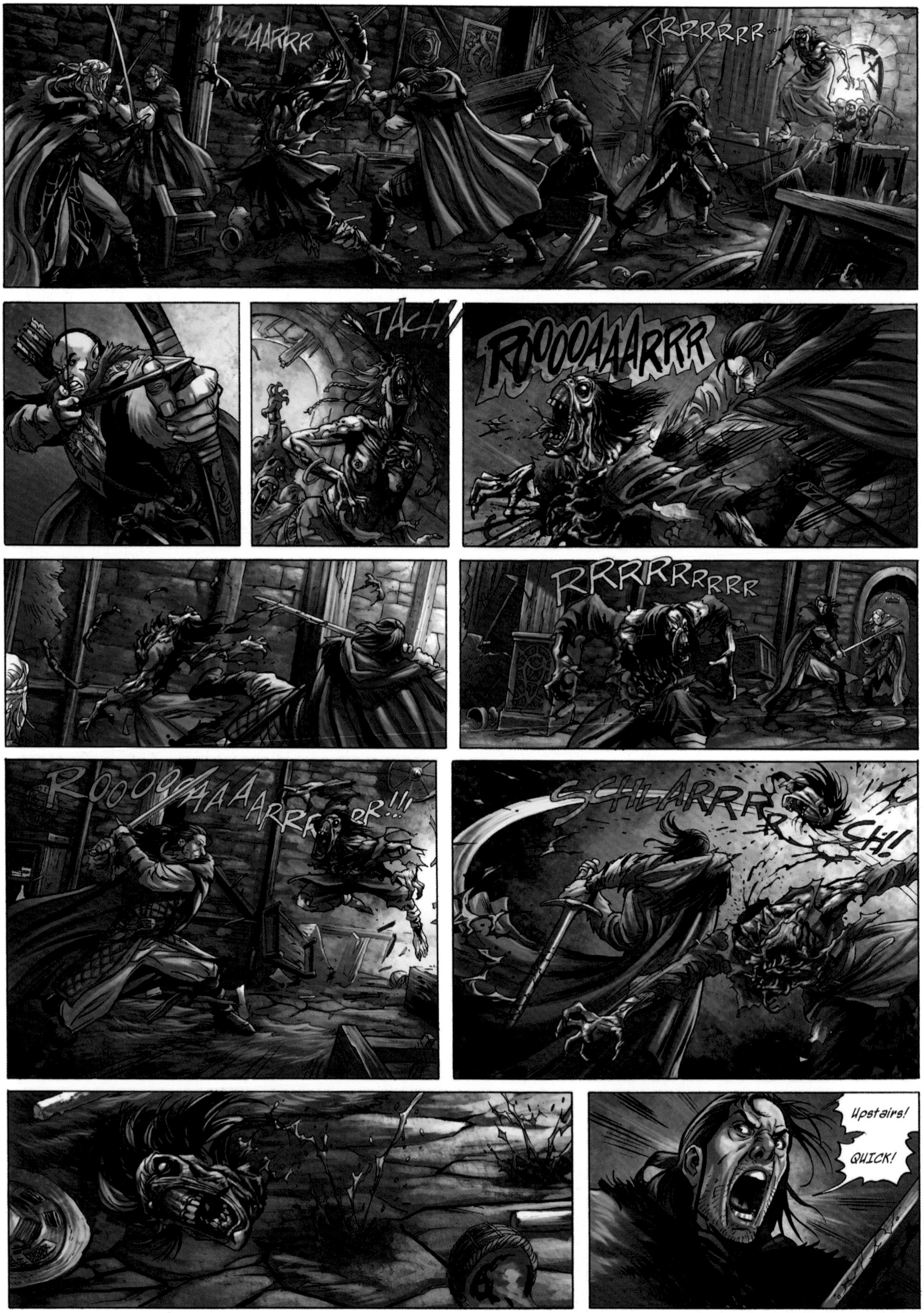

ROOOAAARRR
RRRRRRR...
TACH!
ROOOOAAARRR
RRRRRRRRRR
ROOOOAAAARRRRR!!!
SCHLARRRRR
TCH!
Upstairs!
QUICK!

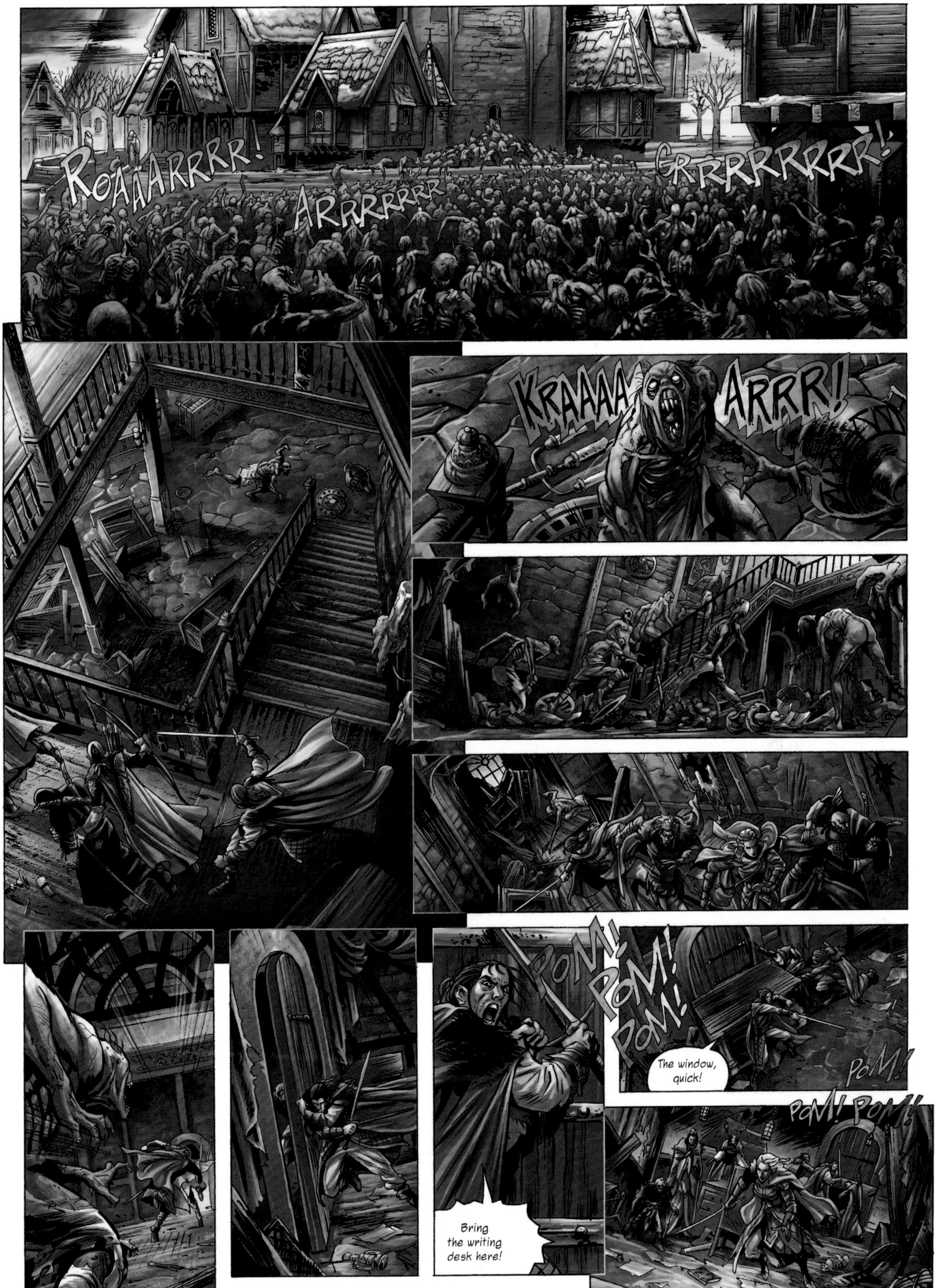
ROAAARRRR!
ARRRRRRR
GRRRRRRRRR!
KRAAAA ARRR!
POM! POM! POM!
The window, quick!
POM!
Bring the writing desk here!
POM! POM!

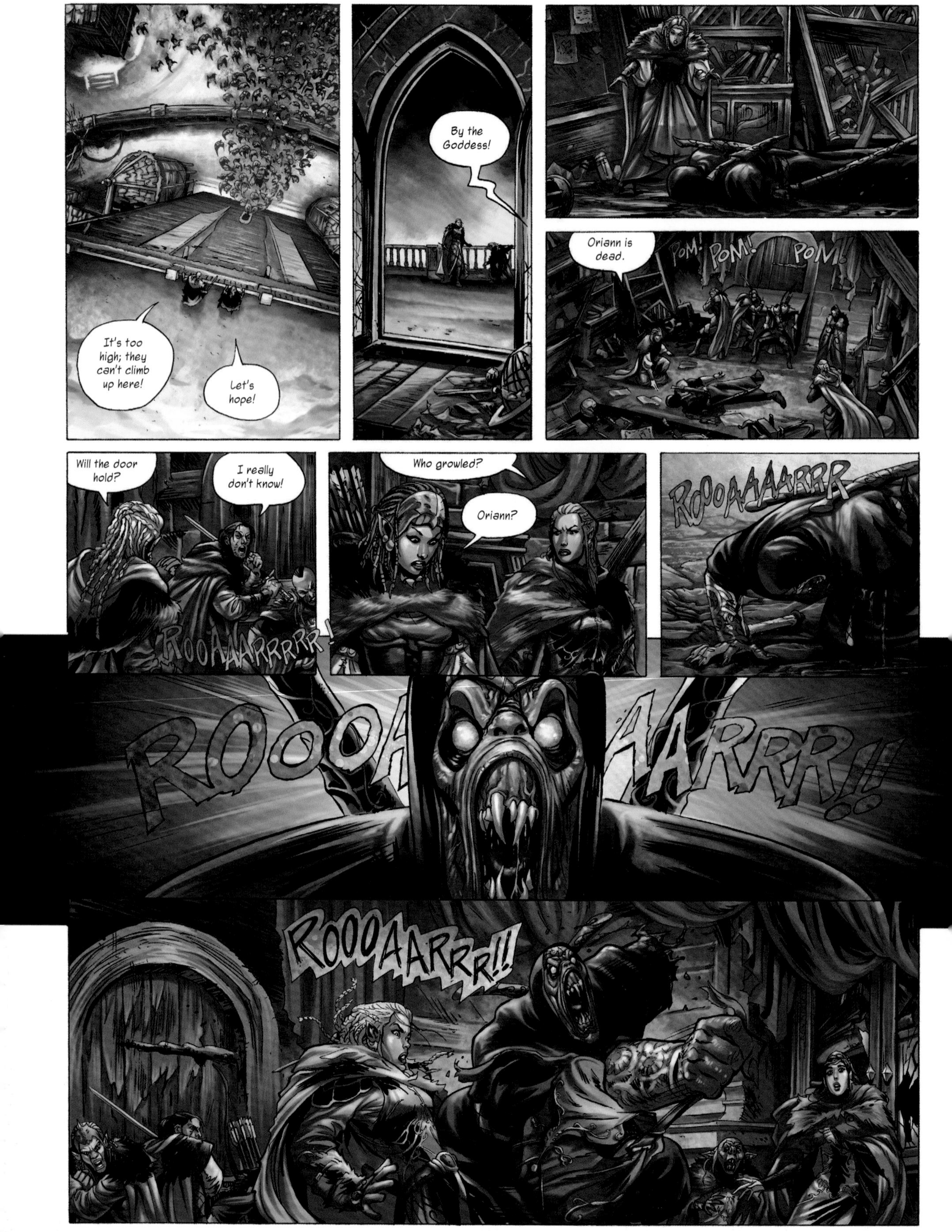
It's too high; they can't climb up here!
Let's hope!
By the Goddess!
Oriann is dead.
POM! POM! POM!
Will the door hold?
I really don't know!
ROOAAARRRRR!
Who growled?
Oriann?
ROOOAAAARRRR
ROOOAAARRR!!
ROOOAARRR!!

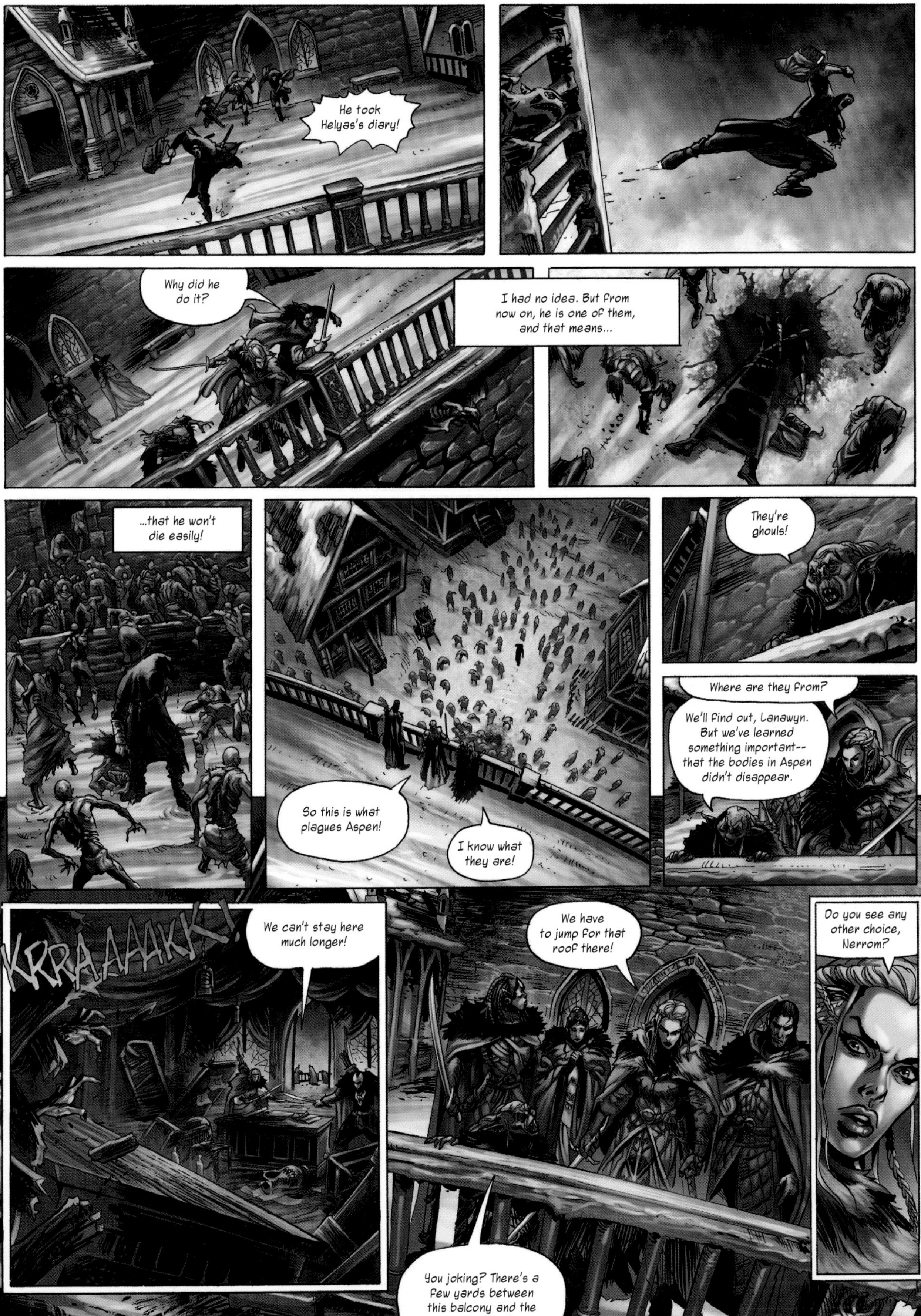

He took Helyas's diary!
Why did he do it?
I had no idea. But from now on, he is one of them, and that means...
...that he won't die easily!
So this is what plagues Aspen!
I know what they are!
They're ghouls!
Where are they from?
We'll find out, Lanawyn. But we've learned something important-- that the bodies in Aspen didn't disappear.
KRRAAAAKK!
We can't stay here much longer!
We have to jump for that roof there!
You joking? There's a few yards between this balcony and the next roof!
Do you see any other choice, Nerrom?

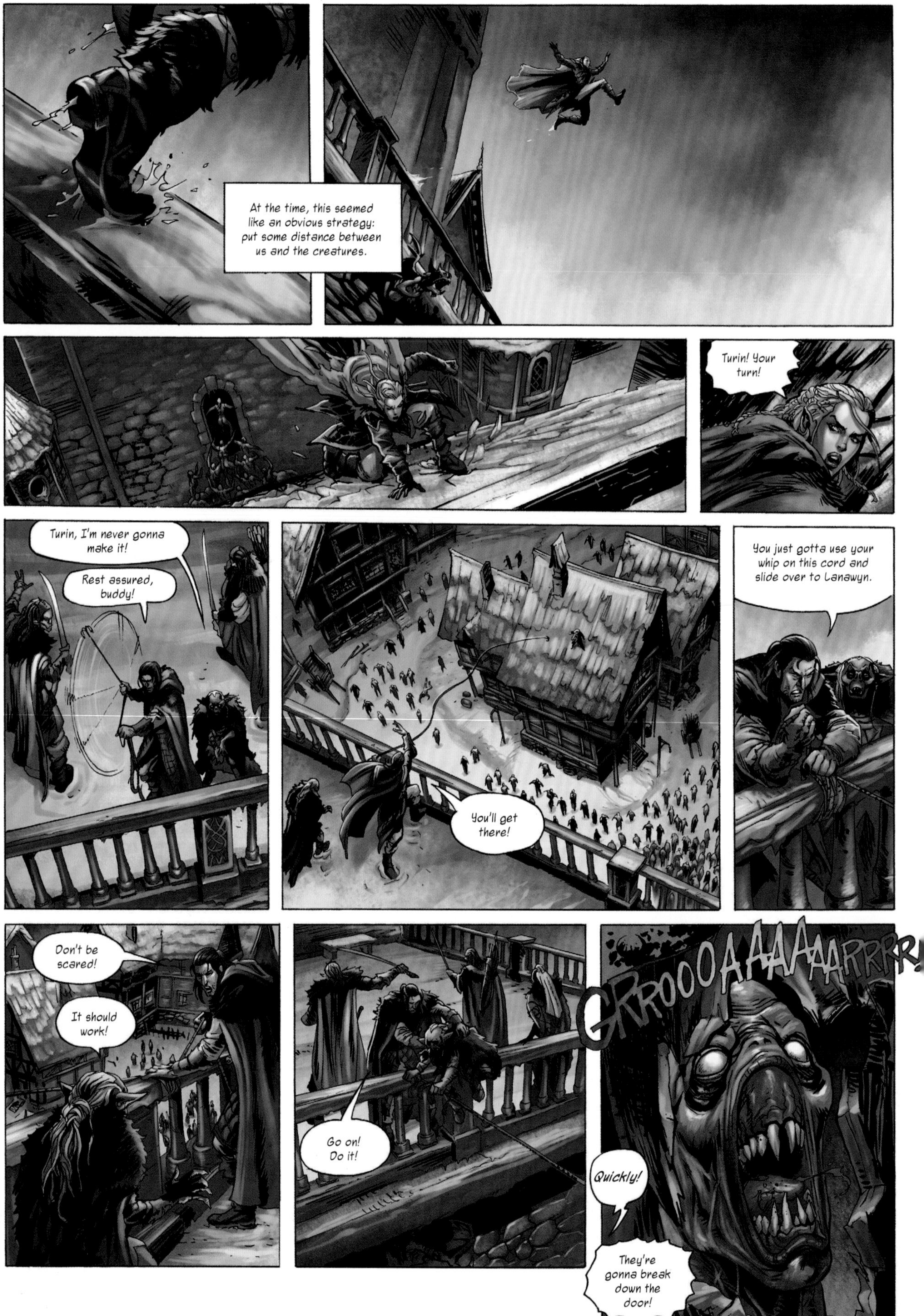
At the time, this seemed like an obvious strategy: put some distance between us and the creatures.
Turin! Your turn!
Turin, I'm never gonna make it!
Rest assured, buddy!
You'll get there!
You just gotta use your whip on this cord and slide over to Lanawyn.
Don't be scared!
It should work!
Go on! Do it!
GRROOOAAAAAARRRR!
Quickly!
They're gonna break down the door!

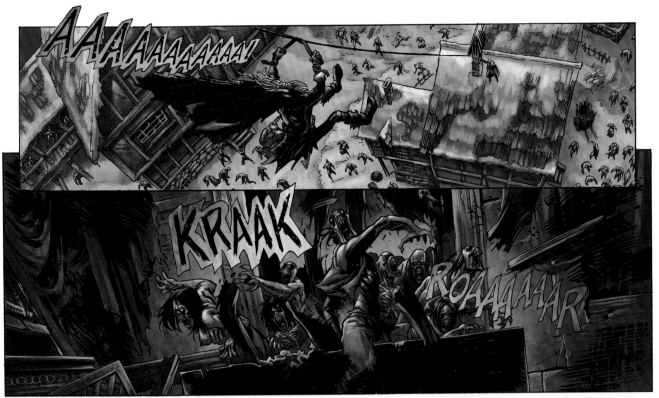

AAAAAAAAAAAA!

KRAAK

ROAAAAAAR

FLEE!

QUICK! QUICK!!

ROOOAAAAAARRRRR

Athé'non! We're all clear!

Athé'non! You scared me, you know that!?

I was scared, too.

I love you!

Putting distance between them and us was the extent of my planning. I wasn't scared to admit...

...that these creatures were terrifying!

Not being able to see more than five steps ahead of us made walking on the roofs a perilous affair.

And we had to do it as quietly as possible.

No point in drawing their attention to us.

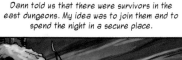

Dann told us that there were survivors in the east dungeons. My idea was to join them and to spend the night in a secure place.

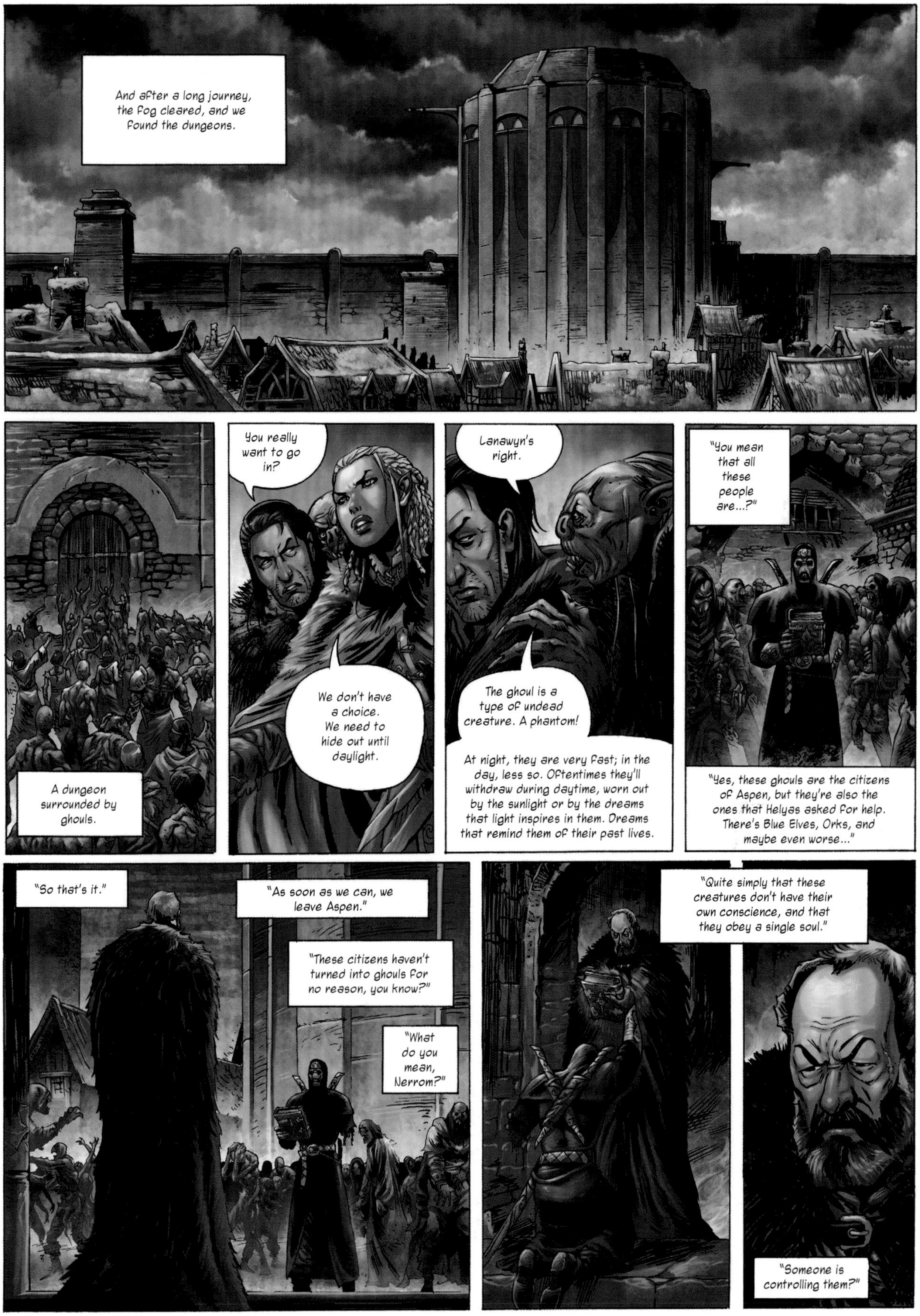
And after a long journey, the fog cleared, and we found the dungeons.
A dungeon surrounded by ghouls.
You really want to go in?
We don't have a choice. We need to hide out until daylight.
Lanawyn's right.
The ghoul is a type of undead creature. A phantom!
At night, they are very fast; in the day, less so. Oftentimes they'll withdraw during daytime, worn out by the sunlight or by the dreams that light inspires in them. Dreams that remind them of their past lives.
"You mean that all these people are...?"
"Yes, these ghouls are the citizens of Aspen, but they're also the ones that Helyas asked for help. There's Blue Elves, Orks, and maybe even worse..."
"So that's it."
"As soon as we can, we leave Aspen."
"These citizens haven't turned into ghouls for no reason, you know?"
"What do you mean, Nerrom?"
"Quite simply that these creatures don't have their own conscience, and that they obey a single soul."
"Someone is controlling them?"

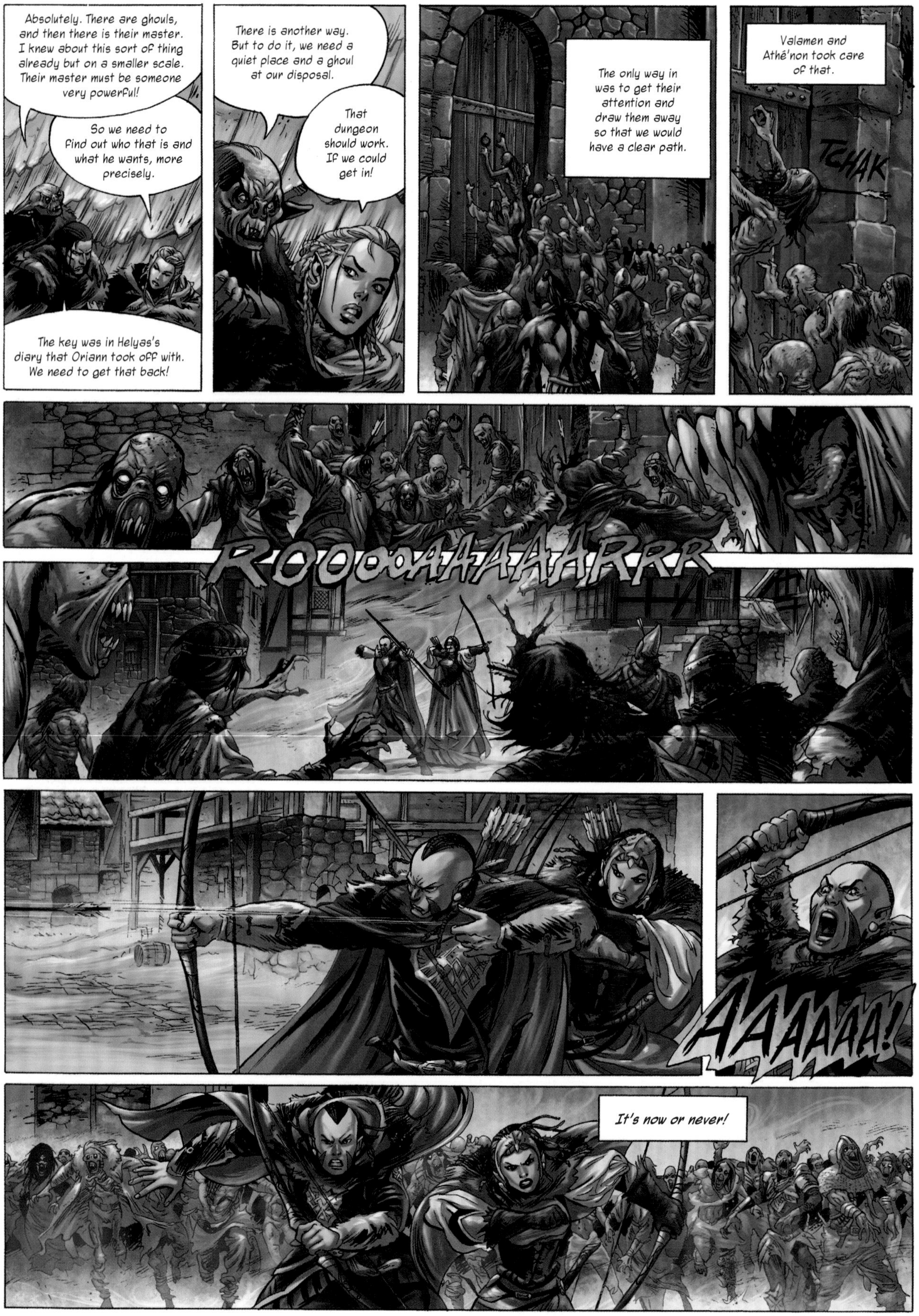

Absolutely. There are ghouls, and then there is their master. I knew about this sort of thing already but on a smaller scale. Their master must be someone very powerful!
So we need to find out who that is and what he wants, more precisely.
The key was in Helyas's diary that Oriann took off with. We need to get that back!
There is another way. But to do it, we need a quiet place and a ghoul at our disposal.
That dungeon should work. If we could get in!
The only way in was to get their attention and draw them away so that we would have a clear path.
Valamen and Athé'non took care of that.
TCHAK
ROOOOAAAAARRR
AAAAAA!
It's now or never!

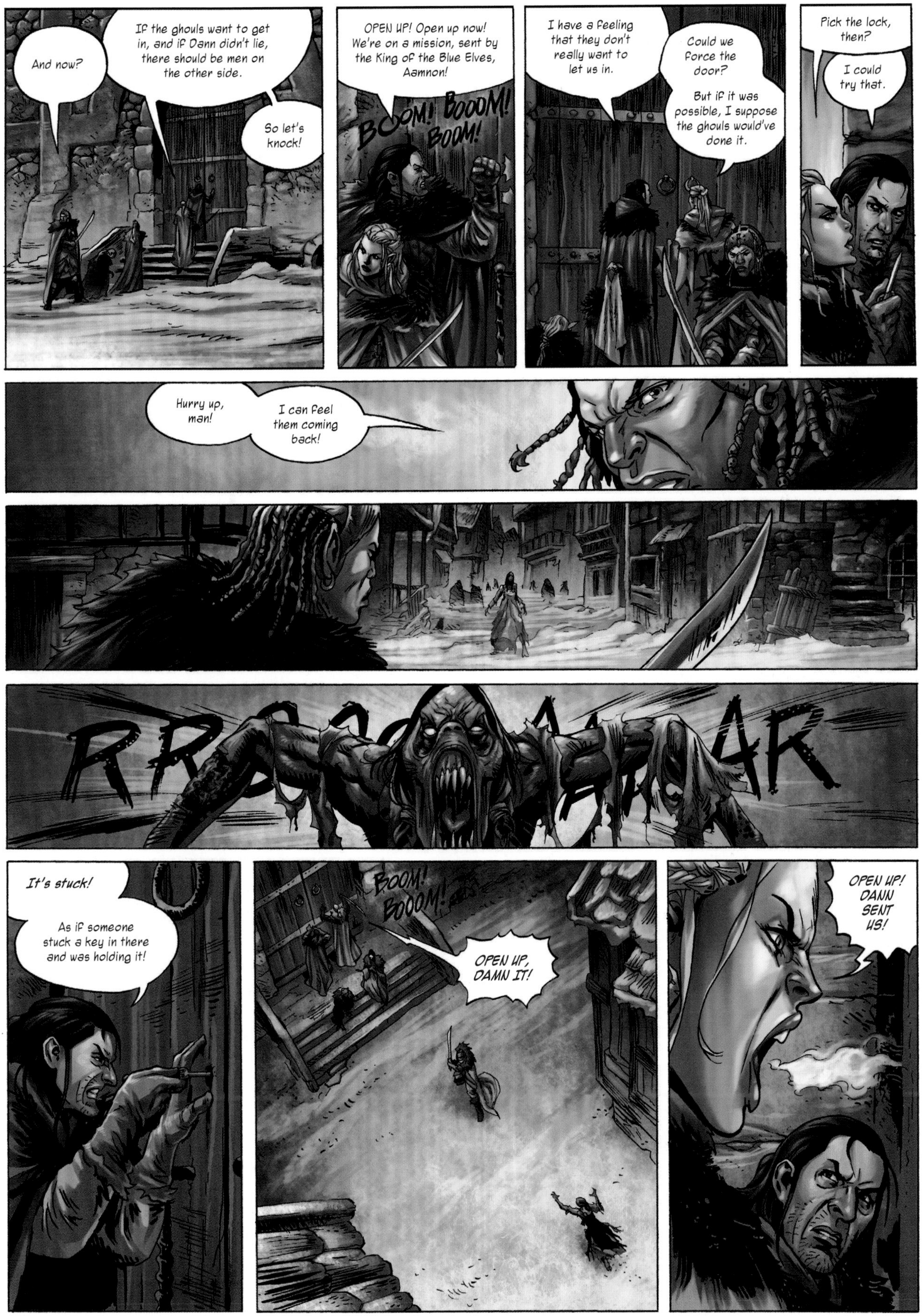

And now?
If the ghouls want to get in, and if Dann didn't lie, there should be men on the other side.
So let's knock!
OPEN UP! Open up now! We're on a mission, sent by the King of the Blue Elves, Aamnon!
BOOM! BOOOM! BOOM!
I have a feeling that they don't really want to let us in.
Could we force the door?
But if it was possible, I suppose the ghouls would've done it.
Pick the lock, then?
I could try that.
Hurry up, man!
I can feel them coming back!
It's stuck!
As if someone stuck a key in there and was holding it!
BOOM! BOOOM!
OPEN UP, DAMN IT!
OPEN UP! DANN SENT US!

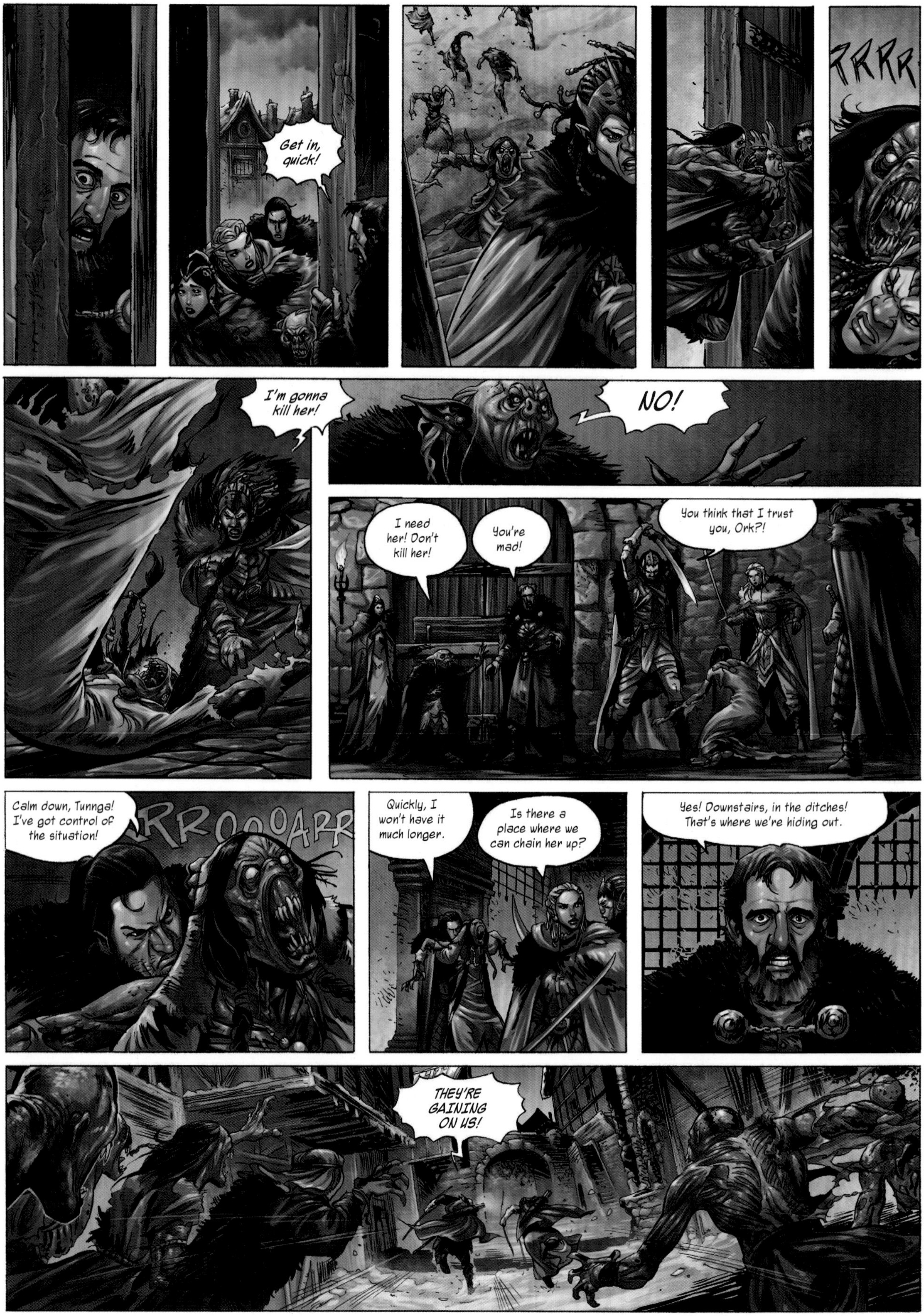
Get in, quick!
RRRR
I'm gonna kill her!
NO!
I need her! Don't kill her!
You're mad!
You think that I trust you, Ork?!
Calm down, Tunnga! I've got control of the situation!
RROOOARR
Quickly, I won't have it much longer.
Is there a place where we can chain her up?
Yes! Downstairs, in the ditches! That's where we're hiding out.
THEY'RE GAINING ON US!

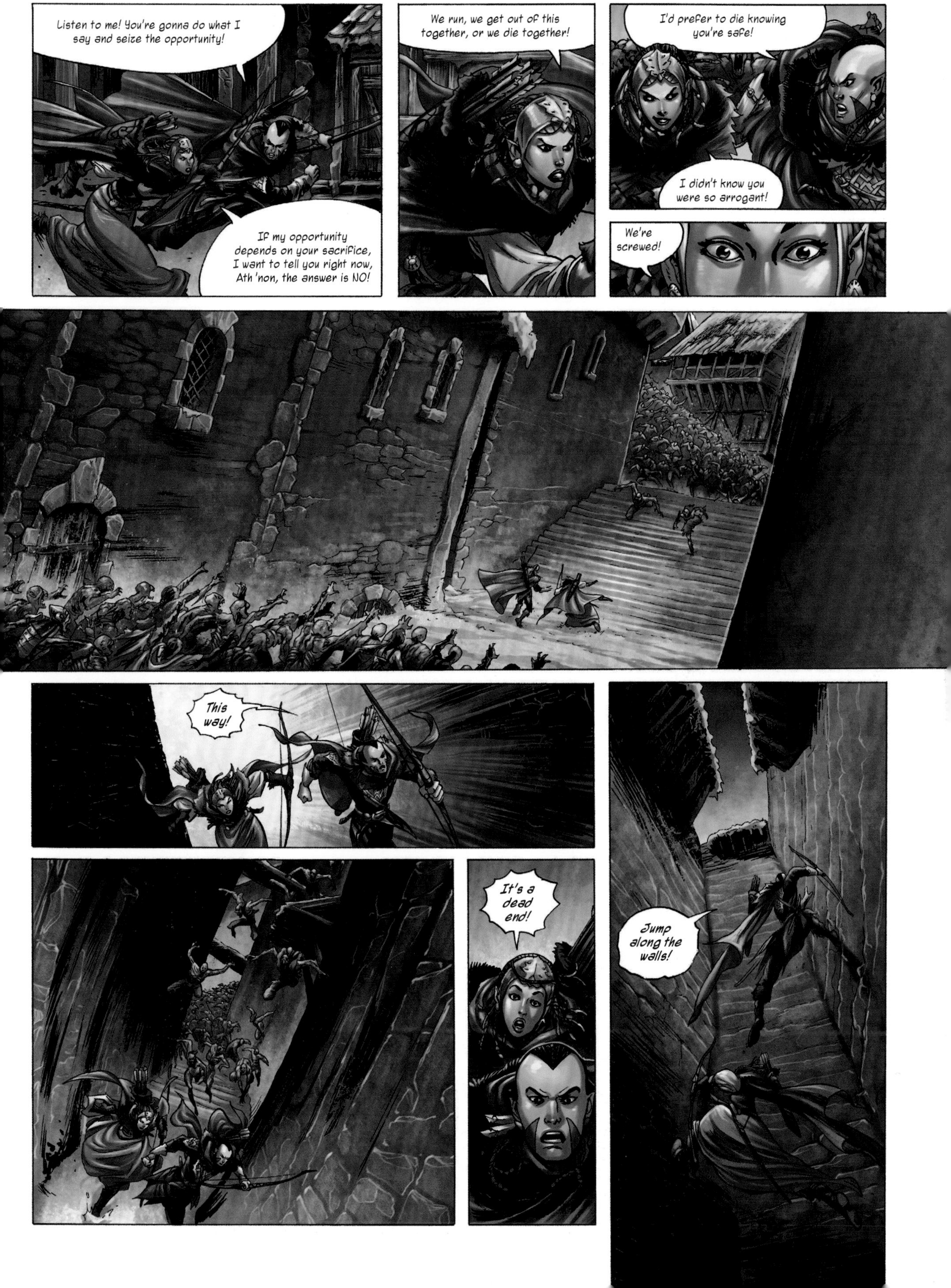
Listen to me! You're gonna do what I say and seize the opportunity!
If my opportunity depends on your sacrifice, I want to tell you right now, Ath 'non, the answer is NO!
We run, we get out of this together, or we die together!
I'd prefer to die knowing you're safe!
I didn't know you were so arrogant!
We're screwed!
This way!
It's a dead end!
Jump along the walls!

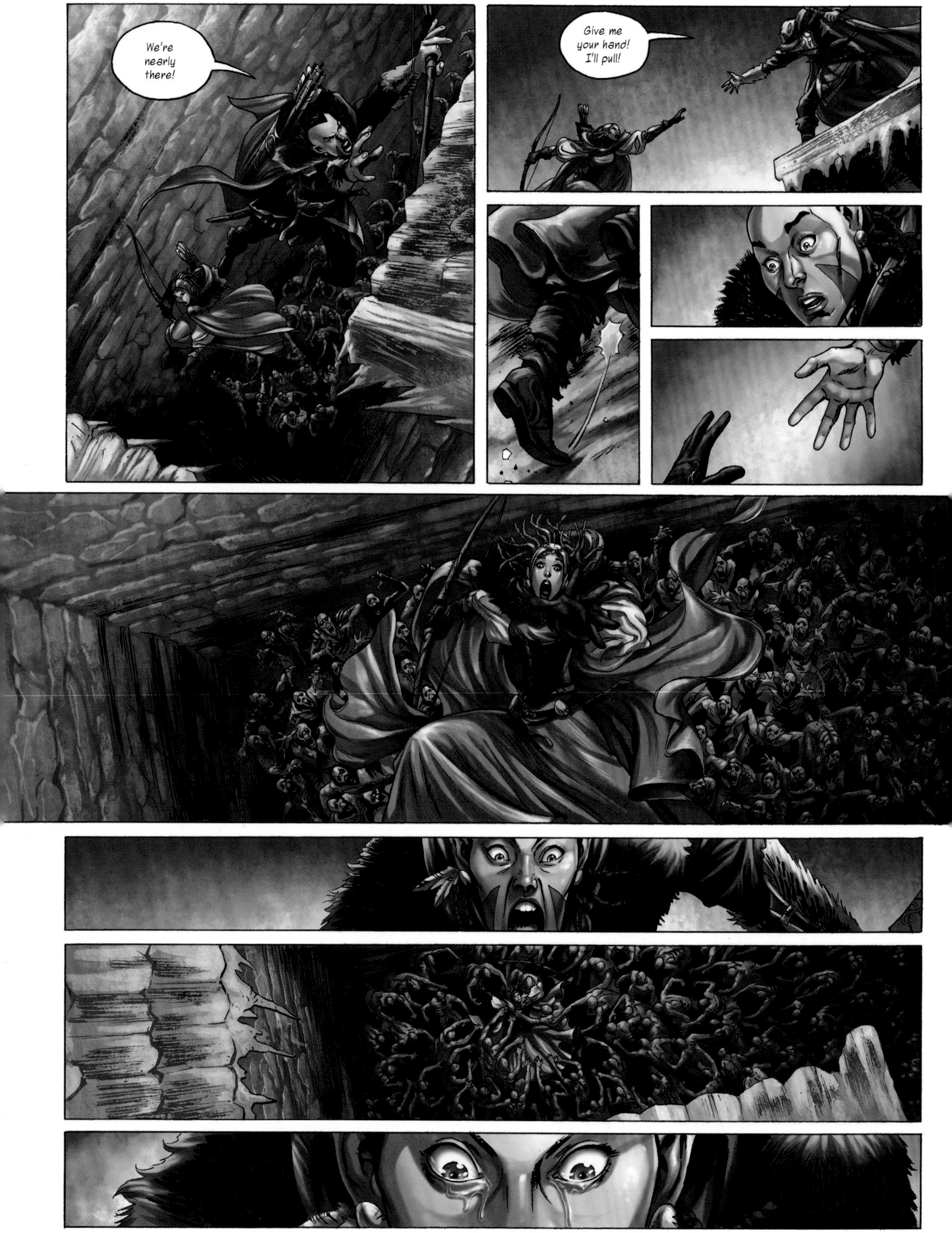

We're nearly there!
Give me your hand! I'll pull!

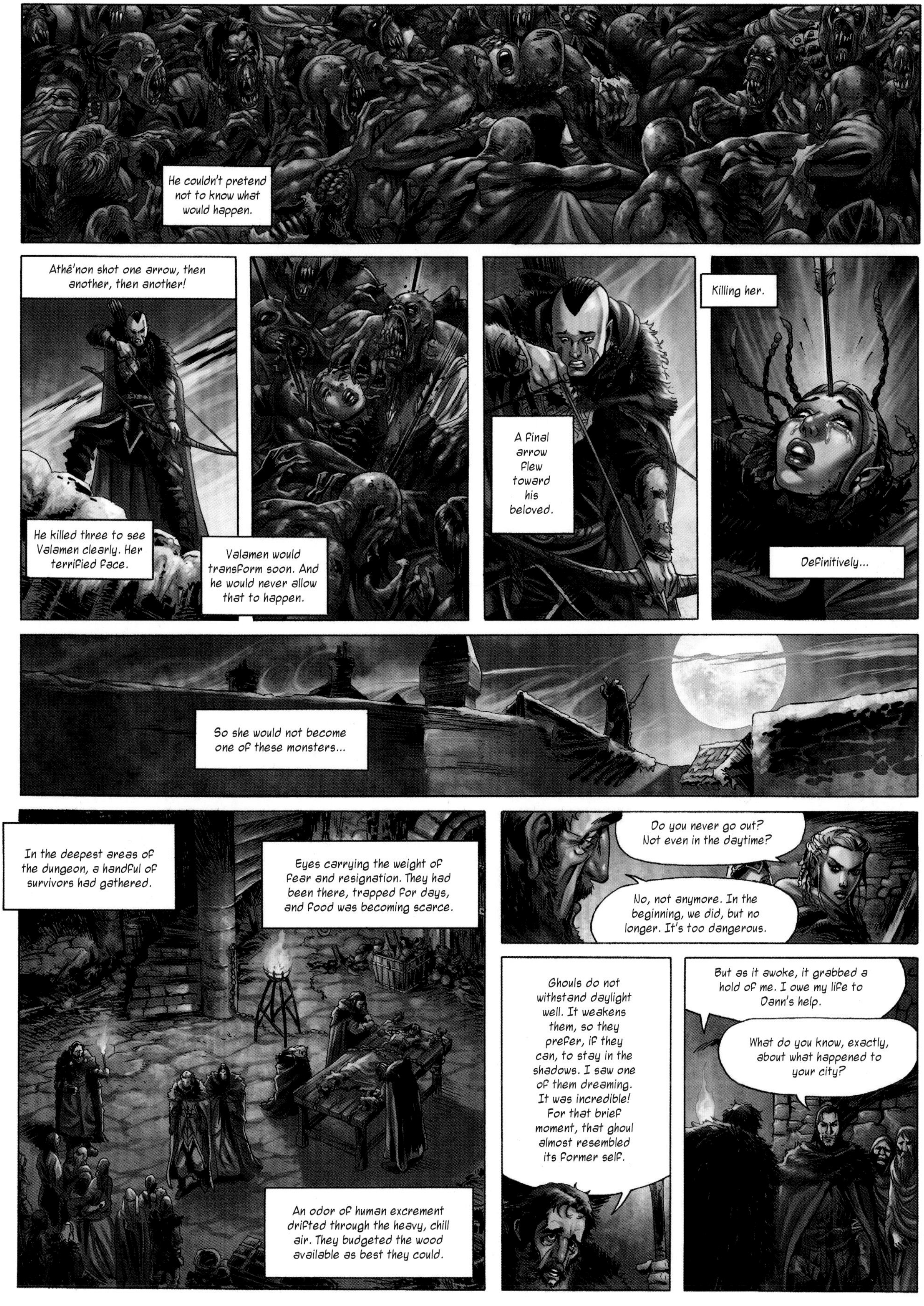

He couldn't pretend not to know what would happen.
Athê'non shot one arrow, then another, then another!
He killed three to see Valamen clearly. Her terrified face.
Valamen would transform soon. And he would never allow that to happen.
A final arrow flew toward his beloved.
Killing her.
Definitively...
So she would not become one of these monsters...
In the deepest areas of the dungeon, a handful of survivors had gathered.
Eyes carrying the weight of fear and resignation. They had been there, trapped for days, and food was becoming scarce.
An odor of human excrement drifted through the heavy, chill air. They budgeted the wood available as best they could.
Do you never go out? Not even in the daytime?
No, not anymore. In the beginning, we did, but no longer. It's too dangerous.
Ghouls do not withstand daylight well. It weakens them, so they prefer, if they can, to stay in the shadows. I saw one of them dreaming. It was incredible! For that brief moment, that ghoul almost resembled its former self.
But as it awoke, it grabbed a hold of me. I owe my life to Dann's help.
What do you know, exactly, about what happened to your city?

Not much. We don't know where this sickness comes from. We just know that these creatures want to spread their contagion.

At first, they hid and dwelled in the shadows. Then, as their numbers grew, they began openly attacking Aspen's citizens. It was a real bloodbath, as many were devoured alive.

What do you plan to do with this creature?

I'll question her.

You? An Ork?

Yes, a necromancer Ork. This Ghoul is an undead. I know how to speak to the Dead. It's even what I do best. And if I'm not mistaken, this creature could teach us a lot.

While our Ork put himself in a trance, I asked the Sister of the Senses to send a message of what we learned, to our king.

We waited for but a moment before Aamnon responded.

"Find the one who controls the ghouls, then flee!"

Lanawyn? You may ask your questions!

Do I ask them to you?

No, to him; he'll respond to you. One of my spells forces it to obey.

Where do you come from? What brought about your arrival?

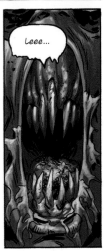

Leee...

Leonaaan...

He freed our mistress.

How?

"There's a strange place in the middle of Nodrënn. An improbable place, yet there it is."

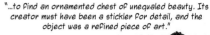

"An almost tropical forest, a sacred place that Leonan discovered after years of research. We call it Ashänn, the Emerald Sanctuary!"

"There, the excavation took place...and he dug, dug a long time, very long, very..."

"...deep."

"...to find an ornamented chest of unequaled beauty. Its creator must have been a stickler for detail, and the object was a refined piece of art."

"What did it hold?"

The Relics of Lah'Saa.

Who is Lah'Saa?

He doesn't want to respond.

Force him!

It's exhausting!

Pointless to ask him. I know the answer.

Lah'Saa is an ancient Elf who took part in necromancy. They say that she was so ambitious, long ago, that she started a huge war, in the hopes of conquering the lands of Arran.

We owe our survival to Slovtan the Wise, a mage who used his knowledge and power against Lah'Saa.

I didn't know that story.

Not all Elf stories are written in your books!

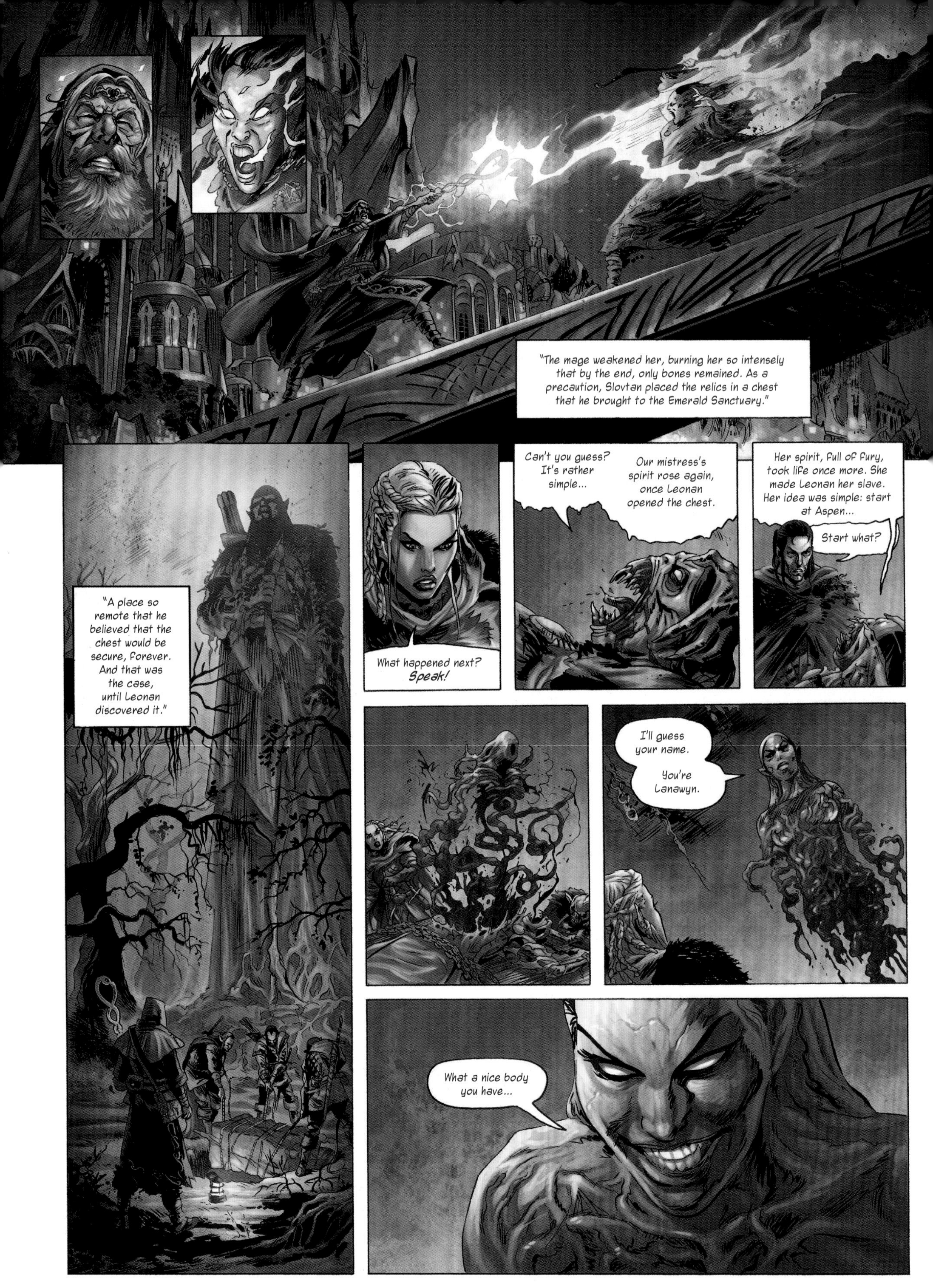
"The mage weakened her, burning her so intensely that by the end, only bones remained. As a precaution, Slovtan placed the relics in a chest that he brought to the Emerald Sanctuary."
"A place so remote that he believed that the chest would be secure, forever. And that was the case, until Leonan discovered it."
What happened next? **Speak!**
Can't you guess? It's rather simple...
Our mistress's spirit rose again, once Leonan opened the chest.
Her spirit, full of fury, took life once more. She made Leonan her slave. Her idea was simple: start at Aspen...
Start what?
I'll guess your name.
You're Lanawyn.
What a nice body you have...

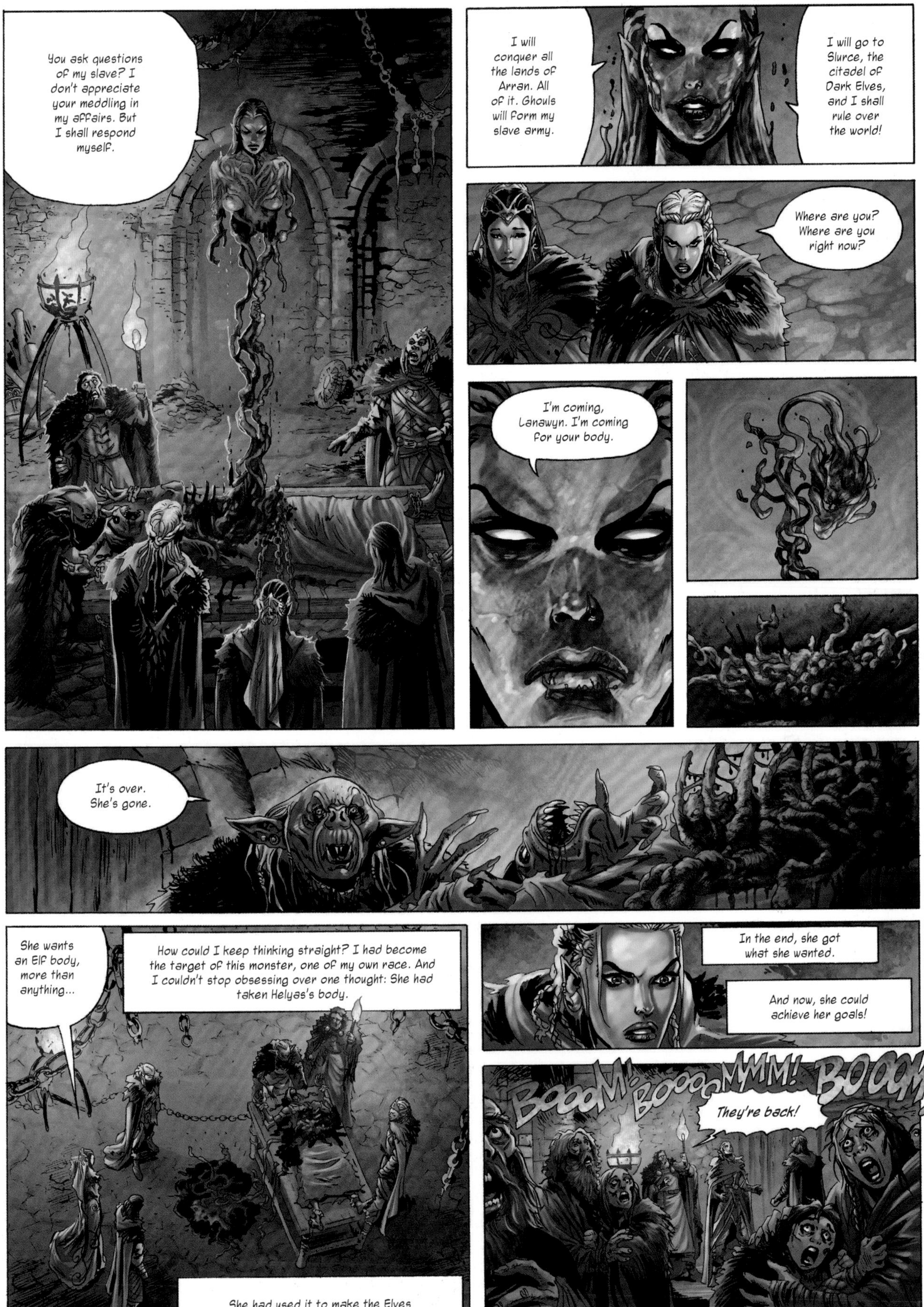
You ask questions of my slave? I don't appreciate your meddling in my affairs. But I shall respond myself.
I will conquer all the lands of Arran. All of it. Ghouls will form my slave army.
I will go to Slurce, the citadel of Dark Elves, and I shall rule over the world!
Where are you? Where are you right now?
I'm coming, Lanawyn. I'm coming for your body.
It's over. She's gone.
She wants an Elf body, more than anything...
How could I keep thinking straight? I had become the target of this monster, one of my own race. And I couldn't stop obsessing over one thought: She had taken Helyas's body.
She had used it to make the Elves come. To find a body to her liking.
In the end, she got what she wanted.
And now, she could achieve her goals!
BOOOM! BOOOOMMM! BOOOM!
They're back!

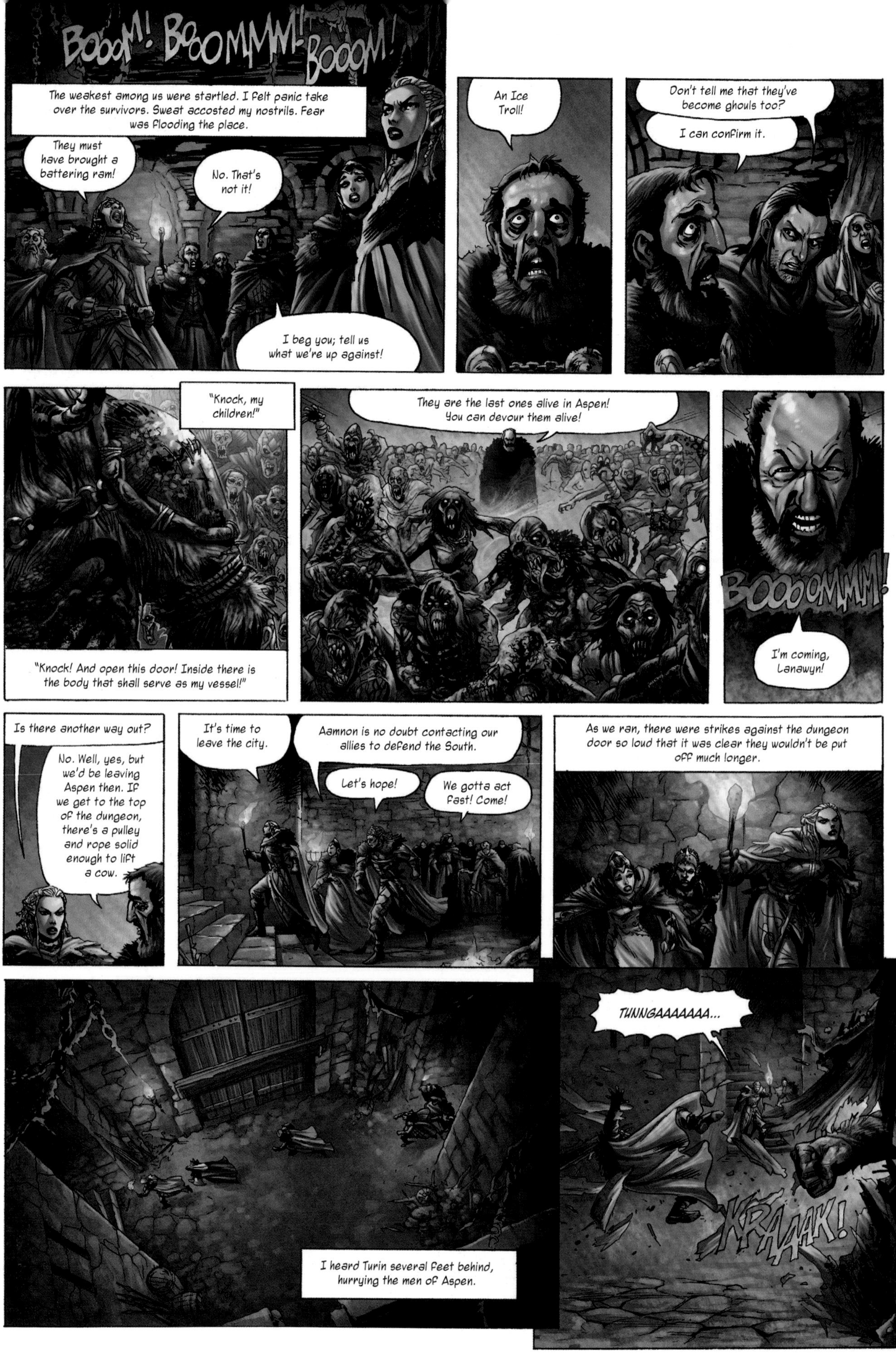
BOOOM! BOOOMMM! BOOOM!
The weakest among us were startled. I felt panic take over the survivors. Sweat accosted my nostrils. Fear was flooding the place.
They must have brought a battering ram!
No. That's not it!
I beg you; tell us what we're up against!
An Ice Troll!
Don't tell me that they've become ghouls too?
I can confirm it.
"Knock, my children!"
"Knock! And open this door! Inside there is the body that shall serve as my vessel!"
They are the last ones alive in Aspen! You can devour them alive!
BOOOOMMM!
I'm coming, Lanawyn!
Is there another way out?
No. Well, yes, but we'd be leaving Aspen then. If we get to the top of the dungeon, there's a pulley and rope solid enough to lift a cow.
It's time to leave the city.
Aamnon is no doubt contacting our allies to defend the South.
Let's hope!
We gotta act fast! Come!
As we ran, there were strikes against the dungeon door so loud that it was clear they wouldn't be put off much longer.
I heard Turin several feet behind, hurrying the men of Aspen.
TUNNGAAAAAAA...
KRAAAK!

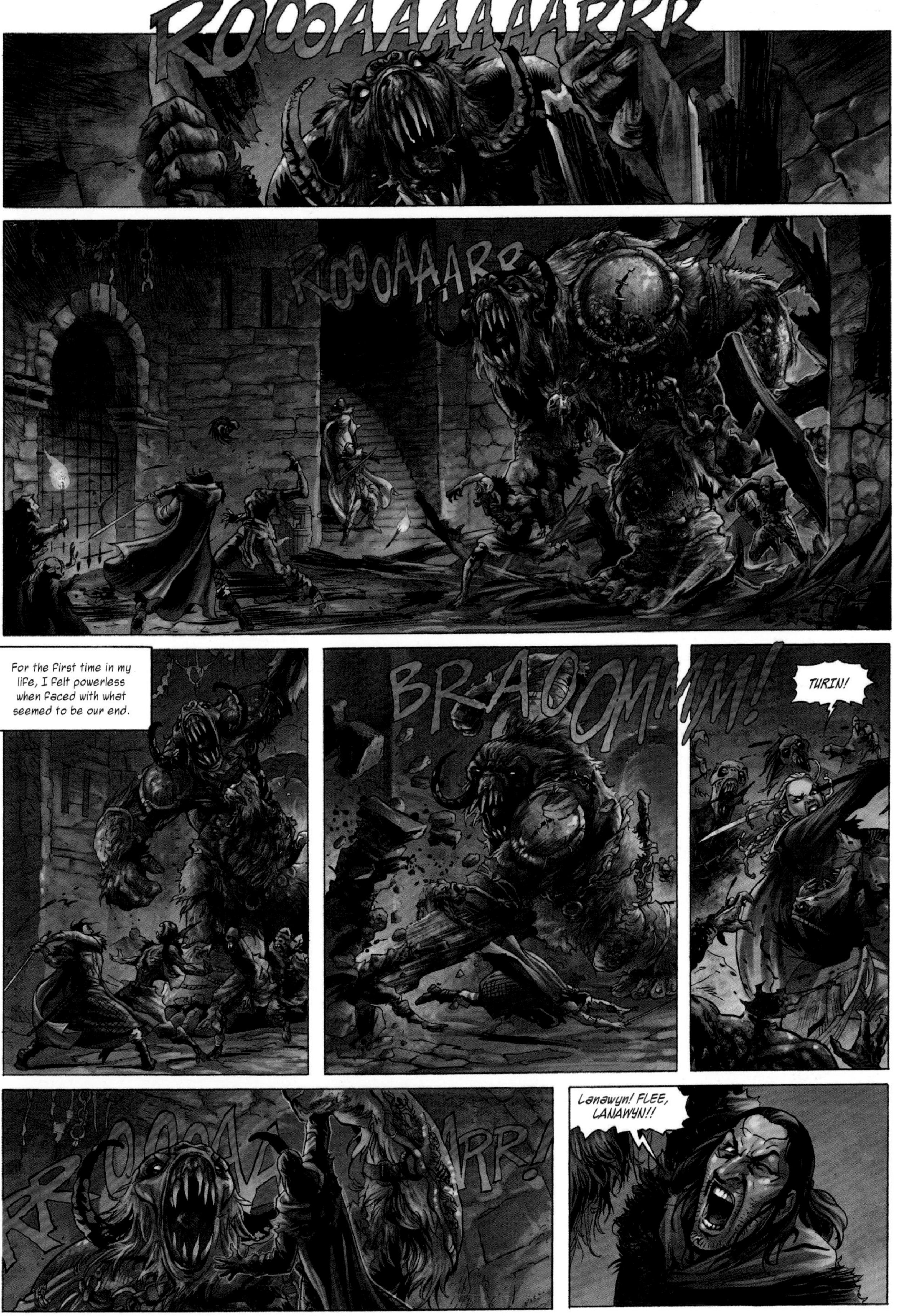
ROOOAAAAAARRR
ROOOAAARR
For the first time in my life, I felt powerless when faced with what seemed to be our end.
BRAOOMMM!
TURIN!
Lanawyn! FLEE, LANAWYN!!

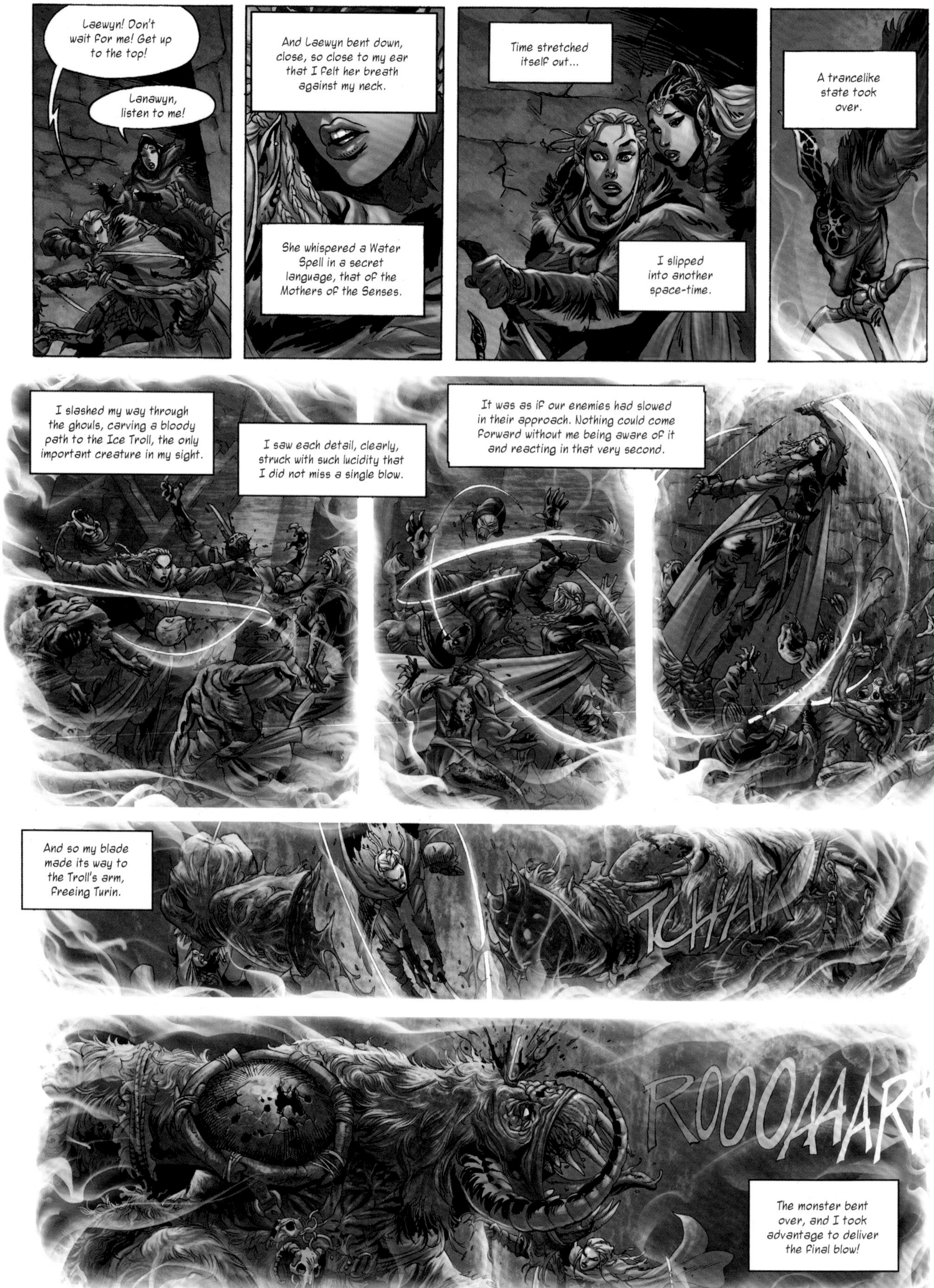
Laewyn! Don't wait for me! Get up to the top!
Lanawyn, listen to me!
And Laewyn bent down, close, so close to my ear that I felt her breath against my neck.
She whispered a Water Spell in a secret language, that of the Mothers of the Senses.
Time stretched itself out...
I slipped into another space-time.
A trancelike state took over.
I slashed my way through the ghouls, carving a bloody path to the Ice Troll, the only important creature in my sight.
I saw each detail, clearly, struck with such lucidity that I did not miss a single blow.
It was as if our enemies had slowed in their approach. Nothing could come forward without me being aware of it and reacting in that very second.
And so my blade made its way to the Troll's arm, freeing Turin.
TCHAK
ROOOAAAR
The monster bent over, and I took advantage to deliver the final blow!

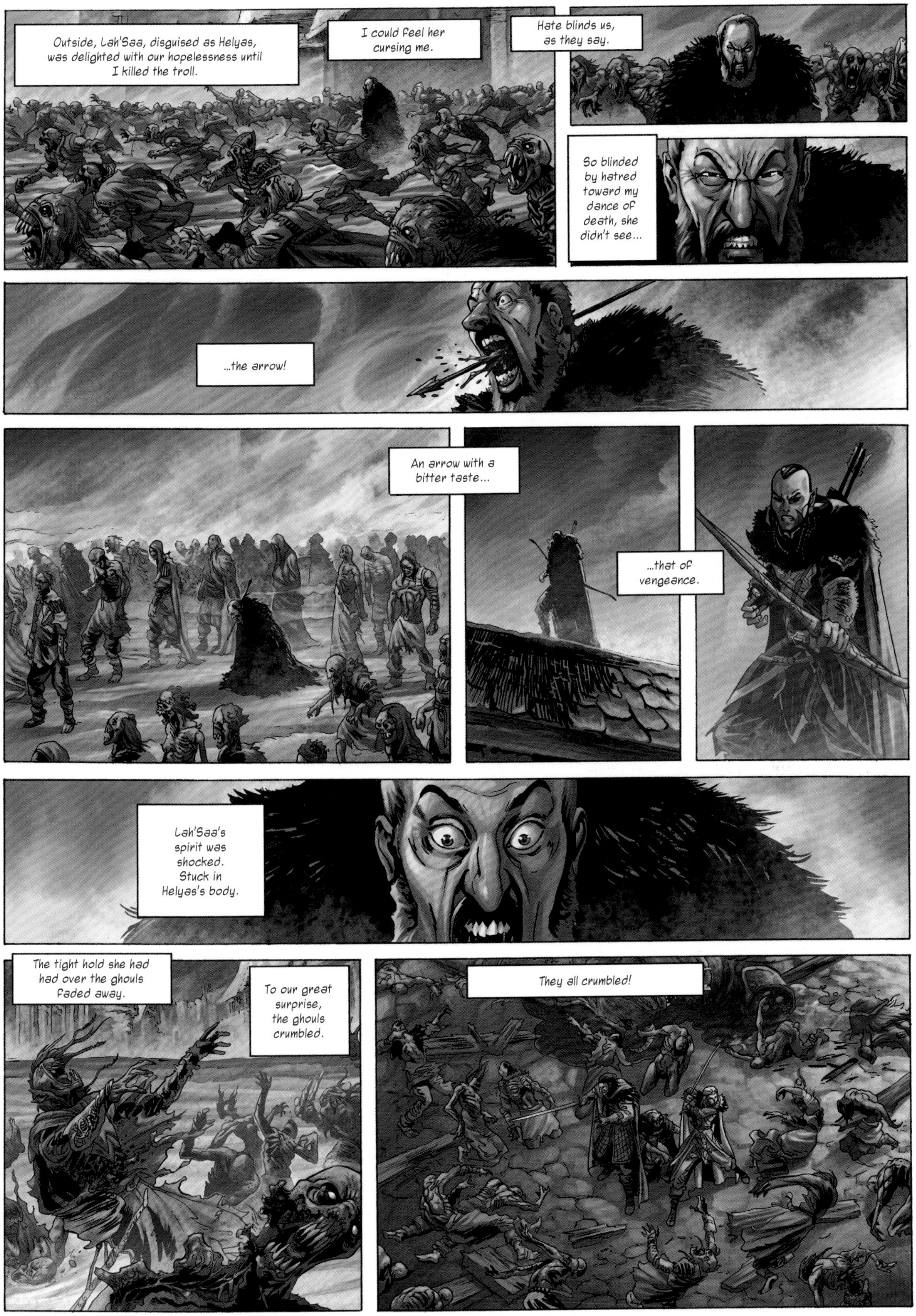
Outside, Lah'Saa, disguised as Helyas, was delighted with our hopelessness until I killed the troll.
I could feel her cursing me.
Hate blinds us, as they say.
So blinded by hatred toward my dance of death, she didn't see...
...the arrow!
An arrow with a bitter taste...
...that of vengeance.
Lah'Saa's spirit was shocked. Stuck in Helyas's body.
The tight hold she had had over the ghouls faded away.
To our great surprise, the ghouls crumbled.
They all crumbled!

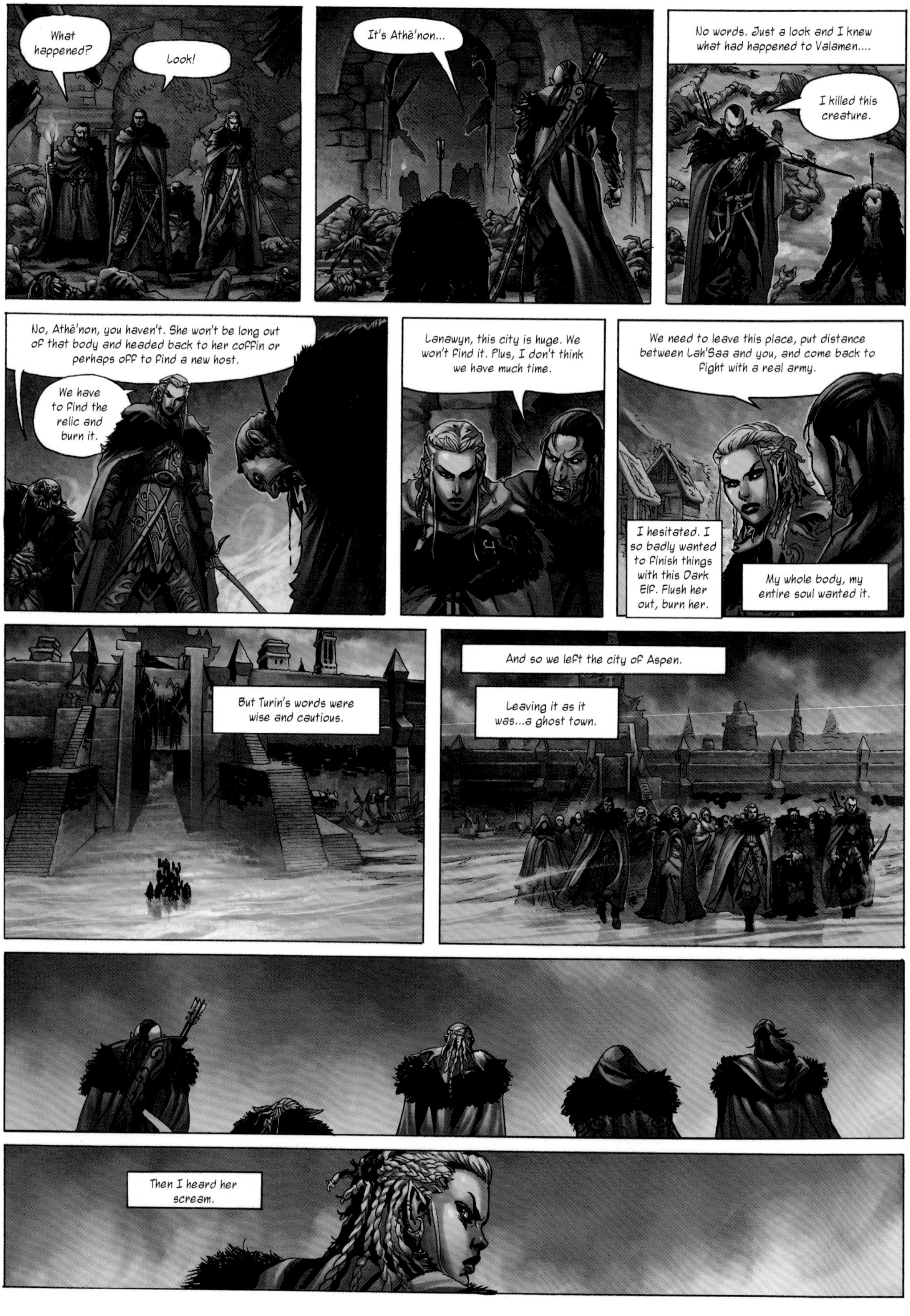
What happened?
Look!
It's Athê'non...
No words. Just a look and I knew what had happened to Valamen....
I killed this creature.
No, Athê'non, you haven't. She won't be long out of that body and headed back to her coffin or perhaps off to find a new host.
We have to find the relic and burn it.
Lanawyn, this city is huge. We won't find it. Plus, I don't think we have much time.
We need to leave this place, put distance between Lah'Saa and you, and come back to fight with a real army.
I hesitated. I so badly wanted to finish things with this Dark Elf. Flush her out, burn her.
My whole body, my entire soul wanted it.
But Turin's words were wise and cautious.
And so we left the city of Aspen.
Leaving it as it was...a ghost town.
Then I heard her scream.

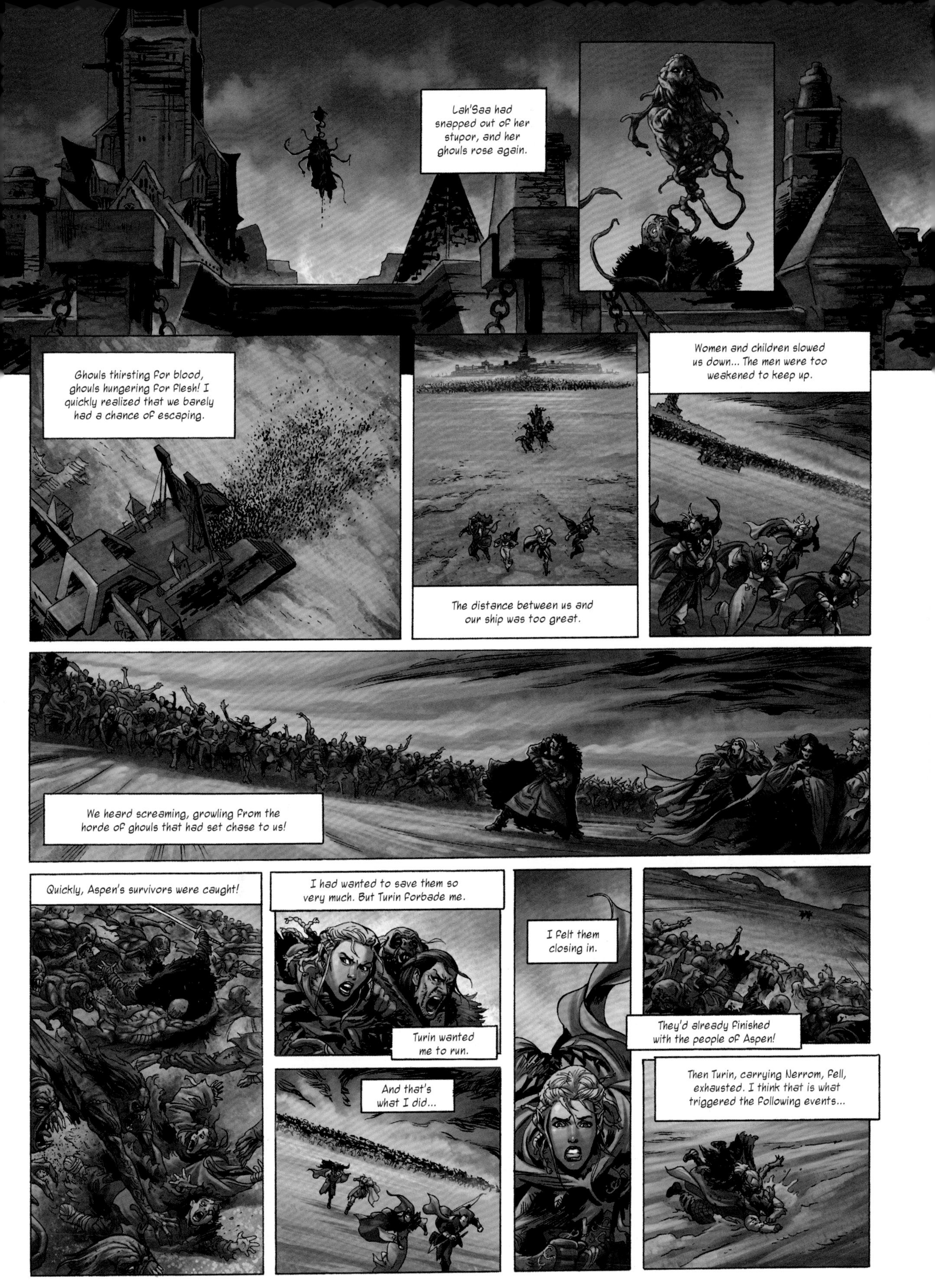
Lah'Saa had snapped out of her stupor, and her ghouls rose again.
Ghouls thirsting for blood, ghouls hungering for flesh! I quickly realized that we barely had a chance of escaping.
The distance between us and our ship was too great.
Women and children slowed us down... The men were too weakened to keep up.
We heard screaming, growling from the horde of ghouls that had set chase to us!
Quickly, Aspen's survivors were caught!
I had wanted to save them so very much. But Turin forbade me.
Turin wanted me to run.
And that's what I did...
I felt them closing in.
They'd already finished with the people of Aspen!
Then Turin, carrying Nerrom, fell, exhausted. I think that is what triggered the following events...

It was as if I were dreaming, awake.

I saw the Crystal. And the Crystal called me.

It needed me. But I felt that our need was mutual.

And yet, the Crystal was far, very far. I had been rid of it, scared by what it did to me, by the desire it inspired within me.

For months, I had the feeling that I was carrying it. That feeling when a limb has been cut off...

I had had the Crystal cut off from me. Since then, it called. Every night, tirelessly...

And so I understood that a part of it was still inside me.

Lanawyn!

Lanawyn, you have to run!

Turin, no!

What is she doing?

She's saving us, human!

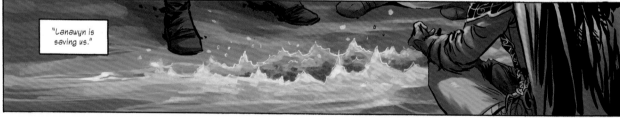

"Lanawyn is saving us."

The far-off cries disappeared. Calm spread from the depths of my soul. My breathing, like the wind across a summer sea, soothed the rest of my body.

Fear disappeared.

I felt its power grow.

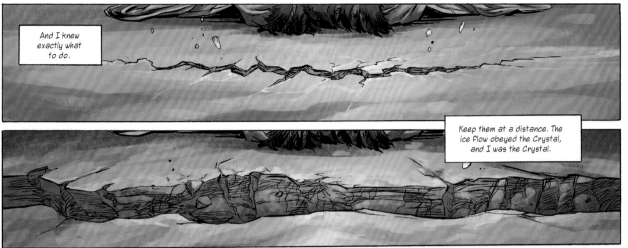

And I knew exactly what to do.

Keep them at a distance. The ice flow obeyed the Crystal, and I was the Crystal.

The ghouls rushed toward the gap...

...without stopping, leaping and falling into the abyss that I had created. Until Lah'Saa ordered them to stop.

I felt her presence across the way. She watched me, impressed but also jealous of this power.

Her voice rushed to my mind.

She said, "One day, you will be mine, Lanawyn! And that day, your power will be mine..."

"I want you!"

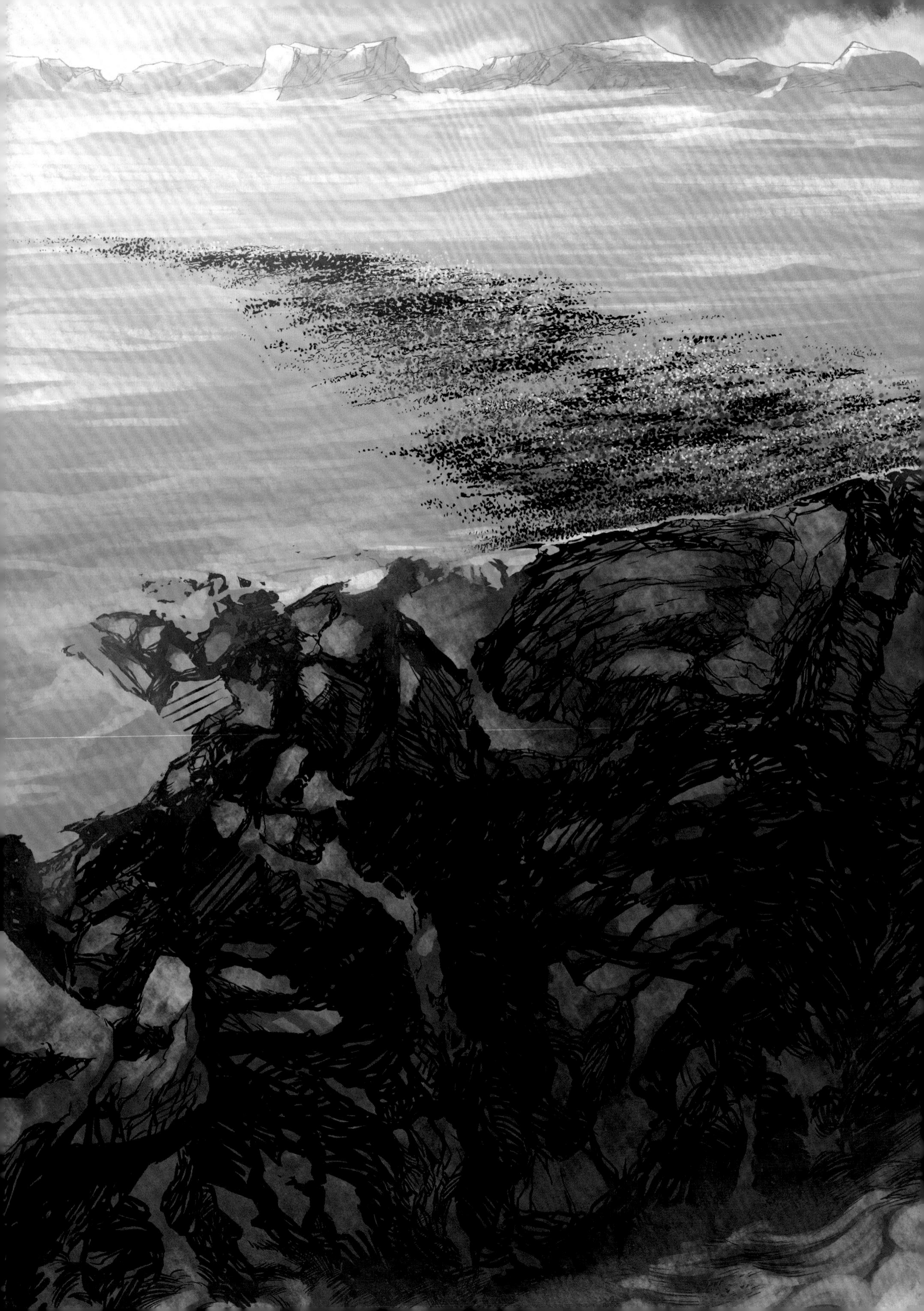

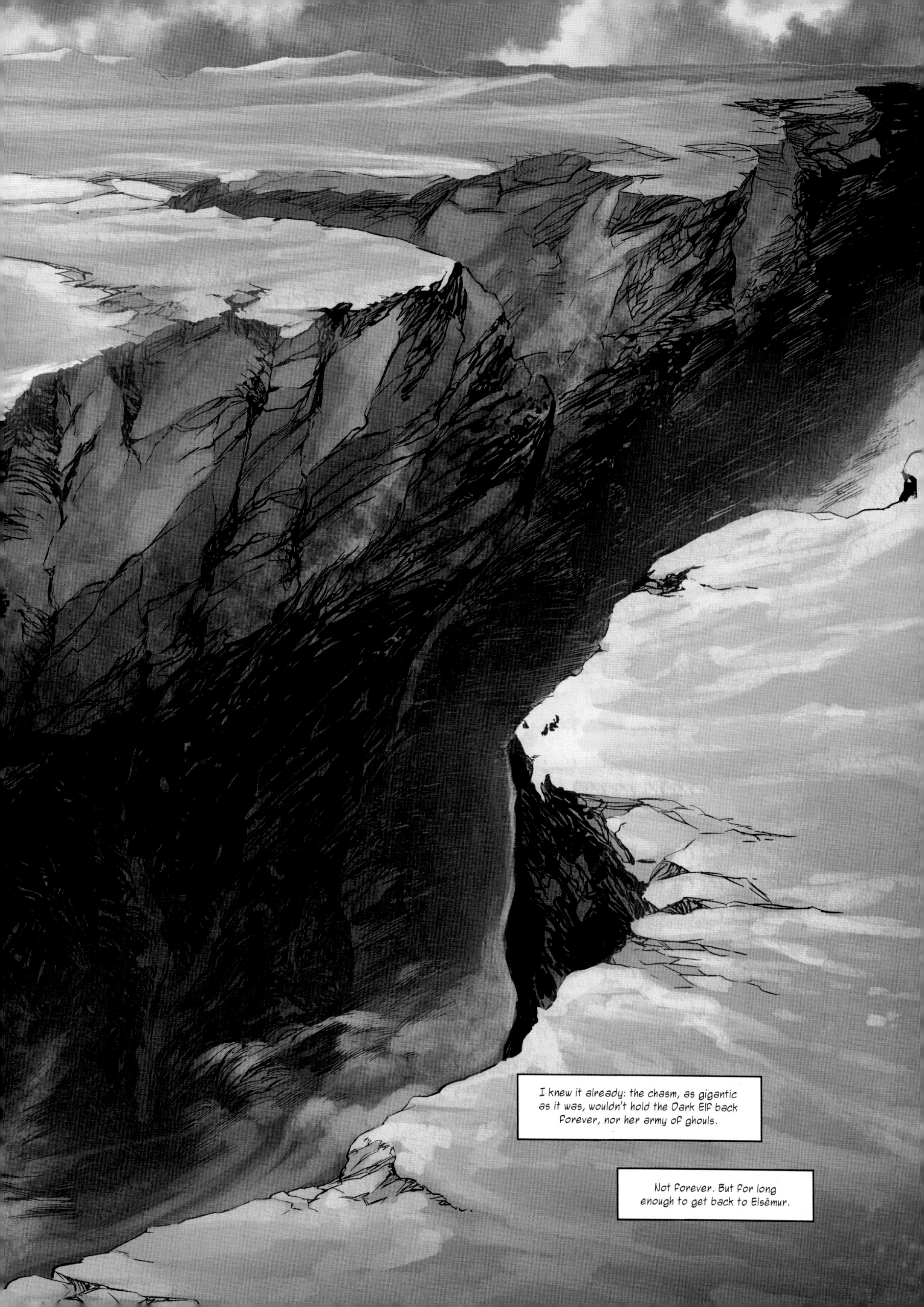
I knew it already: the chasm, as gigantic as it was, wouldn't hold the Dark Elf back forever, nor her army of ghouls.
Not forever. But for long enough to get back to Elsëmur.

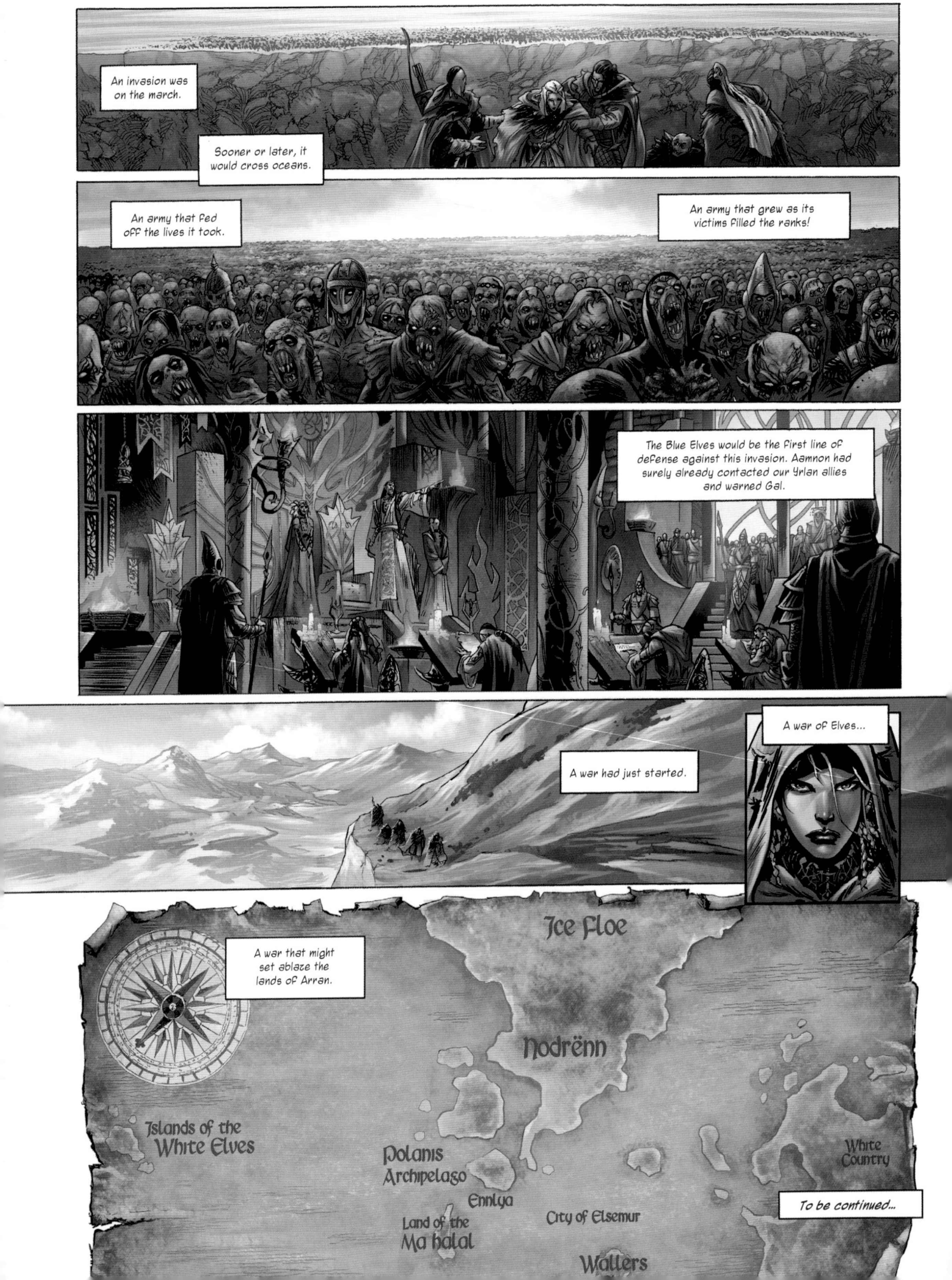
An invasion was on the march.
Sooner or later, it would cross oceans.
An army that fed off the lives it took.
An army that grew as its victims filled the ranks!
The Blue Elves would be the first line of defense against this invasion. Aamnon had surely already contacted our Yrlan allies and warned Gal.
A war had just started.
A war of Elves...
A war that might set ablaze the lands of Arran.
Ice Floe
Nodrënn
Islands of the White Elves
Polanis Archipelago
Ennlya
Land of the Ma halal
City of Elsemur
White Country
Wallers
To be continued...

WWW.INSIGHTCOMICS.COM

Find us on Facebook: www.facebook.com/InsightEditionsComics

Follow us on Twitter: @InsightComics

Follow us on Instagram: Insight_Comics

Published by Insight Editions, San Rafael, California, in 2017.

Library of Congress Cataloging-in-Publication Data available.

ISBN: 978-1-68383-105-1

PUBLISHER: RAOUL GOFF
ASSOCIATE PUBLISHER: VANESSA LOPEZ
SENIOR EDITOR: MARK IRWIN
MANAGING EDITOR: ALAN KAPLAN
EDITORIAL ASSISTANT: HOLLY FISHER
PRODUCTION EDITOR: ELAINE OU
PRODUCTION MANAGER: ALIX NICHOLAEFF

ROOTS of PEACE REPLANTED PAPER

Insight Editions, in association with Roots of Peace, will plant two trees for each tree used in the manufacturing of this book. Roots of Peace is an internationally renowned humanitarian organization dedicated to eradicating land mines worldwide and converting war-torn lands into productive farms and wildlife habitats. Roots of Peace will plant two million fruit and nut trees in Afghanistan and provide farmers there with the skills and support necessary for sustainable land use.

Manufactured in China by Insight Editions

10 9 8 7 6 5 4 3 2 1